Praise fo

"*Cross County* is a high-tension, sharply etched supernatural thriller that will tantalize and unsettle you right to the last page."
– Tom Piccirilli, author of *The Cold Spot* and *The Midnight Road.*

"Waggoner is a master of the tightly coiled tale of suspense, his prose a deadly snake waiting to strike."
– Thomas F. Monteleone, author of the *NY Times* bestseller, *The Blood of the Lamb.*

"A fast-paced, over-the-top, blood-and-guts thriller . . . for those who like their horror bloody, their heroes tarnished and their action just this side of unbelievable."
— *Publishers Weekly*

"Tim Waggoner is a magnificent horror writer who will be appreciated by readers who like Douglas Clegg and Bentley Little."
— *Alternative Worlds*

"Tim Waggoner writes with a passion and imagination that demand your attention."
— Ron Dickie, *Horror World*

"Waggoner does a very good job with his characters and an even better one in creating bizarre images and landscapes through which to conduct his readers."
— Don D'Ammassa, *SF Chronicle*

"Refreshingly different from most of what's being published in the horror genre these days."

— *Cemetery Dance Magazine*

"*Like Death* is a stunner. Tim Waggoner's electric prose reads like an unholy collaboration between Gary Braunbeck at his most artful and surreal and Edward Lee at his most grandly perverse and over-the-top. *Like Death* is the early front-runner for top debut of '05."

— Bryan Smith, author of *House of Blood*

"An up-and-comer who's worthy of the hype... Tim Waggoner is well on his way to being proclaimed horror fiction's leading surrealist."

– *Cemetery Dance Magazine*

"Tim Waggoner works some mojo!"

– Douglas E. Winter, Bram Stoker Award® nominated author of *Run*

"Waggoner's work soars with breathtaking surrealism and writhes with human pain almost too much to encounter in the written word."

– Gary A. Braunbeck, Bram Stoker Award®-winning author of *To Each Their Darkness*

"Waggoner is in possession of a talent that should be taken seriously, and I can't wait for his next book."

– Johnny Butane, *The Horror Channel*

"A new force to reckon with."

– *The Horror Channel*

"Waggoner's prose is smooth and infallibly entertaining."

— David Niall Wilson, *Cemetery Dance*

"PANDORA DRIVE moves at a brisk pace and shoots ahead in linear fashion (even though it gets flipping freaky). I like Waggoner's writing and will have to go back and catch his earlier work, such as last year's LIKE DEATH..."

— Tale Bones

"LIKE DEATH is a well-written, unpleasant excursion into insanity."

— Buried.com

"LIKE DEATH is one of the most bizarre serial killer thrillers recently published. Waggoner, unlike some others, never lets anything get in the way of his story, as everything in LIKE DEATH—serial killers, ghosts, killer cannibal police officers, time travel, alternate universes, bizarre sex, and more—all builds to, and supports a spectacular climax. While the suitably hardboiled ending is hardly a 'happy' one, it's the right one. It's hard to say much more about LIKE DEATH without giving away one of the novel's great plot twists. Sex, life, death, reality: all become fluid and all are mixed together to give the reader a wild ride in what may be one of the year's best novels."

— Mark Louis Baumgart, *Cemetery Dance*

"Waggoner delivers a tale of cosmic and body horror at its most disturbing. *The Men Upstairs* is a fascinating study of the ancient tension between repulsion and desire."

– Laird Barron, author of *Occultation*

"In Broken Shadows Tim Waggoner gives us a cornucopia of different tales that are haunting, dark, visceral and will satisfy any short story lover's craving."

– *Literary Mayhem*

"Tim Waggoner is insane! It's like he drinks rocket fuel and shoots streams of fire from his fingertips. Extremely bizarre and magnificently entertaining."

– Andersen Prunty, author of
THE WARM GLOW OF HAPPY HOMES

"Devilishly and deliciously disturbing."

– Shock Totem

BONE WHISPERS

BONE WHISPERS

A Collection of Short Fiction

Tim Waggoner

POST MORTEM PRESS
CINCINNATI

Post Mortem Press - Cincinnati, OH

www.postmortem-press.com

FIRST EDITION

Printed in the United States of America
Library of Congress Control Number: 2013940944
ISBN: 978-0615822327

Original Publication Credits

"The Great Ocean of Truth." Fear the Abyss, Post Mortem Press, 2012

"Thou Art God." Dark Faith 2, Apex Publications.

"Surface Tension." Queen Anne's Resurrection, Dec. 2011

"Do No Harm." Zombiesque, DAW 2011

"Sleepless Eyes." Horror Library vol. 4. Cutting Block Press, 2010

"Bone Whispers." Zombie Raccoons and Killer Bunnies, DAW Books, 2009.

"Skull Cathedral." Squid Salad Press, 2008

"Harvest Time." Bits of the Dead, Coscom Entertainment, 2008

"Best Friends Forever." Imaginary Friends, DAW Books, 2008

"Unwoven." Shroud no.1, 2008.

"No More Shadows." Noctem Aeternus, 2008.

"Some Dark Hope." Horror World, Dec. 2007.

"Country Roads." Legends of the Mountain State: Ghostly Tales from the State of West Virginia, 2007

"Swimming Lessons." Delirium Books website, 2008.

"Conversations Kill." Cemetery Dance no. 60, 2009.

"Long Way Home." Thrillers II, CD Publications, 2007

"Darker Than Winter." Thrillers II, CD Publications, 2007

"The Faces That We Meet." Thrillers II, CD Publications, 2007

This one's for Tom Monteleone, for all his encouragement over the years, but especially for writing "Wendigo's Child."

Table of Contents

Top Five Reasons I Admire the Hell Out of Tim Waggoner

Michael A. Arnzen

1. HE GOES THERE

Ever been in a NYC taxicab? The drivers barrel through narrow roadways, cut across traffic, and generally bob and weave with the devil. You tumble around in the back seat, holding on for your very life -- a life you place in the hands of your bizarrely proficient driver. When I'm in a NYC taxicab, I pretend I'm on a roller coaster, and try not to think about the room for human error -- instead, I imagine the cab drivers are superhuman in their navigational control and that their stunt driving skills could put the entire Andretti family to shame.

That's sort of how I think of Tim Waggoner, when he's behind the wheel of a story. He takes me places my brain doesn't necessarily want to go. No: he barrels right into them. And I hold on for stability, knowing I'm going to be disturbed... and loving every minute of the ride. Because it IS one helluva ride. It's not just the ideas he imagines, which never fail to astound. It's his prose style. It makes me want to keep reading. And it always delivers with surprise, emotional gut-punches, and flair. I admire the hell out of Tim Waggoner because he tells inventive fiction inventively, and blows my mind every time.

2. HE IS PRESCIENT

Since I write horror stories myself, whenever I read them, I always get sucked into this guessing game, where I am matching wits with the author. I do it sort of the same way an obnoxious mystery novel fan might do it, trying to outsmart the author in their clever little "whodunit" games. But when I read horror fiction, I am following the plot logic and paying attention to the foreshadowing, and trying to see if I can figure out how the author is trying to sneak up on me and twist my head around.

I always lose this game when I read Tim Waggoner. His writing is always is one or two steps ahead of me, and I never see what's coming before it's too late. Especially in his endings. And I LOVE that. I prefer to lose these stupid matchwit games I play. It means the writer is good. He knows that there are people out there who read stories straight and others who read them askew, and he deftly outsmarts them both. To call him a "writer's writer" is a bit of a reduction, because he's more than that. He's just a great writer, period. This comes from being very well read in the genre and from sustaining a long career (which he has, and he deserves far more cred for this than I think he gets). But he might just be prescient, too. Perhaps, beyond any given story, he might even be ahead of his time. I admire the hell out of Tim Waggoner because he never takes the easy way out, and because he shows us all how we might be guilty of it...urging us to think beyond our own horizons. Good fiction does that, and Tim's fiction is damned good.

3. HE PUTS THE "SUR" IN SURREALISM

If you look over his publishing history, you'll see that Tim Waggoner has not only been publishing in quality markets for a very long time, but has also been publishing in diverse realms -- from media tie-in books related to everything from Freddy Krueger movies to the Supernatural TV series to vintage video games (yes, he's written a Defender novel!) -- to flash fiction (he appears alongside me in a few of those 100 X Little Y anthos from Barnes and Noble, for instance) to articles about writing and alternative history tales about the Civil War to bizarro erotica to...oh, I give up. He does it ALL. And he does it professionally. The proof is in the pudding, but I also suspect he's on a few editor's speed dials, because he is a VERY productive writer, clearly capable of cranking it out and meeting deadlines better than I can.

But I also think I'm a lot like Tim. We're sympatico. Not just because we both predominantly write horror fiction and have a high affection for the short story, but because we both write for diverse markets and genres and don't put any stock in the idea that a writer has to brand himself by reducing himself to one single pony show. WRITING is what we do, filtered through our weird-colored glasses. But with most writers who do it all, sometimes uninformed readers and even worsely uninformed publicity agents for publishing houses don't know where the heck to "place" us. But the truth is, they simply aren't paying any attention. Read a small sampling of his work -- like you will in this wonderful book -- and you'll see his signature style foment before your eyes.

What distinguishes Tim Waggoner from other writers? His penchant for surrealism. Tim is one of the few writers who is able to merge the setting of a story with the psychological geography of a dream. He gets so deep into the heads of his characters that you slip right inside along with them...and come as close to experiencing a waking dream -- sometimes nirvana...sometimes madness -- as is possible in fiction. He is working in the tradition of the French Decadents, and we're lucky to have writers like Tim still with us today. Even when he's telling a relatively straightforward tale, the surreal is there on the edges of everything. I admire the hell out of Tim Waggoner because he puts the "sur" in surrealism, and he's able to get away with it in the popular marketplace for fiction today.

4. HE'S A GREAT TEACHER

One of my fond early memories of Tim Waggoner is sitting in a workshop he taught at a Horror Writers Association weekend long ago. I got to see the side of Tim that his students get to see at the college where he teaches in Ohio. He was relaxed and eager to help everyone out...and he knew what the hell he was talking about. This was shortly after I myself had started teaching fiction writing, and I remember finding a kindred spirit in Tim at that moment. I asked him if I could have copies of his handouts, and he gladly provided. He remains one of the few other folks in the HWA who are educators as much as they are thrill-meisters...and so when opening came up for an adjunct in horror at our MFA program in Writing Popular Fiction at Seton Hill University, I put his name forward right away as a possible hire. He's still with us, and his students adore him. They ought to call themselves "Timinions" if they don't already. His insights save novels. But he isn't just teaching to make a buck; he teaches because he loves to talk shop, like all genre writers who are fans first do. He is a very generous person, eager to help others become better writers, because he is very secure in his own talents, and sees the potential inside others. Read some of his "how to" articles about the craft of writing and you'll hear his patient, wise voice. I admire the hell out of Tim Waggoner because he just loves the genre so much that he's eager to share his passion with others. He realizes that the genres we write in are kept alive by community -- not competition -- and that once you succeed you have an obligation to help others grow if you want your genre to live on. We're all in hell together, after all.

Or maybe we're just in his hellworld, once we've read one of his books. This collection, in particular, has a lot of lessons to teach. It's also a very sick book, with lots of nasty moments, from encounters with a different kind of god to a peculiar rodent with a message to tell. You'll go from the graveyard to the grindhouse in Bone Whispers, and you'll see what I'm talking about: Tim pushes the genre envelope quite a bit and has lots of fun along the way, but he also tells a good story first and foremost. As I said way up above, Tim "goes there" in his fiction, but he never lets go of the story.

5. HE'S A SWELL GUY

Tim is going to take you to some very dark and dirty placs in this collection, but you can trust him. He's a swell guy. It's obvious by now, isn't it? Tim does it all, and he does it passionately. But he's also just a genuinely good human being. Whenever I see him, he smiles and offers a hug. But usually the first thing he does is get an earnest look on his face and ask: "How is it going?" He cares about his comrades. He cares about his readers, too. You can tell from his writing: he puts the readers' needs first. His care comes through. That's why books like this are such a pleasure to read...even if they are out to get you.

AN INTRODUCTION TO BONE WHISPERS

The best horror writers I know are not "Evil" Knievels -- masochistic daredevils -- and they're not Snarky DeSades -- sadistic snobs -- either. Instead, they're good human beings -- generous, caring people like Tim Waggoner. There's a timeworn belief that horror writers are nice people because they purge all the ugly stuff that's inside of them through their writing...making us some of the most well-adjusted folks you'll ever meet. I believe that's true. We get to have waking nightmares in our fiction and the bogeymen of everyday life are nothing but a joke after that. That's why we read this stuff, maybe, too. But there's something else about the VERY good writers that make them so nice. They've suffered. They've been to the dark side, seen it, and lived (usually scarred) to tell the tale. They've earned the right to talk about it, and you can hear their wisdom in their voice and their sure handed storytelling. Writers like Tim want to disturb you, but they realize the seriousness business behind all this weirdness we write about. Reading Tim Waggoner you get the sense that he is both unleashing the beast and also very aware that the beast is a very dangerous one...and you trust he's got it tamed, even if it bites you on the throat. We're lucky to have this book, which is like a crazy zoo. I admire the hell out of Tim Waggoner because he's a beast-tamer par excellence, as Bone Whispers will prove.

But all this is moot and very personal. You don't need to know why I admire the hell out of Tim Waggoner anymore. You will admire the hell out of Tim Waggoner because of this collection. It shows him at his very best, and it is living testimony to his merit. You'll probably agree with me that this is among the best works of horrific fantasy you've come across in a long while -- a book that contains more amazing surprises and deeper head trips than you might be expecting if you just opened the cover. You've unleashed something here. It's whispering shh-shh-shh. Better go tend to it.

-- Michael A. Arnzen, Pittsburgh, April 2013

Thou Art God

YOU'RE WORKING ON YOUR LAPTOP at a window-side table in a downtown coffee shop when you see the woman in the brown coat outside. She walks past the window where you're sitting, and you have a perfect view of her. She looks to be in her fifties, face weathered and careworn, hair short and straight, the brunette color a shade too bright. You figure it for a bad dye job. Her left cheek is swollen and misshapen, as if something's wrong with the bone underneath, and her right arm is folded to her side, elbow bent, hand jiggling as she walks. She limps as she pushes an empty baby stroller before her, its colors washed out and nearly bleached white, as if it's been left outside too long.

And that's the moment you *know*.

For the last half hour you've been sipping coffee with two shots of caramel flavor while working on client invoices. You could've done it at the office, but you were so sick of staring at those four damn walls that you just had to get out. As you typed on your laptop, you wondered for perhaps the thousandth time if this was why you studied your ass off in law school – so you can input numbers into a computer like a trained monkey.

But now you know, and you stand and walk toward the door. Other customers look up as you push it open and step outside, and you feel their gazes follow you. You step in front of the woman, and for a moment you think that she's going to keep coming until she bumps the stroller into your legs. But then her eyes focus on you, and she stops, startled.

"Wha u wan?"

Her speech is slurred, and on any other day you'd struggle to understand what she said. But not today.

"Just to touch you."

You reach out and brush your index finger against her swollen cheek. Your flesh barely comes in contact with hers, but you can feel the cheek is hard and cold as marble. There is no flash of light, no crack of thunder, no special effects showing how her flesh melts and rearranges. One instant her cheek is swollen, the next it isn't. She straightens her arm, flexes it a couple times, wiggles the fingers and looks at them with wonder, as if she's not quite sure what they are.

She looks down at the stroller and frowns.

"Why in the world was I pushing that? I don't have any children." Her voice is clear, her diction crisp and distinct.

"Does it matter?" you ask.

She considers for a moment, as if you've just asked a profound question. "No, I suppose it doesn't." She smiles and you step aside. She continues down the sidewalk, her gait smooth, almost graceful. Part of you is astonished by what's just occurred, but to another part of you, the woman's transformation seems like the most natural thing in the world.

You watch her go, wondering what lies ahead of her now. You could know if you wanted to. Her entire future could be laid out in front of you as easily as you take your next breath, but you decide not to pry. It doesn't seem polite.

You go back inside, and discover everyone is still looking at you. Business people in suits who up until a minute ago had talked shop, college students who'd pretended to study while texting friends or surfing the Web, pierced and tatted baristas who'd served coffee with memorized patter and frozen smiles, mothers who'd gossiped about their husbands, kids, and each other while their babies-in-tow nibbled gooey biter biscuits. And even those little ones are looking at you, sticky-moist treats clutched tight in tiny hands. Everyone is silent, faces grim, gazes penetrating. Some of them must've witnessed what happened outside, but no one rushes over to ask you how you did it, no one cries out, *It's a miracle!* They just stare at you, and although you wonder what's going on behind their eyes, you're surprised to discover you don't know, *can't* know, even though you really want to. It seems you still have some limits after all.

The silent scrutiny unnerves you, and you close your laptop, slide it into its case, tuck it beneath your arm, and start toward the rear door. You parked out back today, and although you don't relish walking through the coffee shop – past all those *eyes* – you can't bring yourself to stay any longer. Heads swivel to track you as you depart, and you pick up your pace. You push open the door and go outside, forcing yourself not to run.

You head across the parking lot to your Lexus. It used to be your favorite toy, a tangible symbol of your success – or as your ex-wife would say, a stereotypical symptom of male midlife crisis. But now it's just a hunk of metal that can take you away from here, Point A, to a Point B that's yet to be determined. It doesn't really matter where you go – you just want to put some distance between yourself and this place.

You feel a crawling sensation on the back of your neck. You glance over your shoulder, and you see the coffee shop's customers and staff have followed you outside. Their faces still show no expression as they come walking toward you, but you sense strong emotion rolling off of them. Not hostility exactly, but an intensity, one that's growing.

You take your keys out of your pants pocket and thumb the remote to unlock your car. You feel an impulse to run to the Lexus, but you restrain yourself. Partially because you don't want to look as if you're overreacting, but mostly because you fear than any sudden movement you make will set the crowd off, and they'll come racing toward you en masse, their eerie composure broken as they howl for your blood.

As you reach you car and open the driver's side door, you think this is ridiculous. There's no reason for you to flee. All you did was have an epiphany, and what you now know is a wonderful thing. A beautiful thing. Why would anyone wish you harm for that?

You turn toward the crowd and see they're much closer now, and while they haven't started running yet, they're walking much faster.

You grope for words to explain what you now know, and what comes out of your mouth is a simple, succinct phrase.

"Thou art God," you say.

The crowd stops. They look at you for a long moment, and then they speak more or less in unison.

"We know – now. And that's the problem."

They start moving forward again, and fear surges in your gut. You healed the woman in the brown coat, and with your newfound abilities, you could defend yourself from the crowd if necessary. Then again, if they truly know what you know, can do what you can do . . .

You drop your laptop to the ground, and as soon as if leaves your hand, it leaves your thoughts. Work is the farthest thing from your mind right now. You get in the car, slam the door, jam the key in the ignition, and turn it. The engine rumbles to life as the crowd surges forward, and you can feel their power building, like the electric charge in the air before a thunderstorm. You put the Lexus in reverse, back out of your space, slam it into drive, and peel out of there. You look in the rearview mirror as you race away, and you see the crowd following at a run. But they don't follow for long. By ones and twos they stop running until they're all just standing still again, watching you go with their impassive gazes.

As you pull onto the street, you release a shaky breath, and you struggle to understand what just happened. A universe of new information churns in your mind, but your brain is still that of an ordinary human, and trying to sift through the infinite data is like trying to drink an ocean through a straw. You drive randomly, heading in the general direction of your office, but not really intending to return to work today, and probably not ever. You think back to what the crowd said in its single voice.

We know – now. That's the problem.

How could knowing the truth be a bad thing? You know the answer to the question human beings have been grappling with since they first became capable of conceiving the notion that there might be something bigger than themselves, something more to existence than simple survival and procreation. You understand the true nature of God.

How it happened, why it happened, you don't know. Sometimes it just does. You should feel exhilarated, ecstatic, should want to share the good news with the entire world. But if the crowd back at the coffee shop is any indication, people don't want to know. And it seems that they don't want *you* to know, either. But it's not like you told them, not like you *made* them know. You just healed the woman in the brown coat, and when you went back inside, they just knew – as if their mere proximity to your little miracle was enough to jumpstart their own epiphanies, But if that's the case, why did they react so differently than you? They didn't stand up and go off in search of miracles to perform. They came after you, and who knows what they would've done if they'd caught you?

Actually, you have a pretty good idea what they'd have done: nail you to the nearest tree. It's not like it hasn't happened before. But *why?*

You're so caught up in your thoughts that you don't realize you're approaching a stoplight. The light's red and there's a line of vehicles waiting for it to turn green. The last car in line is a red Volkswagen with a personalized plate that reads LUVBUG1. You come flying up on it way too fast, and when you realize what's about to happen, it's too late. You stomp on the brake but although your tires squeal as they attempt to grip the asphalt, you slam into the back of the VW with undiminished speed.

Thoughts flash through your mind with such rapidity, it's as if time is standing still. *There's a mother and baby in there,* you think, and you can almost see them. The look of panic-stricken terror on the woman's face, the baby's doughy features scrunched up, mouth opened to wail. Then time starts moving again, and you hear the sickening sound of crumpling metal and shattering glass –

– and then you blink and you're sitting behind LUVBUG1, three feet of space between you, both of your vehicles whole and undamaged. You can picture the mother and her child as clearly as if their car is made of glass. She's texting on her phone, unharmed, unconcerned, her baby in the back, nestled in his car seat, sleeping peacefully. But then the mother looks up, puts the VW in park, tosses her phone onto the passenger seat, and steps out of the car. The baby's awake now, and although he remains buckled in his car seat, his eyes are wide open, his soft features formed into an impassive mask.

You see the mother with your eyes now. She's standing outside her car, looking at you. She's soon joined by the other drivers and passengers in line. Men, women, a few children. You look around, and you see that all traffic in the vicinity has stopped, and everyone is getting out of their vehicles. They're all looking at you, all wearing the same emotionless expression that the people back at the coffee shop wore.

It's quiet, deathly still – and don't you just hate that phrase now? You realize that you can no longer hear the sound of traffic, any traffic, in the area. You stretch out your senses, and you become aware that vehicles for miles in every direction have stopped, and the people inside have stepped out. All of them with strange non-expressions on their faces, all of them facing toward you, and you can feel that, despite the distance that separates you, they can see you just fine. You sense that the number of those touched by knowledge, who now understand the true nature of God, is growing, as if this awareness is contagious, a divine virus passing swiftly from one person to another, ignorance toppling like row upon row of dominoes. How many now know? Hundreds? Thousands?

You fix your attention on the driver of JUNEBUG1, and you speak to her, sensing that whatever she hears, all will hear.

"Its *good* to know. We can do anything, make anything, be anything! Don't you see? We don't have to live like *this* anymore!" You slap your hand against your chest for emphasis. "We don't have to be imprisoned in cages of meat. We can be free. Truly, absolutely *free*."

The woman stops and regards you for a moment. When she speaks, she speaks alone, but you know she's speaking for all of them, all the people who've gotten out of their vehicles, stepped outside of businesses where they were working or shopping. All who, like you, now know.

"Absolute freedom is Hell," she says.

She continues toward you, as does everyone else, and they all speak now, saying a single word in unison, repeating it over and over as they come.

"Forget . . . forget . . . forget . . ."

A warm flush of panic washes over you. You might be God – or part of God, at least – but so is every one of *them*. You don't see how can can hope to stand against them, not all of them, not as long as they act as One, and your reaction to this realization is far more human than godlike.

You run.

You dash across the street into the parking lot of a shopping center. There's a Wal-Mart, a Petsmart, a Subway, and a half dozen other businesses. And from each one people walk forth, exiting the buildings in droves, all of them expressionless, all heading toward you. People who were getting into or out of their vehicles as they went about their errands have – like the drivers on the road – abandoned their cars and minivans and joined the throng. Men, women, children, all ages and ethnicities, united in their single-minded drive to reach you. All speaking at normal volume, all repeating the exhortation for you to forget, forget, forget, their combined voices making the word into an echoing refrain that seems loud enough to shake the very foundations of the world.

You stop in the middle of the lot. You're surrounded. You have nowhere to go, and the others keep coming, not running, for they have no need to. The first of them will reach you in mere moments.

The knowing *is* like a disease, you realize. You're the carrier, and the others are like antibodies, God's immune system activated and ready to do battle. Unless *they're* the disease and you're the cure. You were the first to know, and the only one who believes this to be good and right. Maybe it's up to you to help the others, to make the scales drop from their eyes so they not only know the truth about God, but so they can see that truth for the wondrous gift it is.

But how can you accomplish this before the others get hold of you, before they force you to forget – one way or the other – and afterward, presumably, choose to forget themselves?

The circle of chanting others closes in around you, and those at the forefront raise hands and reach for you, the tips of their fingers only a few feet away now and coming closer with each passing second.

"Forget . . . forget . . . forget . . ."

Then it comes to you. So far, only a relative handful of people on the planet have been "infected" by the knowing. But what if there was a critical mass of awareness on Earth? What if *everyone* knew?

You close your eyes, reach out with your mind, and you broadcast a thought to every human throughout the world.

Thou art God.

Silence. No one speaks, no one moves.

You open your eyes.

Everyone is smiling, their gazes bright with newfound understanding. They turn to one another and begin speaking again, voices jubilant as they exchange greetings.

"Thou art God!"

Across the world, in myriad languages, each and every human expresses the same sentiment, acknowledging what they now know in the deepest parts of their being to be true. Those closest to you catch your eye and give you a nod, as if to say thank you. Your heart soars with joy, and you think that a new day is dawning for creation, that God – once slumbering, fragmented, incomplete – is now fully awake and whole again. *What wonders will we work together*? you ask yourself. *What sort of paradise will we make of the universe?*

And as if the thought gives birth to the action, all of existence suddenly ceases to be, collapsing with all the rapidity of a bubble no longer able to sustain itself. One instant it's there, the next gone. Everything becomes Onething, and that Onething is You.

You dwell in light . . . *are* light: pristine, pure, perfect, endless. You're complete for the first time in untold billions of years, and now that you are no longer bound by the physical limitations of a single human mind, you truly know everything. And in that knowing, you remember. Remember what it was like to be All, to be One . . .

To be alone.

And perfection, not to put too fine a point on it, is dull. Without limitations, without need, without variety, how can there be new ideas, new thoughts, new sensations, new experiences of any kind? Even God wants to grow, and you know you can't do it like this.

You remember when you were separate, just a single human who'd had an epiphany, and you remember what that one woman – the owner of JUNEBUG1 – said to you.

Knowing is Hell.

Indeed it is. But you can fix that. It's simple, really. All you have to do, as the others tried to tell you, is forget. And once again, you speak the same words you did at the Beginning.

Let there be dark.

* * * * *

You're working on your laptop at a window-side table in a downtown coffee shop, but this time, you don't look up, and so you don't see the woman in the brown coat pass by outside. You just keep typing, sipping coffee to keep yourself awake, and although you aren't exactly thrilled to be doing mindless scut work, you tell yourself that really, it's not so bad a life.

Not so bad at all.

Bone Whispers

KEVIN BLANCMORE SLOWED as he approached the old graveyard. It had been almost forty years since he'd been here last, and the place looked as if it hadn't changed in the slightest during that time. It was not a thought that provided comfort.

Kevin braked and pulled his Nissan Altima – on which he was two payments behind, not that it mattered anymore – onto the side of the road in front of the graveyard's black wrought-iron gate. There was no parking lot – the graveyard predated the road by nearly a century, he guessed – and Kevin scarcely had enough room to get his car off the road. There wasn't a lot of traffic out here in the country, and he doubted he'd have to worry about someone coming along too fast, not seeing his car, and broadsiding the damned thing. But even if they did, what did he care?

Kevin turned off the engine and pulled the keys out of the ignition, but instead of getting out of his vehicle right away, he sat for a moment, staring out the windshield and listening to the car's engine tick as it began to cool. He wasn't sitting there because he was afraid, though he supposed he had good reason to be. And he wasn't nervous, not even a little. He felt nothing, and that was the reason he sat behind the wheel of his car, hesitating. Considering what he had come here to do, or more to the point, to *find*, he should feel something. A moment like this . . . well, it was why the word *momentous* had been created, wasn't it? It was potentially life-altering in the profoundest of ways and should be marked as such, if only inside his own heart. But just because he was aware that he should feel something didn't mean he would. It seemed he was as dead inside as any of the graveyard's residents, and all that remained was for the rest of him to catch up.

He unlocked the driver's side door and climbed out of the car.

The weather in southwest Ohio in early June could range from cool and mild to hot and sweltering. But that was Ohio, where the weather changed as often as people's minds. Unfortunately for Kevin, it felt more like mid-August, the air steamy, thick and damp. Even worse, he still had on the suit he'd worn for Nancy's graduation, and the instant he emerged from the Altima's air-conditioned environment, sweat began beading on his forehead and pooling beneath his armpits. He considered leaving his jacket and tie in the car and rolling up his shirt sleeves, but even though he would be more physically comfortable, he decided against it. A momentous moment like this called for a certain level of formality, so the suit would stay on and he'd just have to endure the discomfort. He could do that; after all, he'd had a lot of practice. An entire lifetime's worth it seemed sometimes.

Let's have a pity party for Kevvy-wevvy, he thought. *One, two, three – awwwww!*

Half amused and half disgusted at himself, Kevin walked across the uneven grass that covered the small strip of land in front of the graveyard – *Looks like the county's behind in their mowing* – and stepped up to the gate. The graveyard was enclosed by a salmon-colored brick wall that measured five feet high, nine feet on either side of the gate and at the wall's four corners where conical black-brick turrets pointed skyward. Kevin thought the graveyard's designer must've been going for a somber yet dignified effect, and he couldn't say the man had missed. The gate was in fact a pair, held shut by an ancient rusted padlock. Not locked, though. The padlock hung open on the gate, just as it had done during Kevin's childhood. He wouldn't have been surprised to learn that the padlock rested in the same exact position that it had then, untouched by hands all these long decades. Human hands, anyway.

A metal plaque was bolted on the turret to the right of the entrance, its surface dingy, the letters worn some but still legible.

QUAKER BRANCH MEMORIAL BURIAL GROUND
EST. 1957.

Kevin knew the date referred to the construction of the wall. The graveyard itself was much older.

He took hold of one of the gate's bars, careful to grip a section where the black paint hadn't flaked off too much – *Didn't come all the way here to get tetanus,* he thought, almost smiling – and pushed. The gate resisted at first, the bottom edge digging into the ground, and he gave it a bit more muscle. Finally, the gate budged a few feet, giving him enough space to slide through, even with his less-than-modest gut. The gate hadn't made a sound when it moved, no slow creaking or harsh grinding, and Kevin recalled that it had been similarly silent the last time he was here. Now, just like then, he was vaguely disappointed. A proper cemetery gate should open with some manner of sinister sound to establish the appropriate atmosphere.

Once inside, he paused to look around. Large oak and elm trees bordered the outside of the graveyard, making it impossible to see what, if anything, lay beyond, There were no trees inside, no bushes, no greenery of any kind save grass. Just as outside, the grass was uneven, almost a foot high in some places, in others trimmed so close to the ground that bare patches of dry earth peeked through. There were a good number of gravestones, over a hundred, he estimated, and they were roughly divided into two even sections. On his left were the newer stones, dating from around the time the outer wall had been constructed. They were larger, more varied in type, and the legends engraved upon them were still readable. To Kevin's right was what he thought of as the old section. Here the headstones were much smaller, set closer together, and more uniform in shape. They were colored either stony gray or chalk-white, their edges softened by the passage of one season after another and the elements' less-than-tender ministrations. Kevin knew from previous experience that the inscriptions – those that remained legible, that is – were both simpler and somehow more elegant than those in the newer section. WILHEMINA MOTE, B. 1834, D. 1867. JACOB HOBBLIT, B. 1856, D. 1859. The birth and death dates were almost always closer together in that section, as well. Sometimes too close.

Past the newer section, nestled against the graveyard's east wall, sat a simple wooden building, its sides gray, boards fraying in places as if the structure had been fashioned from cloth instead of wood. Two windows were visible from this angle, a door set between them, a small plaque affixed to the right of the door. Kevin couldn't make out the words from where he stood, but he didn't need to. He knew what the plaque said, could recite it from memory. THIS BUILDING IS A REPLICA OF A QUAKER MEETING HOUSE THAT STOOD ACROSS THE STREET FROM 1803 TO 1849. ERECTED BY THE BOY SCOUTS OF AMERICA, ASH CREEK TROOP, 1962.

The plaque didn't mention the fate of the original meeting house, and Kevin had always wondered what had happened to it. Had it burned down? Or simply grown old and fallen apart? *Happens to the best of us,* he thought. *The worst of us, too.* He also wondered why the scouts had chosen to reconstruct it. It seemed like a rather morbid project to Kevin, but then he'd never been a boy scout. Maybe it had been a jolly good time for those young upstanding citizens-to-be. Or maybe it had just been one more damn thing to do to earn another meaningless badge.

Looking at the meeting house – the *replica*, he reminded himself – Kevin experienced a flash of memory, so intense and visceral, for an instant it was as if he'd traveled back in time forty years. He was inside the meeting house, sitting with his back against the door, tears streaming down his cheeks. On the other side of the door was an excited snuffling accompanied by the sound of claws scratching against wood. From time to time there came a *thump*, both felt and heard, as something heavy shoved its body against the door in an attempt to force it open. And of course there were the sounds of his sobs and his plaintive whispered pleas. *Go away, please go away . . .*

Kevin gave his head a single sharp shake to dispel the memory, but while it retreated, it didn't go far. He felt moisture on his face, and he reached up and wiped it away, telling himself that it was only sweat and almost believing it.

The memory reminded him, as if he needed to be reminded, that there was one part of the graveyard he had up to this point assiduously avoided looking at: straight down the middle, back against the south wall. It wouldn't here now, not after all this time. So there was no reason not to look, right?

But the hole was still there, looking just as large as he remembered it. A three-foot circumference around which were scattered a number of old broken headstones, looking as if at some point they'd been flung forth from the hole and allowed to lay where they landed. And next to hole, sitting back on its hind legs and gnawing a length of bone held clutched in its front paws, was a groundhog the size of a sheep. The creature looked at Kevin with its glossy black eyes, completely unfazed by the human's presence, regarding him impassively as it chewed on the bone, its teeth making soft *shhh-shhh-shhh* sounds.

Up to this moment the air had been still, but now a breeze moved through the graveyard, causing the branches in the trees that surrounded the outer walls to sway. The soft rustling of their leaves sounded to Kevin's ears like a chorus of whispering voices all saying the same thing.

Welcome back.

* * * * *

Kevin pedaled his bike faster, not caring that he couldn't see the road clearly through the tears in his eyes. Maybe if he went fast enough, the wind he kicked up would dry them. Or maybe he'd end up getting creamed by a car because his vision was blurred. Either way would be fine with him right now.

Houses flashed past: trees in the yards, cars in the driveways. Ranches, two stories . . the same sort of homes that you'd find in town, except there was more space between them out here – sometimes as much as an acre or two. Though Kevin technically lived in the country, it was still close enough to town that there weren't many farms around, certainly none within a mile or so. It was late August and he'd be starting fourth grade next week, not that he cared. He'd used to look forward to the beginning of the school year, but not anymore. Now he didn't look forward to anything.

The wind blowing against his face was hot and dry, and while it blew the tears from his eyes, its heat stung his face. He wondered if he was sunburnt. Probably, he figured. He'd been out long enough. He couldn't decide whether he liked the pain, couldn't decide whether to keep feeling it or ignore it. He decided to worry about it later.

He'd been out riding since breakfast, and his Yellow Submarine t-shirt was soaked with sweat and clung to his scrawny body like it was glued to him. His shorts were damp too, and he could imagine another kid seeing him, calling out, "Hey, did you pee your pants?" and then bursting out with mocking laughter. Kevin would have to toss his clothes into the washer whenever he finally got home. He had to wash all his clothes, his sheets and pillow cases, too. And he had to do the dishes, both his and his mother's. If he didn't, the sink would become so full that cups and plates would slide off the mound and crash to the kitchen floor.

He wondered if his mother had any idea he'd been out this long, and if she did, was she worried? Not that she'd get out of her chair, let alone leave the house, if she was. Sometimes Kevin wondered what would happen if the house caught on fire. Would his mom just keep sitting in that old chair of hers, staring at the TV even after the air had become so filled with smoke that the screen was no longer visible? Would she sit there while the flames drew ever closer and began licking at her flesh? Maybe.

She hadn't liked leaving the house when Dad was alive, but he usually had been able to coax her outside. But now . . .

Kevin didn't want to think about *now*, so he pedaled faster and concentrated on the stinging wind biting into his face.

Eventually he realized he was hungry, and he figured he might as well go home and make himself some lunch. He didn't care about food anymore; it was all so much tasteless mush to chew and swallow. But if he didn't eat, he'd become so hungry that he wouldn't be able to ignore his growling stomach, shaking hands, and throbbing head. It was easier to just eat and get it done with so he could avoid the annoyance. He'd ridden that day without any particular destination, just traveling up and down country roads, riding just to ride, pedaling so he wouldn't have to think or feel. But he was on Jay Road now, only about a mile from his house. He could be home in only a few minutes – if he took the shortest route. Unfortunately, that would be riding past the old Quaker graveyard, and Kevin wasn't sure he wanted to do that.

He'd been to the graveyard a few times before, but always with his father, never alone. It had seemed scary back then, but because he was with his dad, it was fun-scary, not scary-scary. But since his father died – almost a year ago, now, though it sometimes seemed to Kevin to be much longer – he hadn't wanted anything to do with graveyards and cemeteries, or anything else that related to death in any way. But if he wanted to get home fast, he'd have to go past Quaker Branch.

He almost took the long way. But it *had* been almost a year since his dad had succumbed to lung cancer, and Kevin *was* going to be in fourth grade, was practically a fourth-grader already. He figured it was time he started acting his age. He bet when Dad was a kid, he wouldn't have been afraid to ride past the graveyard.

That settled the matter. Kevin turned off Jay Road onto Hoke. His road – Culver – branched off from Hoke . . . right after the graveyard. He thought about pedaling his ass off and flying by the graveyard at super-speed, but if he did that he'd zoom right past Culver. There was no way he'd make the turn going fast; he'd end up in a ditch or sprawled on the street, scraped up and bleeding. He didn't care if he got hurt, but if he were injured, he'd have to clean and dress his own wounds, and he didn't feel like doing all that work. So he slowed as he drew near Quaker Branch, telling himself to keep his gaze fixed straight ahead and not look as he went past. But the graveyard was on his right, and it was set so close to the road that it was hard not to look. And there were memories within those walls . . . memories of him and his dad. In the end, he couldn't *not* look.

When he did, he braked to a stop in front of the black gate without being aware he was doing so. Through the gate's bars, on the far side of the graveyard, a large animal sat back on its haunches, its round head turned toward Kevin, wet black eyes staring at him. Its fur was brownish-gray shot through with coarse silver-white hairs, and it held something in its forelegs . . . something curved, white and smooth. At first Kevin thought it was a giant rat – the creature looked to be three feet tall, if not larger – and it was plump, almost round as a beach ball.

Kevin's imagination whispered through his mind. *You know how it got so fat, don't you? It's got tunnels all through the graveyard. It's broken into the graves, gnawed through the coffins, and –*

Kevin clamped down on those thoughts, clamped down hard. It wasn't a rat, it couldn't be. Rats didn't get that big . . . did they?

The creature, whatever it was, continued sitting there and staring at him, completely motionless. Kevin might have thought the animal was some kind of statue, or maybe stuffed and mounted by a taxidermist, so still was it. But despite the absence of movement, he knew it was alive. He could feel intelligence looking out at him from those wet-black eyes, gauging, judging . . .

Then Kevin realized what it was that he was looking at. Not a rat, but a groundhog. Still a damned big one, though.

So it's a groundhog, his imagination said. *It still could've dug tunnels in the graveyard, still could be feeding here. Look at what it's holding . . . does that look like a rib to you?*

The idea was ridiculous. Groundhogs didn't eat meat . . . did they? Kevin wished his dad were here. He'd know. More, he'd tell Kevin that the groundhog had probably just burrowed its way underneath the wall around the graveyard, and or maybe squeezed its furry bulk between the bars of the gate. It was just curious, just exploring. It didn't live here, didn't have tunnels here, and it certainly wasn't eating the remains of people, some of whom had been dead for more than a century. But Dad wasn't here to tell Kevin these things, and for some reason, they didn't sound as convincing when Kevin told them to himself.

The groundhog continued sitting and staring, but now it began to move. It brought the smooth white curved thing it held toward its mouth and – eyes still fixed on Kevin – began to chew on one splintered end. Even though the groundhog was at least two hundred feet away, Kevin could hear the sounds it made as it chewed as clearly as if it were sitting right next to him. Soft *shh-shh-shh* sounds, almost like someone brushing their teeth.

It wasn't a bone, couldn't be!

Before he realized he was doing so, Kevin started yelling at the groundhog.

"Get out of here! Go!"

He expected the animal to startle, drop the bone, and go running off in the galumphing-undulating way groundhogs had when they really wanted to move. But this groundhog just continued to sit, stare, and chew.

Shh-shh-shh, shh-shh-shh, shh-shh-shh . . .

Kevin opened his mouth to yell again, but before he could, the groundhog stopped chewing. It looked at Kevin for a long moment, and Kevin looked back, unable to tear his gaze away from the strange animal. And then the groundhog dropped the bone – if that's what it was – then fell forward onto all fours and began slowly coming toward Kevin.

Kevin's trance broke then, and he lifted his feet off the ground, jammed them onto the pedals, and got the hell out of there as fast as he could. He pedaled madly and by the time he reached his house, sweat dripped off of him like rainwater, and while he had no memory of doing so, he realized he must've taken the corner turn onto his road at full speed and not wrecked somehow. He remembered something his father had once told him.

It's amazing what people can do when they're motivated, Kevin.

"No shit," Kevin whispered.

* * * * *

Kevin went out riding again after the first day of fourth grade. He didn't even bother going into the house after he got off the school bus. He just dropped his book bag onto the front porch, hopped on his bike, and took off down the driveway. He doubted his mother would know that he'd gotten home, let alone that he'd immediately left, and even if she did, he didn't care.

Kevin didn't have many friends, and none of them were in his class this year. He'd seen Mike Todd and Steve Tomlinson out on the playground at recess, and while he'd been tempted to tell them about the groundhog in the graveyard, for some reason he hadn't. It wasn't that he feared they wouldn't believe him – although Steve could be skeptical at times. It just felt like he should keep the experience to himself, as if what had happened was private, just between him and the groundhog.

He hadn't been able to stop thinking about the giant groundhog, kept hearing the sound of the creature gnawing on its bone, kept seeing it coming toward him across the graveyard grounds . . . The whole thing had been scary, sure, and he was scared now as he pedaled down Culver Road toward Hoke and the Quaker Branch Memorial Burial Ground. But he felt something else, too, something he hadn't felt in a long time: hope.

He remembered staying up one Saturday with his dad about six months ago to watch the late-night horror show, Shock Theatre hosted by Dr. Creep. They watched on the TV down in the basement because Mom was watching another movie upstairs, and she didn't want to change the channel. But that was okay. Kevin liked being down in the basement, alone with his dad, just the two of them. The film that evening had been *Thirteen Ghosts* with Vincent Price, and while Kevin didn't remember much of the story, he'd never forgot one scene where a skeleton came out of a pool to stalk a pretty blond woman in a nightgown.

During a commercial, Kevin had turned to his dad. "I don't like ghosts. They're creepy."

His dad put his arm around Kevin's shoulders and gave his son a gentle squeeze. "Yeah, that skeleton was scary, huh? But you know, I think there's something nice about ghosts, too. At least, about the idea of them. If you ever saw one, then you'd know that spirits were real, and that there's something more to life than just physical existence."

Kevin hadn't had any idea what his father was talking about, so he didn't say anything. But he understood now that his dad had already been sick and knew that he was going to die. He also understood what his father had been talking about. He didn't know if there was anything like a heaven for him to go to once he was gone. He'd been scared.

That was why Kevin hadn't been able to stop thinking about the groundhog. The damned thing was weird, no doubt about that, but if it was supernatural somehow, that meant that there was more to life than most people thought, that magical things could happen. The groundhog wasn't a good thing, Kevin was sure of that, but if bad magical things were real, good ones had to be too, right? He remembered something else his father had once said.

Where's there's shadow, there has to be light.

Kevin was headed back to the graveyard to see if he could find that light, even just a hint of it. Because if he could . . . it meant that his father was maybe still alive somewhere, and not just a body sealed inside a coffin covered with dirt.

This time when Kevin reached the graveyard gate, he put down his bike's kickstand and climbed off. He walked up to the gate, shivering despite the temperature. He expected to see the groundhog come running toward him across the uneven grass, launch itself at the gate, claws scrabbling in the air as it tried to grab hold of him, curved flat teeth gnashing, eager to take a chunk out of his skin, tear away flesh to reveal the gleaming white bone beneath. Hard, fresh, young bone, so good for gnawing . . .

But there was nothing. The graveyard was empty.

For a moment Kevin considered getting back on his bike and leaving. Instead, he pushed open the gate, which made no sound as it moved, and walked inside. He expected to experience some sort of eerie feeling – a chill rippling down his spine, maybe a sense that he was being watched. But he felt nothing beyond the heat of the day and a slight breeze that moved the air around without cooling things off. Well, he was here. Might as well take a look.

He started walking toward the spot where he'd seen the groundhog sitting.

He saw the hole long before he reached it. It was so big, he was surprised he hadn't seen it from the road. It was located only a few feet from the graveyard's southern wall, and the ground here was mostly bare, with only patches of dry, dead grass. The edges of the hole were rounded and worn smooth from years of use. How old could the groundhog be? Kevin had looked up groundhogs in an encyclopedia at the school library, and according to what he'd read, the animals usually lived two to three years in the wild, but they could live as much as six years. But somehow the hole looked older, much older, as if it had predated the burial ground, a natural formation that had been here since long before any humans had ever set foot upon the continent. It was a crazy thought, of course, but he couldn't shake it.

Kevin walked up to the edge of the hole and peered down. It measured nearly three feet across, he estimated, and there was no telling how far down it went. He couldn't see further than a few inches down. After that, the dry earth of its walls gave way to inky shadow that seemed so thick Kevin wondered if a beam of direct light would penetrate it. He wished he'd thought to bring a flashlight. Then he could've checked for himself. He was thinking about riding home to get one when he felt cool air emanate from the hole. It wasn't a breeze, exactly; more like air leisurely wafting forth from somewhere far away. It was cool and musty-smelling, kind of like a basement but more so. A basement built deep within the earth. Miles deep. Miles *upon* miles. A soft sound accompanied the air, kind of like the hush of ocean waves breaking on a distant shore. No, more like the whispering of voices. Hundreds, maybe thousands. So soft that Kevin could almost but not quite make out the words.

He lost track of time as he stood there, looking down into the darkness, listening to the voices as they continued whispering, more urgent now, as if they were desperate to impart a message to him, but whatever it was, he wasn't getting it. Maybe if he stepped closer to the hole, leaned down, cocked his head to the side so that his ear was nearer the source of the whispering . . .

He got as far as sliding one foot forward when he heard a rustling in the grass off to this right. He snapped out of his trance and turned in time to see the giant groundhog running toward him. He had no idea where the creature had been hiding, but that wasn't important now. All that mattered was the damned thing was attacking. The voices grew louder then, and Kevin thought he might have been able to make out what they were saying, but he was too terrified by the creature coming toward him. He screamed, his voice drowning out the whispers, and he whirled around and ran toward the Quaker meeting house. He didn't look back to see if the groundhog pursued. He didn't have to.

He reached the house, grabbed the metal handle bolted to the front door, and prayed it was unlocked. It was. He ran inside, slammed the door shut behind him, and dropped to the floor. He pressed his back against the door just as the groundhog slammed into the other side with a heavy thump. Kevin sat there, listening as the groundhog began scratching at the wood, tears streaming down his face, and he begged the creature to go away and leave him alone. But the scratching didn't stop. It continued and on and . . .

* * * * *

Adult Kevin walked up to the groundhog. The damned thing was even larger than he remembered. He didn't question whether it was the same creature. Of course it was. The beast sat only a couple feet from its lair. The hole looked the same as it had the last time he'd seen it, with the exception of the headstones scattered about. After he'd escaped the groundhog by breaking one of the meeting house's windows, climbing through, and running like hell for his bike, Kevin had returned to the graveyard one last time. He'd knocked down some of the older, smaller headstones – ones he felt confident he could carry – and brought them over to the hole. He tossed them inside, wedging them into the hole, stomping on them to pack them down tight. He'd known it wouldn't stop the creature, which he'd decided might *look* like a groundhog but was undoubtedly something else, but he had to do it, if for no other reason than he could pretend that he'd stopped the thing. He'd expected the beast to come after him at any moment, but the groundhog didn't show, and he'd left the graveyard safely, telling himself that he'd sealed the creature off from the world and no one need ever fear it again. He'd known even then that it was bullshit, but it was bullshit he needed to believe.

Now, four decades later, he walked up to the groundhog and crouched in a squatting position in front of it. The creature made no move against him, nor did it seemed fearful. It continued gnawing on its bone as it regarded him with its wet black stare. Kevin stared back, gazing deep into the darkness within those eyes, and for a few moments he did nothing more. But eventually he began speaking in a soft, tired voice.

"My daughter Nancy graduated high school today. I didn't stay for her party, though. I . . . Her mother and I divorced when she was little, and Nancy's been uncomfortable around me ever since. Can't say as I blame her. I inherited my mother's less-than-sunny disposition, and I've battled depression all my life. And I don't think I ever recovered from the trauma of losing my father so young. At least, that's what all the therapists I've seen over the years tell me. It's been so hard for me. I can barely bring myself to talk with other people and, I can barely get out of bed in the morning. Medicine doesn't help. Just makes me groggier. But that's not the worst of it. A few months ago, I found out that I inherited something from my father, too. His cancer."

The groundhog remained motionless, but it stopped chewing the bone, and Kevin had the impression that it was paying attention to him. More, he had the feeling that it understood his words.

"No one knows. I didn't tell anyone at work. Didn't tell my ex-wife or Nancy. I wasn't planning on doing anything about it.

Doctor says there's nothing *to* do. But as I was driving home from the graduation ceremony, I passed the highway exit for my hometown and remembered this place. Remembered you. So I turned around, got off the highway, and came here."

The groundhog cocked its head slightly to one side.

"To tell you the truth, I'm not really sure why I came here. Maybe I'm hoping that this time I'll finally find out whether there's anything beyond this life or not. Or maybe I'm just hoping that you'll make a fast end of me and spare me weeks of painfully withering away to nothing in hospice." He paused. "I guess the real reason I'm here comes down to one thing: I've got nowhere else to go."

The groundhog stared at him for a long time and Kevin stared back, sweat rolling down the sides of his face and the back of his neck. He wondered if he'd try to run this time if the groundhog attacked, or if he'd just stand here and let the creature do what it would to him.

Finally, the groundhog dropped the bone to the grass and fell forward onto all fours. Kevin's stomach clenched in anticipation of the beast running toward him, but he held his ground. Whatever was to come within the next few seconds, Kevin had at least answered one question for himself: he wasn't going to run.

The groundhog looked at him a moment longer, as if it were trying to come to decision of its own. Then it slowly turned away and began walking toward its hole. When it reached the edge, it stopped and turned back to look at Kevin, and then it crawled in, its large, furry body sliding into the opening with ease. And then it was gone.

Kevin stood there for a moment, trying to understand what had just happened. When he'd been a child, the groundhog had attacked, clearly trying to kill him. But this time it hadn't displayed even a hint of aggression. He was sure it was the same creature, no matter how impossible that might be, so why hadn't it come after him this time? Was he too large to be considered prey now? Too old? And then it came to him. It was neither of those things. The creature hadn't attacked him because there was no reason to. He was for all intents and purposes already dead, both inside and out. He was no longer an intruder to be run off. He belonged here.

Kevin walked over to the edge of the hole – which was larger now, to accommodate the groundhog's increased bulk – and peered into the darkness within. He felt the same cool air on his face as he had when he was ten, smelled the same basementy odor, heard the same soft whispers. Only this time, he understood their message clearly. It was an invitation.

Kevin thought it over for a moment, then he removed his suit jacket, folded it neatly, and lay it on the ground next to the hole. Then he got down on his hands and knees and followed the groundhog into darkness. As he made his descent – fingers clawing moist soil, hard-shelled insects scuttling through his sweaty hair and beginning to crawl beneath his damp clothing – Kevin realized that his father had been wrong about one thing. Where there was shadow, there wasn't always light.

Sometimes there was just deeper shadow.

Some Dark Hope

***HE LIES ON THE BED**, writing in discomfort as cold, greedy-hungry hands slide over the mounds of his sweaty naked flesh. The sheets beneath him are stained with irregular splotches of perspiration, and he sees nostrils flare as those gathered around the bed inhale the stink of sweat both old and new, He hears them sigh in contentment, sees them lick their lips in anticipation.*

They know he's almost ready.

They rub faster, kneading his fat rolls as if he were a giant mound of dough they're trying to shape before baking. He feels their fingernails dig into his pale snail-belly skin, and he draws in a hiss of breath. It won't be much longer, just a . . . few seconds . . . more . . .

* * * * *

Greg saw her walking on the side of the road, painted pale yellow-white in the wash of his headlights. He took his foot off the accelerator, and as his VW began to slow, he wondered if he was going to find the courage to stop or if he'd just coast on by. His heart thudded in his chest with flabby wet squlerches, and cold sweat formed beneath his sagging man-boobs. His moved his foot over the brake, hesitated for a half-second, then slowly began to press downward.

I'm doing it, I'm actually doing it!

She stopped and turned around to face him as he pulled the VW onto the gravel shoulder, tiny rocks pinging and popping beneath the tires. She wore jeans and a long-sleeved pink pullover, cut low to expose the smooth white flesh between the hollow of her throat and the beginnings of her smallish breasts. She was slim, with straight blond hair that hung just past her shoulders. No makeup; that surprised him, though he wasn't sure why. It was mid-April, and a bit too chilly to be walking without a jacket – especially at night.

Probably wants to show off her shape, he thought. *A working girl's got to advertise, right?*

Greg stopped and put the Volkswagen in park, but he didn't switch off the headlights. She stood looking at him for a moment, and though she couldn't possibly have made out his features given the way the lights were shining in her face, he had the impression that she was gazing deeply into his eyes and taking his measure. He didn't like the feeling, and he almost put the car back in drive and pulled away, but then she was walking toward his passenger-side window, and he knew it was too late to leave.

She bent down and tapped on the window with her index finger, smiling as she did. There was no warmth in that smile, but no coldness either. The expression was completely devoid of emotional content, like the flexing of an elbow joint or knee, a purely physical action and nothing more.

He thumbed the switch to lower the window. Cool air wafted in, carrying with it the sounds of passing cars and the scent of a perfume he didn't recognize. It reminded him of honeysuckle, with an unpleasant underlying odor of rotting vegetable matter. *Eau de* pond scum.

Even so, the smell of it made his dick twitch.

"How you doin' tonight, Sugar?"

The words were clichéd, but they sounded natural and unforced coming from her, and the way she said *Sugar* made it sound as if it was his name rather than a generic endearment, like he was a jazz musician or a famous athlete: Greg "Sugar" Lochte.

His mouth felt as if it were stuffed full of rusty brillo pads, and he feared he wasn't going to be able to get a reply out. But when he spoke, he was surprised how relaxed he sounded. Almost suave, really.

"I'm all right. How's your evening going?"

"Can't complain. I'm a little late for work, though. I could use a ride – *if* you've got the time, that is."

Greg couldn't believe it – the stories were true.

"I've got nothing *but* time." He resisted calling her *Baby*; he didn't think there was any way he could pull it off without sounding like a jerk. His hand was trembling so much, it took him two tries to unlock the car doors. He hoped she didn't notice.

"Hop in."

She slid inside and closed the door behind her with a hollow chunk.

She showed her teeth with another of her not-quite-smiles. "Let's roll, Sugar. South Dixie Avenue."

"Yes, ma'am." He almost added, *You didn't have to tell me; I know where we're going.* He put the VW in drive, signaled, and then pulled off the shoulder, all four tires kicking up sprays of gravel.

Greg couldn't believe it; he'd just picked up the Union Street Whore.

* * * * *

"I'm serious, man. No shit. Every night she starts walking on Union Street, hoping that some guy is gonna drive by, see her, stop and offer to give her a ride. If you take her all the way downtown to Dixie Avenue – that's where the house she works at is, see – she'll give you a blowjob to pay for the ride."

"You're full of it.

"No, he's telling the truth. My cousin told me the same thing."

"Then your cousin is full of it, too."

Greg sat alone at a table in the break room, eating a soggy tuna fish sandwich he'd gotten from the vending machine. He'd been working at the hospital cafeteria for three years now, and though he knew the other three men who made up the kitchen staff well enough to say hi, he wasn't friends with any of them. They'd never invited him to sit with them, and he'd never asked if he could join them. They might let him, but he knew he wouldn't be welcome, so he just ate alone night after night, kept quiet, and contented himself with eavesdropping on the others' conversations.

Greg swallowed another mushy lump of tuna, washed it down with a gulp of lukewarm Dr. Pepper, and continued to listen while the guys talked.

"You know anyone who ever picked her up?"

Silence.

"You guys are so fucking full of shit."

"If you're so goddamned smart, why don't you drive down Union tonight and see if you can find her?"

"Hell, Jim's so ugly that if he picked her up, she'd probably just give him gas money."

Jim's "fuck you" was drowned out by the laughter of the other two. But Greg wasn't paying attention anymore. He was busy thinking: maybe the stories *were* full of shit. But maybe they weren't.

* * * * *

"I'd like to put you in, Greg, I really would. But the game's just too close to risk it. You understand, right?"

Greg doesn't look up at his coach as he answers. "Sure." He's only ten, but he tries to keep the disappointment he feels out of his voice. He's afraid that if coach knows how he really feels, he'll reconsider his decision and put Greg onto the field, and if that happens, they'll be sure to lose and the other boys will blame him. And the hell of it is, Greg would blame himself too. He's a sucky baseball player – he's fat, slow, uncoordinated, and timid – but he loves the game so much that he keeps pestering his parents to sign him up for little league year after year. Besides, he's still part of the team even if all he gets to do is sit here in the dugout. He can still root for the others, still cheer when one of them throws a runner out or hits a home run. And that's almost as good as playing.

That's what he tells himself, anyway.

* * * * *

Zephyr was a small town in southwestern Ohio, barely a speck on the map. A rundown, lower middle-class bedroom community where the men went shirtless whenever the weather was halfway decent, and the women's ratty jeans weren't conscious fashion statements. Greg knew South Dixie Avenue well because that's where the porn shops and "gentlemen's clubs" were located, establishments that he'd been visiting regularly since turning twenty-one. He was forty-three now, and he'd never touched a girl, let alone had sex with one. He knew he could've paid for it, but he'd always been too afraid. Not so much of catching AIDs or anything, but afraid of how a woman would react when she saw his small penis. Would she laugh? Grimace in disgust? Refuse to take his money because she couldn't bring herself to touch the tiny pencil nub that was his dick? He imagined what she might say.

Christ, did you have some kind of childhood disease or something? Or did you, like, get in a wreck and most of it got cut off?

He'd read in a porn magazine that women were capable of having anal orgasms. *I sure hope so,* he'd thought after finishing the article. *I'll never be able to make a woman cum any other way.*

He glanced sideways at the Union Street Whore. What if *she* laughed? The way the story went, the woman blew anyone who gave her a ride downtown. But what if, once she saw his micro-dick, she changed her mind? He remembered something one of the guys in the break room had said.

Hell, Jim's so ugly that if he picked her up, she'd probably just give him gas money.

Greg hadn't thought much about the comment at the time, but what if that happened to him?

Here's five bucks. Thanks for the ride, Sugar.

"What's your name?"

He'd almost forgotten she was there, and the sound of her voice startled him so much that when he turned to look at her, he jerked the steering wheel, causing the VW to swerve. He corrected in time to avoid slamming into an oncoming SUV, and the driver blasted his horn in anger as he sped by.

"Sorry about that," Greg mumbled. "Guess I'm a little nervous."

"Hello, A Little Nervous. I'm Lourdes." She pronounced it *Lord-Ess*.

At first he didn't know what she was talking about, but then he got the joke. He let out a too-loud laugh, then said, "I'm Greg." He almost told her his last name, but he held back. This wasn't the sort of situation where people exchanged surnames. Hell, he doubted *Lord-Ess* was her real name, but at least it was more original than Trixie D'Lite or Peaches Lamour.

This time her smile seemed more genuine, but there was still a hint of wrongness to it, like the smile painted on a mannequin's face. "What do you do for a living, Greg?"

He'd liked it better when she'd called him *Sugar*. He thought about lying to her, telling her he was an architect or an accountant, but he'd never been good at lying, could never look anyone in the eye when he tried. Besides, if he had a good job, he could afford to be driving her downtown in something classier than a used beetle, and she'd know it.

"I work in the hospital cafeteria. In the kitchen."

"I think men who cook are sexy."

Greg spent more time scrubbing pots and pans than he did cooking, but he didn't feel a need to be *that* truthful. "How about you? What do . . ." He trailed off as he realized what he'd been about to ask.

Lourdes' smile was the real deal this time. "What do *I* do? Sugar, you play your cards right, and it just might be *you*."

* * * * *

"Look at that gut! Jesus Christ, Lotche – lay off the donuts for a change, huh?"

"He's not fat, he's pregnant! He's gonna be the first man in history to have a baby!"

"He's gonna have twins!"

"No way. Triplets!"

The boys laugh, and Greg forces a smile, hoping they'll see that he can take a joke. Hoping that'll end the taunting and he can take a quick shower in peace. He skipped showering last week, and Mr. Storer had lectured him about going back to class smelling like a "hog's ass." If Greg misses showering this week, he'll get detention, and while it would be worth it to avoid listening to the other boys rag him about his body, the grief he'd get when his dad, the ex-marine, found out about it would most definitely NOT be worth it. So Greg walks past the other boys – all of whom have already showered – wearing only a towel around his waist and his forced smile. He intends to hose off fast, just enough get the worst of the sweat off him, then he'll dry quickly and get dressed, hopefully before any of the guys can see –

He feels a tug at his waist, and then a cool draft on his wobbling flesh as his towel is yanked away. Panicked, he reaches down with both hands to cup his genitals, but it's too late. Fresh laughter echoes through the locker room, and then the taunting truly begins in earnest.

"Shrimp-dick!"

"Cocktail weenie!"

"It's the amazing Gerkin Boy!"

Greg tries to hold back the tears, knows what will happen if he cries, but he can't stop himself. Tears run down his flabby cheeks, and the boys' laughter turns to muttered disgust, and they moved toward him, hands curling into fists, eyes filled with loathing.

* * * * *

"This is it," Lourdes said, pointing.

There was nothing about the house to set it apart from the others on this end of South Dixie: a narrow white two-story with flaking paint and black shutters faded gray by decades of sunlight, and a postage-stamp sized yard with scraggly grass that badly needed trimming. The fours cars parked in the driveway – BMW, Cadillac, Lexus, and Saab – didn't match the house's humble appearance, and Greg figured they belonged to customers rather than residents. The girls who worked here must be awfully good at what they did, Greg thought, in order to attract customers with that kind of money. His anticipation of what Lourdes would do to repay him for the ride went up several notches. But he also started to wonder. If Lourdes was *that* good, wouldn't she make more than enough money to afford her own car? Why would she need to bum rides in exchange for blowjobs? *Maybe she gets off on it,* he told himself. Maybe she was a big-time nympho, which was why she worked here in the first place. She couldn't get enough.

Maybe. And maybe this was some kind of scam. Maybe Lourdes let guys pick her up and she had them bring her downtown and then she robbed them, or more likely a couple of her friends – big, *mean* friends – showed up to do the robbing for her, and then they split the money later. No one would tell the cops. You'd have to admit that you picked up a prostitute and besides, getting tricked like that would be too embarrassing. The victims would just go home and never say anything about what happened to them on South Dixie Drive.

Maybe they do worse than rob you, Greg thought. *Maybe they* kill *you* . . . Those cars sitting in the driveway could belong to their latest victims, and they just hadn't gotten around to disposing of them yet. They –

"You can park at the curb."

Greg almost let out a yelp when Lourdes spoke. For an instant he was tempted to hit the gas and speed on past the house. But he told himself he was being stupid, and besides, he *really* wanted that blowjob. He pulled his VW to the curb – almost but not quite too close to a fire hydrant – and put the car in park.

He turned to look at Lourdes, still holding tight to the steering wheel to keep his hands from shaking. He tried to swallow, but his throat felt caked with hot sand and all that he managed to do was make a soft *glurk* sound.

"Thanks for the ride, Greg."

Her tone was friendly, but not *that* friendly, and Greg had the sinking sensation that she was about to reach into the pocket of her jeans and hand him a few dollars for gas money.

"You want to come in for a bit, Sugar? If you don't have anything better to do, that is."

For a moment all Greg could do was stare at Lourdes and replay her words over in his head to make certain he'd heard her right.

"Sure." Getting the word out was the most difficult thing he'd ever done in his life, but somehow he managed. If she was just going to blow him, she could do it right here in the car, but she'd invited him inside, and that meant she wanted to do more, and she both wanted time and privacy to do it. He was so hard he thought he might cum in his pants.

They got out of the VW and Greg followed Lourdes up the driveway to the side of the house. He kept his gaze fixed on her ass the entire way, and though her jeans were slightly baggy in the seat and she didn't sway her hips as she walked, he enjoyed the view just the same. There was no garage, just concrete steps and a black metal handrail that led to a side door. Lourdes mounted the steps and walked up, not bothering to use the handrail, and Greg trailed after her, like an over-eager puppy being brought home for the first time by its new mistress. Lourdes opened the door, and Greg was surprised to see it wasn't locked. What if the cops showed up and just walked on in? He decided the police were probably paid off – in barter if not cash – and so they left the house alone.

They entered a small kitchen, and Greg shut the door behind them. There was a strange scent in the air, one that he couldn't place at first. It wasn't altogether unpleasant, but it seemed out of place, like . . . And then it came to him: it was the smell released when you lifted a large rock and exposed the wet, black soil underneath, tips of earthworms peeking out of the ground, small black beetles scurrying to seek shelter from the light's violation. He wondered if the smell was the result of water damage to the basement, but then he remembered that it hadn't rained for several weeks.

So they're not the greatest housekeepers here, big deal, he thought. But he breathed through his mouth so he wouldn't have to smell the odor anymore and worry about what might really be causing it.

The kitchen was unremarkable. The counters were spotless as was the floor, though the latter's tiles were yellowed and warped with age. There were no dishes in the sink, and the metal basin was shiny and bone-dry, as if no water had ever been run into it. Greg looked at the wooden cupboards and the humming refrigerator, and he wondered that, if he should walk over and begin opening them, whether he'd find anything inside. Or if, like in Mother's Hubbard's house, the cupboards would be bare.

"C'mon, Sugar. Our room is on the second floor, first on the left, just after the stairs." Lourdes reached out and took hold of his hand, and though his fingers were pudgy and his palm coated with clammy sweat, she didn't seem to notice or, if she did, she didn't care. She led him out of the kitchen and down a short corridor to a set of wooden stairs. They saw no one else, but the wet-soil smell was stronger here, and Greg thought he could hear noises coming from upstairs. Muffled voices, furtive movements, cries of pleasure, whispers of pain.

Lourdes continued holding onto Greg's hand as she began walking up the stairs, and though she held onto him gently, he had the sensation that if he tried to turn and flee, her fingers would clamp down tightly onto the skin of his hand, nails digging into the flesh, breaking the skin and causing blood to well forth. He realized then that he wasn't being escorted upstairs so much as taken. Lourdes wanted him to follow her, and she intended to make damned sure he did so.

Greg expected the stairs to creak beneath their feet as they ascended, but they made no noise. The people in the other upstairs rooms were a far different story, however. Their voices and cries increased in volume, almost as if they were aware of a newcomer's approach and were trying to put on a good show for him. There was something wrong about those sounds, though. They didn't resemble expressions of pleasure. A few times Greg had been assigned to deliver meals to patients when they'd been short-staffed at work, and the sounds he heard now reminded him of the pained moaning and demented muttering he'd hear as he pushed the meal cart through the hospital corridors.

He felt fear-sweat pool at the base of his spine, felt his shrimp-dick wilt until it was only a small lump of Play-Doh in his pants, and he knew that if it could, his micro-cock would recede into his body cavity like a tiny turtle head withdrawing into its shell.

"It's getting kind of late, Lourdes, and I have to be at work early in the morning." His voice was strained, his tone pitched too high, but at least he was able to get the words out. "So I'd better, uh, take a rain check . . ."

She didn't tighten her grip on his hand, but neither did she loosen it.

"Relax, Greg. I think you're going to enjoy this." She gave him another of her joyless smiles. "I know *I* will."

They reached the top of the steps, and Greg was just about to pull his hand free from Lourdes' and run down the stairs when she turned and kissed him. Her lips parted, her tongue darted out to seek his, and he forgot all about fleeing.

* * * * *

Greg at sixteen. It's Monday morning, and he's standing in a high-school hallway, near the drinking fountain next to the band room. He's waiting for someone – someone special. In the pocket of his corduroy pants (his mother won't let him wear jeans) is a jewelry box, and inside is a necklace: a small silver heart on a chain. He doesn't know for sure if it's real silver or not, but since it only cost him nine dollars at K-Mart, he figures it probably isn't. But it LOOKS like real silver, and that's all that matters. He hopes Debbie will like it.

She sat next to him on the band bus Friday night. Not on purpose, he knows that. The bus was crowded and she'd gotten on late and there was nowhere else left for her to sit. No one ever sat next to him if they could avoid it. But Debbie was nice, and after a little bit she started talking to him, and even better, she listened to him too. He'd hoped maybe she'd sit next to him on the stadium bleachers, but she'd sat with some of her friends. He saved her a seat on the bus for the ride home – which wasn't all that difficult since no one else wanted to take it. But once again Debbie had sat with her friends. He was disappointed, but he understood. Debbie was too nice a person to neglect her friends. He admired her for that.

He bought the necklace the next day.

Kids are walking past him, talking and laughing as they head from one class to another. Debbie has trigonometry next with Ms. Raisor (she'd told him this Friday night), and her room is just down the hall from the band room. He figures this is the best place to catch her before –

And then he sees her walking down the hall toward him . . . walking alongside Steve Donaldson, a senior in the trombone section. And they're holding hands.

Before they reach him, Greg walks over to the drinking fountain and slurps water even though he's not thirsty. Part of him hopes that Debbie will notice him anyway and stop to say hi. But she doesn't. She just walks on by, her hand in Steve's, smiling as if she's the happiest girl in the world.

After lunch Greg will flush the necklace down a toilet in the boy's room, and he'll discard the empty box in the waste basket before leaving.

* * * * *

He lay naked on the bed, his tiny cock erect, not that he could see it past the mound of flab around his waist. Lourdes was naked, too, and while she didn't have a super-model's body, she had large dark nipples and a surprisingly thick thatch of pubic hair and he found the combination erotic as hell. But then, considering his lack of success in the sex department, he'd probably find a ninety-year-old double amputee erotic too.

Lourdes stood next to the bed, gazing down upon his body. *Not* at his tiny penis. She didn't seem to be aware that he even *had* one, small or not. He had the sense that she wasn't looking *at* him so much as *inside* him. He had no idea what she saw there, but whatever it was made her eyes shine with hunger.

When she spoke her voice was husky with desire. "Can I . . . touch you?"

Greg couldn't believe it. He would've begged her to touch him, and she was asking permission!

"Please."

Her hands trembled as she reached down and began massaging his rolls of flab. Her breathing quickened and she began to croon softly to herself. "Oh, yeah . . . that's good. That's *real* good . . ." Greg figured she must have some kind of fat fetish, because the way she was acting, it was like they were screwing, but all she was doing was kneading his bloated flesh. What the hell, different strokes . . . as long as he got to bust a nut eventually, what did he care? Lourdes' massage felt good at first, though her hands were a little cold. She began to rub and squeeze him more vigorously, moaning all the while like she was getting ready to cum, but despite her exertions her hands grew continuously colder, so much so that her touch began to burn. Greg wasn't enjoying this anymore. He didn't know what the hell she was doing, but while she might be getting off on this weird shit, he sure as hell wasn't.

He started to sit up, but Lourdes shoved him back down onto the bed with surprising strength for such a slender woman, and then she jammed her hands into his gut – literally reached inside him. It hurt like a motherfucker and he screamed, but when she pulled her hands free, he saw there was no blood, and his skin was whole and unmarked. He also saw that Lourdes hadn't come away from him empty-handed. She held a slimy dark thing that looked like a huge bloated slug. And as Greg watched in horrified disbelief, Lourdes lifted the writhing slug to her face and shoved it into her mouth. She swallowed the disgusting thing whole and her body trembled and bucked and she cried out in release.

* * * * *

"There's always one: the kid with the funny-shaped head, greasy hair, and body odor redolent of stale cheese and old people's feet. The kid that's always the last to be picked for kick ball – if he's picked at all . . . the kid that gets called *lard-fuck* and *no-dick*. That's you, Greg."

Lourdes lay on the bed next to Greg, cuddling against him as she lightly traced his flabby pecs with her index finger.

"People like you store up such delicious hurts in your souls. Humiliations, disappointments, and self-loathings galore. You're a banquet of pain, Greg, and people like me live to feast on what you can provide. We'll pay for it too, and quite handsomely, I might add. Someone as delectable as you can command quite a price for his services. You see, Sugar, I don't work here. I *own* the place. That story about how I'll blow anyone who gives me a ride? *I* started that rumor to attract luscious bags of soul-filth like you. Congratulations, Greg. You not only passed your audition, you're one of the best I've encountered in a long time. Come work for me . . . work here, in a place where you'll not only be accepted for what you are, you'll be desired almost to the point of worship. Please say yes." Her grin this time was completely genuine. "I think my clients will just eat you up!"

* * * * *

"What's going on with Greg? Is he sick or something? He hasn't been into work for days."

"Didn't you hear? He quit last week."

"No shit? What happened, did he suddenly win the lottery?"

"He got a better job. Least, that's what he said. He didn't tell me where, though, and to be honest, I wasn't all that interested."

"I feel kind of bad. I know Greg kept to himself, but we should've done something, maybe had a little goodbye party for him here in the break room."

"I suggested that to him, and you know what he did? He gave me a weird little smile and said, 'I shouldn't start making friends now. It'd be bad for business.'"

Harvest Time

"How about this one?'

You stop and look at the skeletal thing your sister has pointed out. Mottled flesh hanging loose on bones, mouth gaping, thick gray tongue protruding between cracked, leathery lips. The thing's jaws work mechanically, teeth gnawing on the fat worm-tongue. It moans as it chews, pus-colored eyes rolling back in their sockets in a kind of ecstasy.

After a moment's thought you say, "Too skinny."

Your sister looks at you as if you're crazy. "What does that matter? We don't want the body."

As if you need her to remind you of that. You've both been coming here to gather heads for Dire Harvest since you were children. And even if you'd never been here before, the headless bodies lying scattered around the orchard – on their backs, knees in the air, foot-roots still buried in the rich soil – would make it obvious. But she's always been one to argue for the sake of arguing.

"I mean its face is too narrow. Besides, it'll chew that tongue completely off before long, and how will that look?"

The dead thing moans once more, as if to underscore your point.

"It'll look gross," she says, "which is what we want."

You sigh. "A *proper* Dire Harvest head should express the insignificance of life compared to the profound beauty of Oblivion. This –" you gesture toward the tongue-chewer – "expresses only one thing: 'I'm especially stupid, even for a dead man.'"

You turn away and look around the orchard, searching for something better, but before you can spot anything, you sense movement. You turn back around and see your sister step close to the dead thing. She bats away its weak, clutching fingers with one hand and raises the hacksaw to its neck with the other.

"This one will do," she says as she starts sawing. "And don't start in with your unholier-than-thou attitude. One corpse head is as good as another." She shakes her own head. "I wish I hadn't come home for Dire Harvest this year. I should be spending it with my friends back at college instead of with my pain-in-the-butt brother."

The dead thing looks at your sister as she saws at its neck. It moans louder, but whether in plain or pleasure it's hard to say.

You make a decision. "I know we haven't always gotten along," you say through gritted teeth, "but I'm glad you came back." You step toward her and reach for the hacksaw. "Here, let me help you."

* * * * *

As you leave the orchard, a young married couple pulls up in their Accord. When they see you heading alone to your car, the husband looks admiringly at the Dire Harvest head you've collected – red blood dripping from the ragged neck wound – and turns to his wife.

"Wow, they're really fresh this year!"

Surface Tension

You're sitting at a window-side table in your favorite coffee shop. You've been here for – you check your cell phone for the time – almost three hours. You've had three cups of coffee (half-caff, two sugars, three creams) and two scones (one cinnamon, one blueberry). You brought a book with you, the latest volume in your favorite mystery series, but it lies on the table, unopened.

You stare out the window, as you've done for the last two-and-a-half hours. Since the rain began. You checked a weather report on the Internet before you left home. Forecasters called for only a twenty percent chance of showers. Hardly a chance at all, you figured. Certainly low enough to risk a trip out. But somewhere along the line twenty percent began a hundred, and showers became a downpour. Now you're trapped. It's not the rain itself that you're afraid of, not really. It's the water covering the parking lot. So much of it that you can't see the asphalt at all. It looks like the surface of a pool, a pond, a lake, an ocean. Raindrops hitting with enough force to cause constant eruptions on the surface. And you think, anything could be beneath the water. Anything at all.

* * * * *

"Have you ever stopped to look at a rain puddle? I mean *really* look at it?"

You're four years old and you're walking down the sidewalk with your grandfather. He's an old man, older than Time itself, it seems, thin and bony with baggy elephant skin and tufts of wispy white hair dotting his liver-spotted scalp. He walks slowly, which is good because your legs are so short. You don't need to run to keep up with him.

Grandpa's taking you to the playground at the recreation center near where you live. Your parents are both at work, and he's watching you today. It rained overnight and there are puddles on the sidewalk, in the gutters and street. You've never given them much thought, other than to avoid stepping in them. Other children like to splash in puddles, but not you. You don't like to get your shoes and socks wet, don't like the way the sodden cloth feels next to your skin – thick, cold, heavy.

Grandpa crouches next to the puddle, the joints in his knees making soft popping sounds. He motions for you to join him, and you do, although you stay farther from the puddle's edge than he does.

"The wonderful thing about a body of water is that you can't tell how deep it is just by looking at the surface." He smiles. "Not unless the water's crystal clear. And this isn't."

You look at the puddle. It's not clear, not at all. It's black and smooth as glass.

"If you put your finger in it, you might find it's so shallow, there's hardly any water there at all. But sometimes . . ."

Grandpa holds up his hand and extends his index finger toward the sky, and then – with motions as precise and deliberate as any stage magician – he turns it downward and moves it toward the puddle.

You hold your breath as his finger descends, the top of it touching the surface so gently it doesn't make a ripple. He pauses then, and you think that's all there is, but you're astonished when he continues to push his finger into the puddle up to the first joint, the second, all the way to the knuckle. You will think of this moment many times throughout your life, and as an adult, you'll tell yourself that it was just a trick, that Grandpa simply bent his finger bit by bit as he lowered his hand, creating the illusion that his finger was sinking into a puddle deeper than the level of the sidewalk. You were only four, and therefore easy enough to fool. But at this moment, it looks so real, and you have no trouble imagining Grandpa's hand sinking all the way into the puddle and continuing on up to his elbow, his shoulder. The puddle isn't all that wide, but you're skinny, with a narrow waist, hips, and shoulders. You wonder if you step onto the puddle if you'll sink, and if so, how deep you'll go.

A startled cry escapes Grandpa's mouth and he yanks his hand away from the puddle. Droplets splash your face and you want to scream, but all you do is make a little mewling sound.

Grandpa grins. "Something nipped me. Probably a little minnow or something."

He looks at your expectantly, waiting. He wants you, his audience of one, to let him know you've enjoyed the show. You do your best to fake a smile for him.

"Let's go, sweetie. The playground awaits."

He stands with a little *oof* of effort and holds out his hand – the one that touched the puddle – for you to take. You hesitate, but you stand, take his hand, and allow him to lead you away from the puddle. You're grateful for this, but you can't help thinking about his words.

Probably a little minnow . . .

. . . or something.

* * * * *

That night your mom makes you popcorn, and your parents and you sit down to watch the Disney version of *Twenty Thousand Leagues Under the Sea.* It's kind of a slow movie, and your attention wanders. You don't like the idea that so much of the movie takes place underwater. At one point, the crew of the *Nautilus* find themselves battling some kind of monster – a huge, sea-dwelling beast with long tentacles, plate-sized eyes that appear to have no intelligence, and a sharp parrot-like beak for a mouth.

That night you dream of tentacles hiding within an endless expanse of water, stretching upward, ever upward, reaching for you. It's the first time you have this dream. But unfortunately, it's nowhere near the last.

* * * * *

The rain shows no sign of letting up. You wish you'd parked closer to the coffee shop's entrance, but those spaces were taken when you arrived, and you were forced to park on the far side of the lot, and if you want to get to your car, it'll mean a sprint across a body of water that could be as shallow as a quarter of an inch or untold fathoms deep. And anything could be swimming within those depths, waiting for someone foolish enough to step outside.

You know this is ridiculous, that your fear is a delusion bordering on the psychotic, and you force yourself to take deep, even breaths until your pulse slows. You check the time again. You have places to be, things to do, *important* things. You can't afford to sit here all afternoon scared of *water,* for godsakes!

It takes another five minutes for you to work up the nerve to stand. You throw away your empty coffee cup and walk toward the exit. You leave your mystery novel on the table, forgotten. When you reach the door, you there stand there a moment, your hand on the metal bar. *You can do this,* you tell yourself. *If anyone notices you running, they'll just think you don't want to get wet.*

You take another deep breath, hold it, and then you open the door.

The wind hits you first, bringing with it a cold misty spray that coats your face. You shudder, but you step all the way outside and start running across the parking lot toward your car. You didn't bring an umbrella, don't even own one. You never go out when it's raining. Except, unfortunately, today.

Rain pelts onto you like ice shards, and the sound of it striking the ground envelops you. You can feel the vibrations from hundreds, thousand of individual tiny impacts, but it's not enough to muffle the sound of your pounding heart. As you run, your feet send up splashes of water, and while the asphalt at first feels solid enough beneath you, halfway across the lot it seems that the water level is rising, and the ground begins to feel like mud. Your shoes and socks are soaked, and you could swear the water has risen past your ankles. Or perhaps, you think with a sting of panic, you're beginning to sink.

The wonderful thing about a body of water is you can't tell how deep it is by looking at the surface.

Grandpa's words echo through your mind, but the falling rain is so damned loud you can barely hear them.

Two-thirds of the way there.

Your car is a gray shape half-hidden by streaming curtains of rain. You focus all your attention on it and tell yourself to keep going, just keep going, no matter what.

The water feels as if it's up to your calves now, and you're not so much running as slogging forward. Still, you keep your gaze fixed on your car, although it's hard to see it with so much water running down your face and into your eyes. You think you see movement in your peripheral vision, and you tell yourself it's an illusion caused by the rainwater in your eyes, but you look anyway, can't stop yourself even though you know you should.

You see a slender undulating shape uncoiling toward you, dark and smooth, an oily sheen on its rubbery flesh. Sucker pads on the underside like small circular mouths gape wide as the tentacle stretches closer, quivering with excited hunger. It's joined by a second, then a third. More appear, too many to count, and then they all reach for you.

You find the scream that eluded you so many years ago when you were a child, and you give voice to it now.

* * * * *

Back inside the coffee shop, you stand before the smooth surface of the bathroom mirror. Your clothes are soaked, your hair's a stringy sodden mess, and your tears aren't making your any drier.

You failed to walk across a parking lot in the rain, something so simple anyone could do it. You turned and ran when you saw the tentacles, rushing back through the door is such a panic that everyone looked up, startled. You ran to the bathroom and locked yourself in, with a vague idea of trying to dry yourself off somehow. But in truth, all you wanted was to get away from the rain, put a few extra walls between you and them . . . it . . . whatever.

You look at your reflection.

"You're pathetic," you say.

The surface of the mirror ripples like water then, and when the glass becomes still once more, your image has changed. In the mirror you're naked, skin rubbery, dark, and glistening. Your eyes are large, unblinking, emotionless. Instead of hair, a nest of tentacles extends from your head, waving back and forth slowly, as if stirred be an underwater current. Your mouth is a hooked parrot beak, and when it opens to speak, the sound that comes out is a high-pitched ululation, but you understand it nevertheless.

You're tired of it. The fear. I can help you. You will never be afraid again. All you have to do is take my hand.

A tentacle stretches forth from the mirror, one terminating in five small tendrils. They wriggle like a clutch of baby snakes, and while the sight of them should cause you to question your sanity, they seem natural somehow. Almost normal. And you're surprised to find yourself reaching out to clasp them. But as your trembling fingertips brush the tendrils, you draw your hand back, uncertain.

There's so much I can show you. I can take you deeper than you ever imagined possible. So deep that we'll leave everything else behind. Worry, pain, sorrow, fear . . . We'll go so deep that there won't be anything but us and vast endless Nothing. And there you will at last know peace.

New tears fall from your eyes. Tears of terror, yes, but there's hope in them, as well as joy.

Still trembling, you take your other self's hand, her finger-tendrils wrap tight around your flesh, and she pulls you forward, in, and down, down, down . . .

Best Friends Forever

"Daddy, is that a stuffed dog on the side of the road?"

Upon hearing his daughter's words, a cold pit opened up in the middle of Ron Garber's stomach. He gripped the steering wheel tight and concentrated on keeping his gaze fixed straight ahead. If he could keep from looking, just for a few more moments, they'd drive past and he wouldn't have to see whatever Lily was pointing at. If he didn't see it, it couldn't be real, and if wasn't real, he could forget about it.

"Daddy! Over there! Look!"

Lily was only seven, still young enough to be relegated to the back and be forced to endure the humiliation of a booster seat. But despite her age, she had a mind sharp as a scalpel. She'd know something weird was going on if he refused to look, and she could be tenacious as a pack of pitbulls when she wanted to. She wouldn't stop asking him why he didn't look until she got a satisfactory answer. He had no choice. He had to look.

It's probably nothing, he told himself. Just a toy some kid had been playing with and left outside, temporarily forgotten.

He turned to look in the direction Lily had pointed. On the opposite side of the road, sitting on the gravel shoulder, was a three-foot high stuffed St. Bernard. Brown and white fur, floppy ears, red-felt tongue hanging out, black plastic eyes. Eyes that did more than not reflect light but which seemed to absorb it, feed on it, drink it in and swallow it down.

Ron hadn't seen the toy dog in . . . in . . . *A while*, he decided. But he recognized it instantly. His nostrils filled with its musty odor – the result of the animal having been left out in the rain overnight once when Ron was only slightly younger than Lily.

Though he continued to hold tight to the steering wheel, his fingers felt the dog's artificial fur, and he whispered a single word.

"Biff . . ."

"Let's stop and get the doggy!" Lily said. "He looks lonely!"

Ron's foot pressed down on the accelerator and their Toyota Sierra minivan flashed passed the toy.

"Daddy, we can't just *leave* him there! Someone might steal him! Or he might get hit by a car!" Lily had always been a sensitive, highly empathetic child, and she sounded honestly worried.

Ron reached up and tilted the rearview mirror so he couldn't look back and see Biff.

"No need to worry, honey. Whoever the dog belongs to will come back and get it soon." He tried to keep his voice as normal-sounding as he could, but his words came out edged with tension. He glanced over his shoulder at Lily to gauge her reaction, but his daughter wasn't looking at him. She was looking at the repositioned rearview mirror and frowning.

"Besides, there's a lot of traffic, Lily. I'm not sure I'd be able to turn around." Only partially a lie. Ash Creek was hardly the largest town in Ohio, but it was almost the lunch hour, and a lot of people had left work to pick up something to eat. There were a number of fast-food joints in this part of town, so there were a lot of cars on the road. Not so many that he *couldn't* turn their minivan around if he really wanted to, but even as smart as Lily was, he hoped she wouldn't realize that. She *was* only seven, after all. Still, before she could say anything, he added, "I have to get to my appointment on time. It's an important opportunity, and I can't afford to miss it."

This *wasn't* a lie. True, he'd made sure they'd left early enough to give him a comfortable cushion of extra time to get to Coleman Publishing, but he didn't want to squander that time by making any unnecessary stops. He glanced at the black portfolio case propped against the passenger seat next to him. *Important opportunity* was an understatement. It was the break he'd worked so long and hard for.

He'd been at his home office earlier that morning, sitting at his drawing board laying out ads for a newspaper insert for a local grocery when he'd gotten the call. Kevin Armstrong, art director for Coleman Publishing, had finally gotten around to reviewing the samples Ron had sent several weeks ago. Armstrong had liked what he saw and told Ron that Coleman had been approached by a local church to print a line of Christian-themed children's books to use in Sunday school. Armstrong thought Ron might be the perfect choice to illustrate them. The gig wouldn't pay much, and Ron wasn't religious by any means, but if he landed the job, he'd get his first professional credit illustrating kids' books. A credit he could use as a calling card when approaching national publishers.

Because Ron was a freelance commercial artist who worked out of his home, it fell to him to care for Lily while her mother was at work. Normally, it wasn't much of a problem. Sure, his productivity had suffered to a degree, but he loved spending time alone with his daughter. Doing design work for ads, pamphlets, and brochures might've paid the bills, but for years he'd dreamed of illustrating children's books. And now that it looked like that dream might be coming true at last, he'd had no choice but to bring Lily with him. They had no friends who were home during the day who could watch her, and Lily was too young to stay home by herself, even if only for an hour or two. Ron had tried calling Growing Minds Discovery Garden (evidently *daycare* was too déclassé a term for them) where they sometimes left Lily. But Lily had a slight cold and was running a low fever, so they wouldn't take her. Ron had told the director of Growing Minds about his meeting with Armstrong and that other than a bit of a runny nose, Lily was acting perfectly fine. The woman had said that while she sympathized with Ron's situation, rules were rules, and there was nothing she could do about it.

Frustrated, he'd called Julia at work and asked her to tell her bosses that she was sick so she could come home and watch Lily for him. *That* had been a mistake. They'd nearly gotten into a fight over the phone. Julie had only recently returned to work as a paralegal, and she didn't want to do anything that might jeopardize her job. She worked for Sloan and Sloan, husband and wife lawyers who shared a practice. While Mr. Sloan was easy-going enough, his wife was a real hard-ass. No way did Julia want to risk the woman's wrath by lying to her so she could skip out of work. Couldn't he call the publisher and reschedule?

No, he couldn't, he told her. That would be unprofessional.

He could almost hear her shrug over the phone. "Then you'll just have to take her along, I guess."

He expected Lily to protest his excuses for not stopping to pick up the stuffed dog, but she said nothing. He thought maybe she was pouting, so – judging they were far enough away from the spot where Lily had spotted the stuffed St. Bernard – he readjusted his rearview mirror so he could see her. But when he saw her reflection, he experienced a shock that was equal parts surprise and stunned recognition. The image in the mirror was Lily, all right, but not the seven-year-old girl with bright eyes, round face, button nose, and curly strawberry-blonde hair. It was Lily as a baby, not quite a year old. Strapped snugly into her carseat, wearing a one-piece outfit that left her chubby pinks arms and legs bare, fine curly wisps of hair on her head, nothing like the thick, rich locks she was destined to have. Lily's pudgy face was red, eyes squeezed close, mouth open wide. She looked as if she was crying, but Ron heard no sound.

He blinked and Lily was suddenly seven again, sitting on her booster seat and looking at him expectantly.

"Didn't you hear what I said, Daddy? I said maybe we could pick up the doggie on the way back."

Feeling disoriented and a trifle dizzy, Ron said, "We'll see,"

He was nervous about meeting with Mr. Armstrong, that was all. Coupled with his artistic imagination, his anxiety had caused him to momentarily "see" a memory. Weird, maybe, but nothing to be worried about.

He faced forward again and concentrated on his driving, but somewhere in the back of his mind, he heard a baby crying.

* * * * *

Ron was too young when he got Biff to remember the first time he saw the toy that, in many ways, was to become the best friend he'd ever had. But his mother had told the story to him often enough over the years that he felt he could recall every detail.

It had been his first birthday, and his parents had done all the usual things. They'd put him in his high chair, turned off the kitchen light, and brought out a cake with a single thick candle shaped like a numeral one on top. The candle was lit and Ronnie's eyes widened as his mother sat the cake down on the table in front of him – but not *too* close. Wouldn't want Baby getting burned. His parents sang "Happy Birthday" to him, and he smiled at the tune, though he couldn't quite understand the words. Then both his Mommy and Daddy blew out the candle flame. Ronnie liked looking at the flickering warm glow, and he was sad to see it go bye-bye.

Mommy cut the cake while Daddy took pictures. Mommy put Ronnie's slice on a tiny paper plate and set it on his highchair tray. He squooshed the cake with his tiny fingers, getting more of it on his bib, face, and in his hair than in his mouth. Mommy spooned a bit of ice cream into his mouth and he dutifully swallowed it, only to make a horrified face at the unfamiliar sensation of cold in his mouth, following instantly by tears. Mommy washed his hands, then Daddy took him out of the high chair and carried him into the living room. A half dozen objects were stacked on the coffee table, all wrapped in brightly colored paper. But Ronnie barely glanced at them. His gaze was drawn to the large brown-and-white thing sitting on the floor next to the coffee table.

Daddy put him down on the floor and Ronnie took several unsteady steps toward the big fuzzy thing before giving up and falling to his hands and knees so he could make better speed. He swiftly crawled over to the fascinating object, reached out, and grabbed a handful of brown-and-white fur. It was so soft . . . He buried his face in its fur and grabbed hold of it, squeezing as hard as he could. It was soft like Mommy, big like Daddy, and warm, too. But it didn't pull away when he squeezed it, didn't say "Ouch, that's too hard, sweetie!" Ronnie instinctively understood that whatever this furry thing was, it was his and it would accept whatever he did without question, complaint, or reprimand.

From that moment on, Ronnie cried whenever anyone tried to separate him from his new friend. It was an "Oggy" he eventually learned, and he wanted his Oggy to go wherever he went, wanted it in the crib with him when he slept, despite how much room it took up, to protect him from the things that moved sinuous and silent in the dark. Wanted it sitting on one of the kitchen chairs when he ate, sitting by his side as they watched cartoons, looking on with its black plastic eyes while he got a bath. If he went outside, Oggy had to go outside. When Ronnie had to come back in, so did Oggy. This meant a lot of extra work for his parents, as Ronnie was too small to carry Oggy around by himself. But eventually Ronnie grew and he was able to drag Oggy along with him, giving his Mommy and Daddy a bit of badly needed relief. But Ronnie didn't notice or care about his parents' reaction. All he cared about was spending time with Oggy.

* * * * *

Ron glanced at the digital clock on the van's dashboard and gritted his teeth. 11:47. There'd been a wreck on Everson Road, not much more than a fender-bender, really – but he'd had to wait in a mini traffic jam until a state trooper and a tow truck had cleared the vehicles involved from the street. He judged he could still make his appointment with Mr. Armstrong, but his margin for error was decidedly thinner than it had been.

"Daddy? I don't feel so good."

Those were the last words Ron wanted to hear. He felt like groaning, but he didn't want to hurt his daughter's feelings, so he worked on keeping his voice calm as he asked, "What's wrong, honey?"

"My tummy feels all shivery."

Ron bit back a curse. Lily had a tendency to get carsick, but usually only on long trips. He'd taken precautions, though. It was hot out today, but he had the minivan's air conditioning on, and though he'd been hurrying to make up the time lost to the accident delay, he'd tried to avoid accelerating or braking too rapidly and cutting corners too sharply when he turned. Still, it looked as if his precautions had failed.

Of course they did, he thought. That's how the universe works, right? The more you needed to avoid something, the more likely it was to happen.

He checked the time again. 11:50. He couldn't afford to stop, but how could he keep going, knowing Lily was in discomfort? And – to be cold-bloodedly practical about it – how could he continue on to his meeting with Armstrong if Lily threw up all over herself? He'd have to take her home for sure then.

He looked in the rearview mirror and saw Lily's pale, frightened face looking back at him.

And even if he was cruel enough to make her sit in her own sick while he kept his appointment, the vomit-stench would attach itself to him. He could just imagine introducing himself to

Armstrong and trying to explain why he stank of his daughter's puke.

"Don't worry, honey. I'll find somewhere to pull over."

He saw a Hamburger Haven coming up on his right. He signaled, eased up on the gas, then gently pressed down on the brake. He turned into the restaurant's parking lot so slowly that the person behind him blasted his horn. Ron was tempted to give the sonofabitch the finger, but Lily was with him, and he didn't want to be a poor role model, so he resisted. There was a parking space near the entrance, and Ron eased the minivan into it and cut the engine. Trying not to think about the time, he got out of the van and hurried around to the side and slid open the side door. He hoped the absence of motion combined with exposure to fresh air would settle Lily's stomach, but it was so damned hot out, he wondered if he should've left the door closed and the AC running. He'd only been outside for a few seconds and already beads of sweat were forming on his skin. He was wearing a nice shirt, tie, slacks, and dress shoes for his interview with Armstrong, and he worried about getting sweat stains on his clothes. Not much he could do about it, he supposed.

"How are you doing, honey?"

Lily was still pale and her breathing was coming in ragged pants. She kept swallowing, too, fighting to keep her stomach from emptying its contents.

"I . . . I'll be okay, Daddy." She attempted a smile, but it came out as a grimace.

Ron was overwhelmed by a sudden swell of both pride and guilt. His little girl was doing her best to be brave because she knew how important his meeting with Armstrong was for her daddy. He was proud of her for trying to act so grown-up, but he felt guilty that he'd been more concerned about wasting time stopping then about his little girl's physical condition.

He unbuckled her seatbelt. "C'mon, let's go inside where it's cool."

Lily was beginning to sweat now too, and she gave him a weak but grateful smile as she climbed out of the van. He took her elbow to steady her, slid the door closed, then locked the van using his keychain remote. Then together they entered the restaurant.

A blast of cold air hit them as soon as they walked in. Too cold, Ron thought. His own stomach lurched at the sudden extreme shift in temperature, and he doubted the transition made Lily feel any better. Worse yet was the smell inside the restaurant – hot grease, smoke, and frying meat. Lily's face went chalk-white. Without saying anything, she turned and fled toward the women's restroom. Ron felt equal amounts of concern and frustration, the latter making him feel even more guilty than he had before.

This Hamburger Haven was set up like all the others Ron had even been in. A front counter where apathetic teenagers and bored retirees took and filled orders, tables and chairs where customers could sit while they gobbled down the muck the place passed off as food, and a play area outside with more seats and a configuration of plastic tunnels for small children to crawl around inside like hamsters. Ron disliked fast food in general – it always upset his stomach – but he had fond memories of bringing Lily here when she was little, of taking her to the play area and letting her explore the tubes. Not too far in, though, for she wasn't even a year yet and just starting to learn to walk.

"Can I help you, sir?"

He turned toward the voice, startled out of his memories. A stout matronly women in her fifties wearing a blue Hamburger Haven uniform stood before him. Her nametag said *Gloria* and beneath that *Manager*.

Ron was puzzled by the woman coming up to speak to him. Since when did Hamburger Haven get so proactive about customer service? Gloria stared at him as if there was something wrong with the way he looked. Her nose wrinkled and she turned her head slightly aside, as if he had offensive body odor. But he was wearing clean clothes, and he'd showered this morning and put on deodorant. Sure, he'd started sweating outside, but not *that* much.

"I'm just waiting for my daughter," he said. "She's in the restroom."

The woman's eyes narrowed with suspicion, and Ron understood why she had come out from behind the counter to check on him. The way Lily had run from him must've looked as if she were trying to escape a captor.

He gave Gloria what he hoped was a reassuring smile. "She gets a little carsick sometimes."

She frowned. "I didn't see you come in with anyone."

"Maybe you weren't looking. There's a lot of people lined up at the counter." Which was true. It was the lunch rush, after all.

Gloria's frowned deepened into a scowl. "Unless you're going to buy something, I'll have to ask you to leave."

Ron was starting to get angry. This woman was acting like he was some kind of dangerous nut instead of a father doing his best to take care of his child.

"As soon as my daughter's okay, we'll get out of here. All right?"

The woman looked as if she were going to say something further, but then she glanced at all the customers waiting to place orders, and she turned away and headed back to the counter.

Ron was glad to see her go, and he'd be even more glad to get the hell out of here, after –

The women's restroom door opened and Lily came out. She was still pale, though not nearly as white as when she'd gone in. Her face was wet, and at first he thought she was dripping with sweat, but then he realized she'd splashed water on her face.

"How are you feeling, sweetie?"

"Better." Her voice was shaky, but not as weak as it had been. "I think I'm okay to go now."

He felt a surge of hope, and he immediately squashed it. Lily was infinitely more important than any illustrating gig he might get.

"Why don't we sit down for a little bit until you feel all the way better? I can get you something to drink, maybe some Sprite to settle your stomach."

"Really, Daddy, I'm okay. Let's –"

"I asked you to leave." It was Gloria again, only this time she wasn't alone. She'd brought a tall, beefy teenage boy with her.

Ron's anger rose, and it was all he could do to keep from shouting at the woman. "I'm not sure my daughter is feeling well enough yet."

The teenage boy – whom Gloria had doubtless brought along for whatever muscle he could provide – gave his manager a confused, questioning look.

Gloria didn't glance back at the boy. She kept her gaze focused on Ron. "I don't want any trouble. Just go. *Now*." She didn't sound mad. She sounded scared, and Ron couldn't figure out why.

Lily tugged at his arm. "Let's go, Daddy? Please?"

Now Lily sounded scared, and though Ron wanted to tear into the manager and give her hell for treating him this way, he didn't want to subject his daughter to any more of the woman's weirdness.

He gave Gloria a parting glare. "Fine. Whatever. But see if we ever come back here again."

As Ron and Lily headed for the door, he heard the teenager say "We?" but he didn't turn back. They exited into a thick, syrupy heat that made Ron feel queasy. He looked to Lily to check how she was handling the abrupt temperature shift and was surprised to see a big grin on her face.

"Look, Daddy!" She pointed toward the van.

Sitting on the sidewalk in front of the vehicle, facing toward them, was Biff.

* * * * *

Ronnie was nine. He sat in his driveway, legs crossed, hands resting limply in his lap, ever-faithful St. Bernard sitting next to him. His Oggy was somewhat worse for the wear after eight years of accompanying Ronnie on his adventures. His colors had faded, and there were bare patches in his fur. A number of his seams had split over the years and had been sewn back up by Ronnie's mother, leaving bits of thread here and there. The plastic eyes had been scratched from too much hard play, giving them a somewhat milky cast, like an old person's cataracts.

He sat there, doing nothing, thinking nothing. Eventually Jerry Klauser came riding by on his new ten-speed. Jerry lived down the block, the youngest of seven kids, though he was a year older than Ronnie. For reasons that Ronnie had never been able to fathom, Jerry thought he was real hot stuff and teased Ronnie whenever he got the chance.

Ronnie hoped Jerry would ride on past, but knew he wouldn't.

Jerry rolled up to the end of Ronnie's driveway and put his feet down to stop.

"Hey, it's Ronnie and his Oggy-Woggy!"

Ronnie didn't feel like talking to anyone right now, especially Jerry Klauser, but he knew the taunts would only continue and get worse if he didn't respond.

"His name's Biff."

As Ronnie had gotten older, he'd come to realize what a babyish name Oggy was. He'd tried out other names: Champ, Killer, and – least imaginatively of all – Bernard. But one day his parents had left him with a babysitter while they went out to the movies. He watched TV while she did homework, and he noticed she'd used an eraser to remove parts of the cover, creating white lines like writing. The lines said SUZE AND BROOKE: BFF.

"What's *Biff* mean?" he'd asked.

Suze had been puzzled for a moment, but when she figured out what he meant, she laughed. "It's B-F-F. It stands for Best Friends Forever."

Ronnie thought that was a great way to describe him and his St. Bernard and so that day Oggy became Biff.

"Biff is a stiff!" Jerry said in a singsong voice. "I'd like to throw him off a cliff!"

Ronnie's jaw tightened and his hands clenched into fists. "Shut up and leave me alone, Jerry."

"What's wrong? The baby can't take a joke? Are you gonna start to cry? Maybe Oggy will give you a kiss and make it all better."

Ronnie rose to his feet. "I told you his name is Biff." He could feel the pressure of tears behind his eyes, and he fought to hold them in. He didn't want to give Jerry the satisfaction of seeing him cry.

Jerry's eyes hardened. "You wanna make something of it, Baby?" His words seemed false somehow, as if he were repeating something he'd heard on TV. Jerry had never tried to pick a fight before, but he sounded serious. Ronnie had never been in a fight, but the way he felt now, he'd almost welcome it. He took a step toward Jerry but then thought better of it.

"Just go away. My grandma died this morning."

Though all Ronnie had done was talk, Jerry reacted as if he'd punched him in the stomach. His eyes went wide and his mouth fell open.

"No shit?"

Ronnie had never used a swear word before, but it seemed only appropriate now.

"No shit."

"Aw, geez. I'm . . . sorry."

Jerry looked at him a moment longer, as if he were trying to think of something else to say but couldn't. Finally he put his feet back on his bike pedals and rode off down the sidewalk.

Ronnie's mom was inside the house, lying on her bed, crying. She'd been there all day, ever since Aunt Karen had called with the news of Grandma's death. Dad was still at work, and though he'd told Mom he'd try to come home early, he didn't know if his boss would let him. So Ronnie had been left alone with his grief all morning.

No, not alone. Never. Not so long as he had Biff. Ronnie sat back down next to his friend – the only *real* friend he'd ever had. He grabbed Biff and held him tight as the tears he could no longer hold back flooded forth.

* * * * *

"It *was* the same dog, Daddy! He followed us!"

Ron drove five miles over the speed limit. It was 11:57, three minutes before he was scheduled to meet with Mr. Armstrong, and he still had several miles to go to reach Coleman Publishing. He was going to be late, there was no helping that now, but maybe he wouldn't be *too* late.

"It *couldn't* be the same one, and it sure as hell couldn't have followed us. It's *stuffed* for Christ's sake!" He instantly regretted using such harsh language when speaking to his daughter, but he was so goddamned pissed off. Over Lily's protests, he'd taken the St. Bernard – which was *not* Biff, he kept telling himself – into the Hamburger Haven to tell the manager that someone had abandoned the toy outside her restaurant. The woman had vehemently refused to take the dog from him, and had shouted for him to get the fuck out before she called the cops. Everyone in the restaurant – employees and customers alike – had looked at him as if he were insane, and so he'd plopped the stuffed down that was *not* Biff down on the counter and left.

"I tell you what, honey. If you really want a stuffed dog, I'll take you to the toy store after my meeting and you can pick out whichever one you want, no matter how big. How does that sound?"

"But I don't want any old dog," she whined. "I want *that* one!"

Ron gritted his teeth and held his tongue. At least her carsickness had passed, he told himself. He thought her heard the sound of a baby crying softly then, but it seemed so faint and far away that it had to be his imagination. The sound soon faded away, as if the child had tired itself out and fallen asleep. He glanced in the rearview mirror. Lily sat looking out her window, lower lip pushed out in a little girl pout. If she'd heard the baby crying, she didn't show it. At least *she* wasn't crying. That was something to be thankful for. It had been a hard morning for her as well. He understood that and vowed to do his best to make it up to her – after his meeting.

They drove on in silence for the next few minutes, and Ron tried to remain calm as the digital clock moved from 11:57 to 58, 59, and then to noon. He was now officially late.

But there, coming up on the right, was the entrance to Coleman Publishing. He remember the blue sign standing up in the grass out front, remembered the white letters that spelled out the company's name, including – in smaller letters below – est. 1967. The colors were a bit faded now, but –

He frowned. What was he thinking? He'd never been here before, had mailed his art samples to Mr. Armstrong. He'd probably driven past on occasion, but he'd never really noticed the place, certainly not to the point where he'd recognize changes in the sign's colors. He was probably remembering a different sign, a different company, getting the memories mixed up. Yeah, that was it. Had to be.

He slowed, signaled, and turned into the entrance.

“Looks like we made it, kiddo!” He felt suddenly light, cheerful, all anxiety drained away. The clock said 12:02. Late, but only a little. Mr. Armstrong probably wouldn’t even notice. He glanced up at the rearview mirror to see how Lily was doing. She stared straight ahead, eyes widening with horror.

“Daddy, look out!”

He lowered his gaze and through the windshield he saw a large brown-and-white shape dash across the driveway right in front of their van. Felt the heavy *thump* more than he heard it. He slammed on the brakes, squealing tires blending with Lily’s screams.

* * * * *

Ron stood in his bedroom, looking at the two suitcases and bulging duffle bag sitting on his bed. For the dozenth time he took a mental inventory of everything he’d packed, and for the dozenth time he decided he hadn’t forgotten anything. He knew he was stalling, and that his mom and dad knew it too, but neither of them had come in to tell him it was getting late and they should get on the road. He appreciated that.

He was excited about leaving for college, was looking forward to moving into the dorm, starting his art classes, getting a chance to see what it was like to live on his own. Finally starting his adult life. He knew he wasn’t leaving home for good, not really. He’d be back for holidays and summers. But this was the last time this would he *his* room, the place where he lived. From now on he’d only be visiting.

He hadn’t thought it would be so hard to say goodbye to a place, to let go of all the memories that filled the room like light and air. But it was. And there was one memory that was hardest of all to let go of.

Biff sat on the floor next to his dresser, a fine coating of dust on his fur. The stuffed dog leaned sideways, head flopped over at an angle, its stuffing having clumped up and settled in odd places over the years. Biff had been sitting in this position since Ron started junior high, and he hadn't touched it since. He'd outgrown the need for make-believe friends. But then again, he hadn't stuck Biff in the closet with all the other toys he never played with anymore. And whenever his mom made noises about giving Biff to Goodwill or worse, just throwing him out, Ron wouldn't hear of it. Maybe Ron hadn't needed Biff the same way as when he'd been little, but that didn't mean he didn't need him at *all*.

Ron went over to the dresser and crouched down in front of Biff, just like he was a real dog. Feeling only a little foolish, but still glad no one was here to see him, he reached out and scratched the top of Biff's head.

"I guess this is it, old buddy. I won't see you again until Thanksgiving. I . . . want to thank you. You've been a good friend to me." He smiled. "Tell you what. I ever have a kid, I'll give you to him or her and you can be their friend. What do you think of that?"

Biff didn't respond. He never had. After all, he was just a stuffed animal. But if Biff had been alive, Ron liked to think his old friend would've been pleased.

* * * * *

Ron stood in front of the van, telling himself that he wasn't seeing what he thought he was seeing. Lily knelt on the ground, holding the crimson-splattered body of Biff to her chest, tears streaming from her eyes, her small body wracked by sobs. The animal that had run in front of the van had been a living dog, a *real* dog, Ron was certain of that. But the tattered wet thing his daughter held was the stuffed St. Bernard from his childhood. The impact had split open the seam that ran from Biff's neck, down his chest, and across his belly. Wads of gray stuffing that looked too much like internal organs protruded from the wound, along with thick red fluid that looked like blood but couldn't possibly be.

"You killed him!" Lily wailed.

Ron struggled to find words to comfort his daughter, but his thoughts were sluggish and he felt a throbbing pain at the base of his skull. Still, he had to say something.

"He can't be dead, honey. He was never alive. You can't kill something that never lived . . ."

Lily kept on sobbing and Ron doubted she'd heard him. His entire head was pounding now and a wave of vertigo washed over him, causing his gut to twist with nausea. Something was seriously wrong here, and he instinctively understood that he had to get Lily away from this place before –

"Mr. Garber!"

Ron turned to see a bald man with a salt-and-pepper goatee hurrying toward them down the driveway, coming from the direction of the Coleman Publishing building. The man was tall, thin, and wore wire-frame glasses. He had on a gray suit and a tie that – even from this distance – Ron could see sported a design of tiny interlocking paint palettes. Ron had never seen the man before . . . had he? But he recognized the voice. It belonged to Mr. Armstrong.

Ron felt a surge of panic. He couldn't let Mr. Armstrong see him like this! How could he ever explain? *Sorry, sir, but I seem to have run over and killed a stuffed animal from my childhood. Most embarrassing.*

He put his hand on Lily's shoulder and gently squeezed.

"C'mon, honey. We have to go. We can't –"

"Mr. Garber!" Armstrong called again. He was much closer now, and Ron's panic gave way to fatalism. It was too late . . . in so many ways. He gave Lily a last squeeze before turning to meet Armstrong.

As the man reached them, sweat running down the sides of his face, breath coming hard from half-running the whole way, Ron said, "I know this looks bad, Mr. Armstrong, but I can –"

"Mr. Garber, when you called this morning, I *told* you not to come. You know I have nothing but the utmost sympathy for your situation, but you *cannot* keep doing this. I don't want to call the police again, but I will if I have to."

The man sounded at once sympathetic and exasperated, and Ron had no idea what he was talking about.

"What happened was a terrible thing, Mr. Garber, but it was six years ago. I'm not going to be insensitive and tell you to get over it. I can't begin to imagine the pain you've experienced. But you've got to come to grips with what happened. Can't you see that?"

Ron felt pressure building inside his head, so intense that he feared it might explode any moment. "I . . . I don't . . ."

And then the pressure, the pain, the confusion vanished, and Ron remembered.

Remembered driving to his appointment with Mr. Armstrong six years ago, on a day even hotter than this one. Lily in the back, not quite a year old, sitting in her car seat, Biff next to her. His childhood friend, now his daughter's companion, confidant, and guardian. Lily with her fever and without a babysitter, crying all the way to Coleman Publishing, falling asleep at last as he pulled into the parking lot. Ron trying to decide what to do: bring Lily inside and risk her waking up and squalling in the middle of his interview with Armstrong? He told himself she needed the sleep, that he wouldn't be long, that he'd leave the windows cracked, that she would be all right. After all, Biff was there to watch over her, wasn't he?

The meeting went well and Ron got the job. But when he returned to the van, Lily wasn't all right. She was never going to be all right again.

Armstrong found him screaming his grief as he tore Biff apart with his bare hands. After all these years, his whole fucking *life*, his best friend had let him down when he'd needed him most. It was Biff's fault, not his. Never his.

Ron realized he couldn't hear Lily crying anymore. He turned to look at her and saw exactly what he feared he would. Nothing. No Lily, no Biff. No stuffing, no blood. Just empty, clear asphalt in front of the van's tires. The van, which looked older, scratched, dented, and badly in need of a wash. Ron looked down at his clothes and saw they were filthy as well, wrinkled and stained. He examined his hands. His nails were long, cracked, discolored. He reached up to his face, felt his unkempt beard, his long scraggly hair. He inhaled and smelled his own foulness. Now he knew why the people in the Hamburger Haven had reacted to him the way they had. He'd gone in alone, looking like this, talking to a daughter who had died long ago.

He ran his fingers over his sweat-slick face. "I'm sorry, Mr. Armstrong."

The profound pity in the other man's gaze was far worse than anger or revulsion. Ron shuffled back toward the van's open driver's door, climbed in, and shut it behind him. Mr. Armstrong stood and watched as Ron put the vehicle in reverse and began to back up.

* * * * *

Ron sat at a picnic table in the park, art portfolio on the seat next to him, sketch paper open on the table. As he drew, he thought. In a way, Biff *had* tried to protect him by preventing him from keeping his appointment with Mr. Armstrong – and from having to remember. Sure, Biff had been a hallucination, just like seven-year-old Lily, the age she would've been if she'd lived. But maybe Biff was the part of his mind that wanted to get better, to break the cycle he was trapped in. Maybe he was ready to go back to therapy, maybe he'd even call his ex-wife. He and Julia had barely spoken since Lily's death. Maybe it was time they did.

His thoughts were interrupted by the deep, sonorous bark of a large dog.

"Daddy, look! I taught Biff a new trick!"

Ron looked up. Lily pointed her index finger at the St. Bernard and said, "Bang!"

Biff fell onto his side and rolled over, tongue lolling from the side of his mouth. Lily giggled in delight and ran over and gave her friend a hug. Bill's tail thumped happily on the grass.

Ron smiled and looked back down at the picture he'd been sketching: a little girl playing with a St. Bernard in the park on a bright summer day. It was just a sketch now, but he thought it was good enough to finish. It might even turn out to be good enough to put in his portfolio. He hoped so. It would be nice to have something new to show Mr. Armstrong at their next meeting.

No More Shadows

Daniel was making his third trip around the parking lot of Electronixx (the Hi-Tech Superstore with More) when his cell phone rang. He didn't feel like talking to anyone – and there was only one person it could be this time of night – but after the fifth ring, just when the phone was about to switch over to voice mail, he snatched it up from the passenger seat and answered.

"Hi, Dan. I hate to bug you again, but I was wondering if you had a chance to pop that check in the mail yet. Lindsey needs a new winter coat, and she has an orthodontist appointment on Monday."

"I get paid tomorrow, Angie." As if she didn't know that. "I'll be able to write you a check then." He paused, not wanting to say the next words, unable to stop himself. "I could come by the house after work and drop it off. If you want."

Her reply came without hesitation. "Thanks, but we're going up to Akron to visit my sister this weekend. We'll be leaving as soon as Lindsey gets out of school tomorrow. Just go ahead and mail the check if you don't mind." No warmth in her voice, all business.

"Yeah, sure." He neared the parking lot's exit, thought about leaving. Instead he turned and began his fourth circuit.

"Are you out somewhere? Sounds like you're driving."

"Just running a couple errands."

"At ten o'clock at night?"

He shrugged, although there was no one to see the gesture. "Got nothing better to do." And wasn't that the sad truth. Even sadder was the fact that his "errands" consisted of driving aimlessly around town, exploring side streets, circling parking lots, driving just to drive, staying out so he wouldn't have to spend any more time then necessary in his crappy one-bedroom apartment. This was his nightly routine, had been ever since he'd moved out of the house two months ago.

"I'd think a lot of stores would be closed by now." An edge of suspicion in her voice, and the subtext of her words was clear: *What are you doing spending money on yourself when you owe your daughter and me a check?*

He wasn't out shopping, hadn't stopped anywhere except at a Burrito Bungalow for dinner, but he resisted the urge to defend himself. He knew it would only end up with the two of them arguing.

"Can I say goodnight to Lindsey?"

"She's already in bed. Sorry."

He doubted Lindsey was asleep. She always read for a half hour or so before turning off the light and snuggling beneath the covers. When she'd been younger – and not so much younger, at that – he'd read stories to her. Only a couple months ago, he'd been the one to check on her and remind her that she needed to turn out the light and get to sleep. Now he was a man who wrote checks to her mother and only saw his daughter every other weekend.

"I just want to say goodnight to her, Angie. I . . ." *Just want to hear her voice,* he finished silently. *Just want to remember that I'm her daddy. That I used to be someone.*

Angie was quiet for several seconds, and he thought she was on the verge of relenting, but before she could speak a short, rail-thin man ran stumbling into the glare of his headlights. Daniel only had enough time to register fragmentary images: a terror-stricken pale face, small round glasses, short blond hair, stubby fingers on the end of flailing hands, right leg twisted at an awkward angle, the limb in danger of buckling any second despite the man's small frame. Daniel dropped his cell, jammed his foot down on the brake pedal of his Jeep Cherokee, and yanked the steering wheel to the left. The vehicle had been traveling less than 20 mph, and his tires gave only a short squeal of protest before the Jeep came to a stop.

Daniel sat gripping the steel wheel with both hands, breath trapped in his throat, heart hammering in his ears. No thump, he told himself. No scream. That meant he hadn't hit the guy. The adrenaline-rush of fear gave way to relief, but that emotion was in turn obliterated by a surge of anger. What the fuck had that stupid sonofabitch been thinking? It was ten o'clock on a Thursday night, closing time for Electronixx, and while the parking lot was half empty, that meant it was also half full. If Daniel had been traveling any faster, he might've slammed into a parked car when he veered to miss the small man. As it was, only sheer luck had kept him from hitting another vehicle; the Cherokee's front bumper had edged into an empty space right next to a pick-up. If he'd been a little slower on the brake . . .

Daniel put the Jeep in park and searched for his cell phone. He found it lying on the floor on the passenger side, and he undid his seatbelt and leaned down to pick it up. As he straightened in his seat he put the phone to his ear, spoke Angie's name twice, but there was no reply. Either the call had been dropped or she'd disconnected. He tossed the phone onto the passenger seat, his disappointment over not getting to talk to Lindsey replaced by anger. He yanked the key out of the ignition, and practically jumped out of the car. He started yelling before he even saw the man.

"Are you crazy? Didn't you see me coming?" A voice in the back of his mind said that he should be checking on the man to make sure he wasn't hurt, and while Daniel felt a twinge of guilt for letting his anger get the better of him, he continued shouting. "Jesus Christ, you could've been killed, or at the very least caused me to wreck!"

During his tirade, Daniel had walked around the back of the Cherokee, intending to confront the small man. He'd forgotten to turn off the Jeep's headlights before getting out of the vehicle, but they were angled off to the side now, and they no longer illuminated the section of the parking lot where the man had been. But there were plenty of light poles stationed at regular intervals throughout the lot, giving off more than enough fluorescence for Daniel to see. It was early November in Southwest Ohio, which meant cold and wet. It had been spitting rain on and off all evening, and a scattering of glistening black leaves were plastered to the asphalt like insects with strange flat carapaces. The small man – he couldn't have been much over five foot – stood almost directly beneath one of the parking lot lights, the fluorescent glow washing him in ghostly blue-white. Now that Daniel got a good look at him, he could see that the man wore a blue windbreaker far too thin for the weather, jeans, and tennis shoes. Daniel's own leather jacket and slacks were only slightly more appropriate for the temperature, but then he hadn't expected to do much walking around tonight.

Despite the fact Daniel had been railing at the man, he wasn't looking in Daniel's direction. Indeed, he showed no sign that he was even aware that he'd almost been hit by Daniel's Cherokee. He kept turning his head as if searching for something, his feet shuffling back and forth in constant movement, as if he were desperate to keep running but unable to decide which direction to go. Daniel's anger ebbed as he realized the man was probably crazy, and he was about to turn around and head back to his vehicle when the man's gaze finally fixed on him, and his panic-stricken eyes widened even further. Not in fear this time, but recognition.

"Daniel? Daniel Symons?"

Daniel was so surprised to hear his name come from the man's lips that for a moment all he could do was stand and stare. And it was in that moment that Daniel realized who the short man in the blue windbreaker was.

"Billy Wallace? Is that you?"

The relief that washed over the man's – over Billy's – face was so sudden it was borderline comical. Billy rushed up to Daniel and gripped him by the shoulders, eyes wide, mouth stretched into an almost maniacal grin.

"My god, am I glad to see you! You gotta help me, Dan! They're after me!"

Too many conflicting thoughts and emotions roiled in Daniel's mind, preventing him from answering right away. He had no doubt that the terrified man standing in front of him, fingers digging almost painfully into his skin, was Billy Wallace. Daniel hadn't seen him since high school, over twenty years ago now, but aside from some wrinkles around the eyes and a hairline that wasn't receding so much as rapidly retreating, Billy looked little different than he had then. Seeing him here, in the middle of Electronixx's parking lot on a cold November night was weird enough, but the basic situation was so eerily similar to the last time Daniel had seen him that he was gripped by an overwhelming sense of déjà vu, one so powerful that for a moment he wondered if he might be dreaming. But then Billy squeezed his shoulders more tightly, and Daniel imagined his fingernails might cut through his jacket's leather. No dream, then. The sensations were too real.

Billy leaned in closer and gave Daniel's shoulders a shake to emphasize his next words. "You gotta get me out of here before they catch up to me!"

Billy's breath, unfortunately, was just as real as his grip. Redolent of days-old coffee and stale cigarettes, it made Daniel's gorge rise, and he had to swallow once before he could speak.

"What the hell are you talking about? There's no . . ."

Daniel's words died as he looked past Billy – over the top of his head, really – and saw a quartet of shadowy figures approaching from just beyond the pool of fluorescence in which Billy stood. They were tall, even taller than Daniel who stood over six feet, and thinner than Billy, almost cadaverously so. They moved slowly, their steps measured and deliberate, and if it hadn't been for the echo of their feet on the wet asphalt – soft plapping sounds, as if they wore swim fins – Daniel might've thought them nothing more than an illusion created by a combination of the night's gloom and exposure to Billy's wild paranoia.

Billy released Daniel's shoulders, took hold of his left arm, and started pulling him toward the Cherokee. "We need to leave – *now!*"

Maybe it was due to seeing Billy again in such strange circumstances, or maybe it was the atavistic crawling sensation on the back of his neck that told Daniel he was shit deep in trouble. But whatever the reason, he didn't question Billy. He started running for the Cherokee, digging in his pocket for the keys, praying they'd reach the vehicle in time, but in time for what, he wasn't certain.

Daniel jumped into the vehicle and yanked the door shut behind him. He jammed the key into the ignition as Billy opened the passenger door and frantically climbed inside. Through the open door Daniel caught a momentary glimpse of four dark figures approaching the Cherokee, a sight that was thankfully cut off as Billy slammed the car door. Daniel turned the key, resisting the urge to look past Billy out the passenger side window to monitor the shadowmen's progress. He didn't need to see them to know they were coming.

The Cherokee's engine growled to life, and Daniel put the transmission into reverse and stomped on the gas pedal. The vehicle swerved backward, and Daniel immediately stepped on the brake to keep from smashing into a parked Saturn behind him. The headlight beams swung around to shine on the shadowmen, and Daniel experienced a surge of irrational hope that the illumination would burn the dark figures out of existence like true shadows. But instead of dispelling the shadowmen, the glare from the headlights horribly accentuated their forms, revealing them to be man-shaped blobs of darkness, the surface of their bodies shiny-slick, like wet sealskin. Daniel saw no eyes, ears, or mouths, but he had no doubt the creatures could sense them and, though he saw nothing specific on which to base this conclusion, there was something about the inexorable way the four continued toward the Cherokee that made them seem *hungry*.

"Go, go, GO!" Billy shouted, and his words goaded Daniel into action. He put the Cherokee in drive and pressed down on the accelerator. Back tires squealed on wet pavement, and the rear end of the vehicle fishtailed before the Cherokee straightened out and roared forward. The shadowmen didn't move at first, and Daniel thought they might hit the damned things, but the dark quartet stepped aside at the last minute – two moving to the right, two to the left – and the Cherokee passed between them without difficulty. Daniel steered for the parking lot's exit, and though he told himself not to, he couldn't keep from looking in the rearview mirror. The shadowmen were there, of course, haloed by fluorescent light, standing motionless, watching as Daniel drove away, taking Billy with him. And then Daniel pulled the Cherokee onto the street and accelerated, determined to put as much distance between himself and Electronixx as possible.

They drove several moments in silence, moving at a good clip through Ash Creek's newly refurbished commercial district, past shopping centers, discount jewelers, upscale coffee shops, and restaurants struggling to look as if they weren't only a step or two above fast food joints. Daniel tried several times to ask Billy what the holy hell those shadow creatures were and what the fuckers wanted, but he couldn't bring himself to speak. He wondered if he might be in shock, but he decided that if he was, that was okay. Fine and dandy, as a matter of fact. He didn't think he was ready to know what the shadowmen were yet, and what's more, he wasn't sure he'd *ever* be ready. And that was cool. Copacetic, as they used to say in the sixties. Just as long as he never had to see the goddamned things again.

It was Billy who broke the silence first.

"Sure was lucky you came along when you did. I owe you my life, man."

Daniel's first thought was *Who says "man" anymore?* But then who was he to talk? He'd just used the word *copacetic* a couple minutes ago, hadn't he? *Least I didn't say it out loud.*

"I don't know if I'd call it luck," Daniel said, surprised to hear his own voice, and even more surprised by how calm he sounded. "I was just out . . . shopping." He didn't want to admit the real reason he was driving around Electronixx's parking lot.

"Didn't find anything, huh?" Billy said, and when Daniel didn't reply, he added, "The backseat's empty."

Daniel thought about making some excuse to explain his lack of purchases, but he couldn't think of anything, so he just kept his mouth shut and continued driving.

"Lucky for me, anyway," Billy said. "Just like that one day back in high school, right? 'cept this time turned out a hell of a lot better." Billy turned toward him, his eyes seeming to gleam in the dim illumination of the dashboard lights. "Kind of weird, huh?" His lips toyed with a smile, revealing teeth in dire need of a dentist's attention. There was something about that almost-smile that disturbed Daniel, a kind of sly knowing that belied Billy's words, as if the man was making fun of him for some reason.

Now that Daniel had the chance to observe Billy up close, he noticed other odd details. The man's hair was so short it was almost a buzz-cut, and his scalp had several bare patches dotted with scabs, as if he'd cut his own hair with an electric razor and done a piss-poor job. The cuffs of his windbreaker were frayed, his jeans were splotched with stains, and only one of his tennis shoes had strings. And then there was the smell . . . not just his coffee-and-cigs breath, though that was bad enough in these close quarters. The ripe-sour stink of a body that hadn't been washed in Christ only knew how long wafted forth from Billy like some olfactory version of radiation. It was so bad Daniel imagined his nose hairs shriveling up with each inhalation. He had no idea what had happened to Billy after high school, but now he wondered if the man was homeless. He sure as shit smelled like he was.

Homeless *and* chased through a parking lot by four shadow monsters, Daniel reminded himself. Wouldn't do to forget that little tidbit.

"You probably don't even remember that day, do you?" Billy said. "I'll never forget it, though. It was sophomore year, and we were in same gym class. With Mr. Briggs, remember? The guy was so fat he couldn't walk more than three steps without pausing to catch his breath. Some example of physical fitness. We weren't doing anything special; it was just open gym time, and the girls were playing basketball at one end of the gym, the boys at the other. I was picked last for a team . . . I always was."

Daniel felt an urge to say something to make Billy feel better, tell him that he hadn't always been the last to be picked, and even if he had, he'd been a decent player. But the truth was that Billy sucked big-time at sports. He'd always been short, skinny, and uncoordinated, but adolescence – instead of granting him height, muscles, and a deeper voice – had instead robbed him of what little grace he'd possessed. The other boys had joked that Billy was the only person they knew who could trip while standing still, and the sad part was it hadn't been much of an exaggeration.

"We were on the same team that day, though you probably don't remember that either, do you? Things went like they usually did for me back then. No one passed the ball to me, and I got a lot of 'intentional fouls,' which meant I got shoved around, punched in the arm, and knocked down."

Billy was right. Daniel didn't remember the details of that particular game, but then he didn't really need to in order to envision the scene Billy was trying to paint for him. Variations on it had been common enough in the gym, on the playground, and after school as far back as Daniel could remember. For some reason, there was always a scapegoat in school, a sineater whose only purpose in life was to take shit from the other kids. Back in the day, it had been Billy Wallace's great misfortune to be elected King of the Shiteaters for Ash Creek High School.

Billy went on. "It wasn't so bad, I suppose. I mean, I didn't get a bloody nose or anything. I figured the worst I'd end up with was some nasty bruises, and I was used to that, so no big deal." Billy fell silent and turned his head to look out the passenger window. They had reached the end of the commercial district and were now traveling down the tree-lined streets of a suburban neighborhood. Mounds of sodden leaves were piled next to the curbs by those residents industrious enough to get an early start on their autumn lawn work. Daniel had once had a yard, and he'd hated dealing with the leaves every fall, even with the aid of a leaf blower. Now he'd give anything to have a home with a lawn that needed tending instead of his cramped, lonely crackerbox of an apartment that needed nothing from him and gave it back in equal measure.

Daniel knew where Billy's story was heading, and it wasn't territory he wanted to revisit, especially right now. He'd recovered enough from the encounter with the shadowmen to finally talk about them, and he thought that subject was a wee bit more important at the moment.

"What were those things back there? Why were they after you?"

Billy didn't answer right away, and Daniel thought maybe he was so lost in his memories that he hadn't heard. That, or maybe he was in shock, too. After all, he was the one the damned things had been chasing. Daniel was about to repeat his questions when Billy spoke once again.

"It was a different story in the locker room, though. Mr. Briggs might've been a lazy fast-ass, but he only tolerated bullying in his gym up to a point. He never came in the locker room, though, so in there, anything went. A few of the boys – Chris Milligan, Bob Lewis, and Douglas Sanderson – started ragging on me for losing the game for them, whip-cracking their towels on my ass. It sucked, but I could handle it. But then their taunts began to turn ugly, and the anger on their faces became hatred. They made a circle around me and started pushing me back and forth between them, like I was some kind of exercise ball or something. Then they started hitting instead of pushing. Hitting hard. The other boys gathered round and started laughing, cheering them on, yelling for them to hit me even harder . . ."

Daniel felt a cold prickly sensation in his gut that had nothing to do with the shadowmen and everything to do with Billy's story.

He had to swallow twice before he was able to speak. "It was a long time ago, Billy."

Billy turned away from the passenger window to face Daniel once more. "Not so long as you think." Then lower, almost a whisper. "Not for me. You were there too, watching with the others, but you didn't laugh or cheer. Do you remember what you did?" Billy rushed on before Daniel could answer. "You told them to stop it and leave me alone."

Daniel remembered. How could he not? He also remembered what had happened next, and that was something he didn't want to think about right then. So he was almost relieved when he glanced up at the rearview mirror and saw a dark shape framed there. At first he thought it was a car running with its lights off, but while it had the general shape of a car, there was something profoundly wrong about it. The edges were too rounded, the proportions uneven, and there was a lack of clearly distinguishable surface details. No dividing line between windshield and metal, no wipers, no visible headlights, no front bumper, and – worst of all – no engine noise. The vehicle, whatever it was, moved swift and silent, and it was right on their ass, the dark machine so close it might as well have been welded to the Cherokee. Daniel knew who rode inside.

"They've found us."

Billy spun around in his seat and looked out the back. "Fuck!" He faced forward and looked out the windshield. "How close are we to the edge of town?"

Daniel couldn't take his gaze off the rearview mirror and the shadowy mass shaped into a crude approximation of a vehicle filling the glass. "About a mile, maybe."

"Head for the country. Once we hit a good long stretch of road we can go fast enough to lose them."

"What makes you so goddamned certain we can outrun the fuckers?" Daniel demanded.

"I've been dealing with them for a while now. They're scary as shit and dangerous as hell, but they're not all-powerful. Trust me."

Everything had gotten strange so fast that Daniel hadn't had the opportunity – let alone the capacity – to think rationally. But he decided to do as Billy said. The man seemed to know what he was talking about, and besides, it wasn't as if Daniel had any brilliant ideas on how to escape the shadowmen.

The suburbs of Ash Creek soon gave way to weathered-gray telephone poles and cornfields bordered by rusty wire fences. The road they traveled was straight and flat, no sign of any other vehicles for miles. The feeble glow of the Cherokee's headlights preceded them and beyond that, only darkness was visible. For a moment Daniel had the impression that nothing existed in front of the Cherokee, except what was revealed – or perhaps brought into existence – by the vehicle's headlights. If that was true, what would happen if he switched the headlights off? Would the road beneath them disappear, sending the Cherokee, not to mention its occupants, plunging downward in an endless descent into nothingness?

"Faster!" Billy urged. "They're catching up!"

His passenger's frantic voice snapped Daniel back to reality – or at least what passed for it this night. He checked the rearview and saw the shadow-car closing fast, its shiny black surface tinted a sinister red by the Cherokee's brake lights. Daniel still couldn't see into the vehicle, but he didn't need to. He knew the four shadowmen were in there; he could *feel* them . . . feel their eagerness, their hunger, almost as if they were broadcasting their all-consuming need on some psychic frequency.

The Cherokee was already doing close to eighty, but Daniel pressed the accelerator down further. The engine resisted at first, but then its rumble deepened and the vehicle slowly began to pick up more speed. In the rearview, the shadowcar receded, but only by a few yards. It still managed to keep up just fine. A terrible thought occurred to him them: maybe the shadowcar wasn't a vehicle after all. Maybe it was the shadowmen themselves, the four merged together as one, disguised, their strength combined so that they could travel swiftly and run their prey to ground.

Beads of cold sweat dotted Daniel's forehead, and he felt a queasy tightness in his jaw muscles, as if he were on the verge of throwing up. "I've had enough of this shit, Billy! I need to know what the fuck's going on, and I need to know *now!*"

Billy didn't respond immediately, and Daniel thought he was going to avoid answering again. But he began speaking in a voice so soft that his words were barely audible over the roar of the Cherokee's engine.

"They don't have a name, at least, not one I know. I've never heard them speak. Maybe they can't." He shrugged. "You know those fish that just lay there on the bottom of the tank, sucking up all the other fishes' shit?"

"Bottom feeders," Daniel supplied. He glanced at the rearview again. The shadowcar was no closer, but it was no farther away, either.

"Yeah. That's what I figure they are. Not fish, of course." He let out a snuffle of a laugh. "But they do the same sort of thing. I guess you could say they eat the garbage of existence. I'm not talking about the kind of crap people throw out of car windows as they drive – empty coffee cups, crumpled fast-food bags, that sort of shit. Not physical trash. They clean up the other stuff we leave behind. Painful memories we try to suppress and forget. Uncomfortable emotions that we struggle to cast out as if exorcising demons. We can't see these things, but they're real. You can feel them. Ever been in an empty room and felt that the atmosphere was emotionally charged? Maybe you sense lingering hostility or a profound sadness. That's what they feed on. Good thing, too, because if all that shit were allowed to build up . . ." He shuddered. "Well, it would be one fuck of a mess, I bet."

Billy's explanation sounded insane to Daniel, but then it was no more insane than the reality of the four shadowmen. Daniel doubted that even the most logical and plausible of explanations – and Billy's didn't count as either – could've satisfied him. How could something like the shadowmen ever truly be explained?

Daniel checked the rearview again, and this time he had to look twice before he could bring himself to believe what he saw: the shadowcar had fallen back at least a dozen yards, maybe more. Wild exultation filled him, and he nearly let out a whoop of delight.

Billy must've sensed his reaction, for he turned around and looked out the back window. "Hot damn, Daniel! You're doing it!" He gave Daniel a congratulatory punch on the shoulder. "Keep it up. If we can put enough distance between us and them, we can cut the lights and pull off onto a side road or maybe into a farmer's driveway. They're simple-minded and act mostly on instinct. Once they set out in a direction, they won't deviate from it without a good reason. If they don't see us turn, it won't even occur to them that we did so. They'll keep on going straight for miles before realizing they lost us. And by then, we'll have pulled back onto the road and hauled ass in the other direction."

Billy's plan seemed like nothing more than wishful thinking, like a child who believes that once he's covered his eyes no one else can see him. But then Daniel remembered something he'd witnessed when he'd been a child himself. He'd spent a week visiting his grandfather at his farm, and he'd watched one day as his grandfather's German shepherd chased a rabbit. Just as the dog was about to move in for the kill, the rabbit veered off at a ninety-degree angle and bounded away in a series of long leaps. The shepherd continued running straight while the rabbit fled. Eventually the dog stopped running and trotted back and forth across the field, confused, sniffing the ground in an attempt to pick up the rabbit's trail. But the rabbit had broken the trail by leaping, and though the shepherd continued searching for the trail for the better part of a half hour, the dog never found it again.

Maybe Billy was right about the shadowmen, maybe they did operate on instinct, just like Grandpa's dog. And if that was true, they maybe Billy's plan had a chance of working. For the first time since he'd gazed up the shadowmen, Daniel began to feel a slight glimmer of hope that he just might survive this night.

Another check of the rearview mirror showed that the shadowmen had fallen so far behind that their dark vehicle was almost lost to sight.

"Now?" Daniel asked.

Billy glanced over his shoulder. "Almost. Give it another minute or so."

Daniel wondered whether his Cherokee would last that long. He kept his vehicle in good condition, but it was overdue for servicing, and any car, no matter how well made and maintained, could only run flat out for so long before something went wrong. A burnt gasket, a leaking hose, a thrown rod – any one of those would put an end to their flight and allow the shadowmen to catch up. And once they did . . . Daniel wasn't exactly sure what the damned things would do, but he doubted it would be much fun. Not for him and Billy at any rate.

"You said those things have been chasing you for a while now. If they feed on leftover emotional gunk, why are they after you?" Daniel had almost said *after us* but he didn't want to put himself into the same category as Billy. Let Billy remain the shadowmen's chosen victim. For as long as he could, Daniel wanted to continue to pretend he was the guy who'd come to Billy's rescue and not a victim himself. And if he didn't believe truly it, at least he could act like he did. It wasn't much, but it was all he had to hold down the ocean of terror roiling beneath the surface of his mind, and it would have to do.

Billy's sigh was heavy with weariness. "There are some people who become a focus for others' negative emotions. They absorb those feelings, whether they like it or not, store them like living batteries." He thought for a moment. "Maybe more like a steak soaking up a marinade before it's cooked." He looked at Daniel and gave him a sickly grin. "Makes for good eating, I imagine."

Daniel's stomach lurched at the imagery Billy's words conjured in his mind. "And you're one of these people, one of these . . . psychic batteries?" But before he finished asking the question, Daniel already knew the answer. Billy Wallace had been a pariah in high school, a punching bag, a dumping ground for any negative emotion someone felt like hurling at him, force-fed like a farm animal bred for slaughter. He was a fatted calf, and to the shadowmen he would be a feast, a banquet of emotions darker than their own ebon substance.

"I didn't do much after high school," Billy said. "But then I wasn't voted most likely to succeed, was I? I worked at a gas station for a few years, but the owner never liked me and eventually I was fired. Same thing happened at all the other jobs I ever managed to land, until finally I couldn't get work anymore. I guess by that time I'd soaked up so much of other people's shit that no one could stand being around me for very long. I was homeless for a while after that, lived right here on the streets of Ash Creek. You probably saw me around a dozen times as you drove around town, but you never noticed me. No one did. Not until *they* showed up. I figure they were drawn by my psychic scent, or whatever you'd call it. That was six months ago and –"

Billy broke off and pointed out the windshield.

"There! See that dirt road up their off to the left? That's perfect!" He turned around in his seat and looked out the back window. "I don't see any sign of them. Now's our chance!"

Daniel checked the rearview one more time and saw only darkness. He knew that didn't mean the shadowmen weren't still back there, though. They weren't on their bumper anymore, but with the way their dark vehicle blended with the night, there was no telling how far behind they'd fallen. Maybe not far enough. Still, this might be the only chance he and Billy got.

"Hold on," Daniel said. He took his foot off the gas, let the Cherokee decelerate for a few seconds, and then hit the brake. He had to resist the urge to jam the pedal to the floor. At the speed they were going, they'd end up in the ditch, maybe even flip over. As it was, the Cherokee's back end shimmied and Daniel had to fight to maintain control of the vehicle. The dirt road – which Daniel knew would in truth be a mud road after the rain they'd had earlier – came up faster than he expected. He yanked the steering wheel to the left, and the Cherokee hydroplaned as Daniel aimed for the entrance. The vehicle slid onto the road sideways, and as Daniel had feared, it was nothing but mud. When the Cherokee hit the road it kept right on sliding, smashing through a wire fence and into an empty field whose crop – wheat or perhaps soybeans – had been harvested some time ago. But even as they slid into the field, Daniel had the presence of mind to flip off the Cherokee's headlights and take his foot off the brake, and they came to a stop in darkness.

Daniel turned off the engine, just in case the sound might attract the shadowmen's attention. Besides, he doubted they'd be able to drive out of this muck anytime soon. They'd probably have to be towed out. Of course, if their ruse didn't work and the shadowmen found them, getting his Cherokee out of the field would be the least of his worries.

Daniel and Billy sat, listening to the ticking of the Cherokee's overheated engine. A faint odor of burning plastic drifted in through the vents, but Daniel barely registered it. He was too busy looking out the windows, searching the night for sign of the shadowmen. He saw nothing, but as he started to feel optimism stirring, he reminded himself that they wouldn't see anything – not until the shadowmen were almost on top of them, and by then it would be too late.

While Daniel feared the shadowmen, for their sheer otherworldliness if nothing else, sitting there in the dark, watching and waiting, he realized he didn't fear dying. He'd been seeing a therapist ever since Angie had told him she wanted a divorce, and he'd just had his latest appointment two days ago. After telling the psychologist how he felt like a failure as a husband and a father – absolutely without worth to anyone, least of all himself – she'd tried to turn the conversation in a more "productive" direction by having him focus on the future.

What are you looking forward to? she'd asked.

After a moment's thought, he'd answered. *Nothing.*

But that hadn't been his first answer. The one that had popped into his head the moment she'd asked the question, the one he'd left unvoiced, consisted of two simple words. *My death.*

Maybe it wouldn't be so bad if the shadowmen found him. Maybe it had been a mistake to run in the first place. A missed opportunity.

Billy spoke then, interrupting Daniel's grim thoughts.

"Do you remember what you did when those boys started to beat me up in the locker room?"

For a moment Daniel had no idea what Billy was talking about, but then it came back to him. He answered without taking his gaze from the windows and the darkness that lay beyond the glass. "I tried to help you."

"You took two steps toward me. Exactly two. Yes, I counted, and yes, I've never forgotten. I also have never forgotten what you said. 'Hey, guys, enough's enough. Leave him alone.' Do you recall what happened after that?" Billy's tone had taken on an insistent, almost demanding edge, which Daniel chose to ignore.

"One of the boys – Chris Milligan, I think – told me that if I didn't stay out of it I'd get my ass kicked too." Even now, sitting in the dark waiting for creatures out of nightmare to come for him, Daniel felt shame at the memory. Shame because he hadn't stood up to Chris and the others. Because he'd backed away and gotten dressed to the sound of the crowd laughing as Chris and his cohorts returned to their fun. They were still at it when he left the locker room and headed off for class, Billy's sobs lingering in his ears.

"None of them – Chris Milligan, Bob Lewis, or Douglas Sanderson – was ever punished." Billy's voice was thick with venom now, so much so that the sound of it made Daniel turn away from the window and look the man in the face. A face that became increasing twisted with hate as he went on. "That fat-ass Briggs never checked to see what went on in the locker room, but I always figured he knew. How could he not? You know gym teachers. They figure shit like that will toughen you up, and if it doesn't, you're a pussy and you deserve whatever you get. I survived, but I lost a couple teeth, and I still walk with a limp on my right side."

Daniel remembered when he first saw Billy tonight, illuminated by the Cherokee's headlights, his right leg looking as if it might buckle any second.

Billy paused then and his mouth eased into a sly smile, though hatred continued to burn in his eyes. "Everything I've told you about the shadow creatures is true. But I never said they were *chasing* me. I said I've been *dealing* with them for a while. I chose my words very carefully, Daniel. They were drawn to me because they wanted to feed on me, but they didn't want to kill me. They wanted to keep me alive so that I could continue to produce negative emotions for them, like a cow giving milk."

"Nothing personal, but that's an image I could've done without."

"Go ahead and laugh if you want, but my friends are plenty satisfied with what I give them. So much so that from time to time they do little favors for me."

Daniel kept his gaze fastened on Billy, but out of the corner of his eye, he thought he saw something dark move outside the Cherokee. No, s*omethings*. Plural.

"I told you they're not very intelligent, at least not in a way you and I recognize, but I've learned to communicate with them over the last few months. Enough to get my ideas across, anyway. We visited Briggs first. He was responsible for making sure students behaved in gym. A responsibility he obviously didn't give a fuck about. The sonofabitch was retired and stuck in a nursing home, but he was still fat as ever. After that, we visited the others – first Chris Milligan, then Bob, then Douglas." His smile became a grin. "Now it's your turn. I saved you for last because what you did was worse than any of the others. As much as I hated them, I understood that they were just acting according to their natures. Not that I forgave them for it – or spared them. But you understood that what they did was wrong, and you even tried to stop it. Except you pussed out in the end. For a moment, I believed there was someone on this sorry shit-pile of a planet who gave a damn about me. But then you turned your back and walked away. That's the worst thing anyone's ever done to me. Worse than all the punches, kicks, and namecalling I endured as a kid . . . worse than all the bosses who yelled at me and told me I was nothing when I became an adult, all the women who wouldn't even waste the saliva to spit on me. And you know what was worst of all?"

There was definitely movement outside the Cherokee now, and it was close.

"Because I gave you hope," Daniel said. "And then I took it away."

"Exactly." Billy glanced out the window, and the venom in his voice gave way to eager anticipation. "It's been a long time, Daniel, but your bill has finally come due." Billy was so excited that he was quivering, nearly bouncing on the passenger seat.

"How many times did you practice that little speech? Nevermind. I've got a serious question: why go to all the trouble of pretending to run away from the shadowmen? They could've just taken me back in the parking lot. No, wait. I get it. You wanted me to see what it was like to have hope taken away."

"Smart man." Billy's grin stretched wider then, assuming a maniacal aspect that Daniel found quite appropriate given the circumstances. "Besides," he added, "it was more fun this way."

"I'm sure. So . . . you hook up with supernatural creatures that are willing to do favors for you as long as you keep supplying them with the good dark stuff, and the best you can come up with is to use them to kill some people who pissed you off in high school?"

The hatred in Billy's eyes dimmed as doubt moved across his face, but a second later a sneer contorted his features, and the fire in his gaze burned strong as ever. "You're just like all the others who made my life miserable over the years, for no other reason than to punish me for the crime of existing."

Movement caught Daniel's attention, and he turned toward the driver's side window to see an ebon hand press against the glass. It was followed by a second hand, and then a dark eyeless face appeared between them and leaned forward. A round orifice gaped open in the middle of the face and affixed itself to the window, the ring of black muscle pulsing rhythmically as if the creature were trying to suck Daniel's psychic energy through the glass. With a sick twist of nausea, Daniel remembered how Billy had described the shadowmen as bottom feeders, and he had to admit the comparison was grotesquely apt.

The remaining shadowmen joined their companion – two on the driver's side window, two on the passenger's – until all four obscene mouths were sealed against glass sucking, sucking . . .

Daniel should've been terrified, and on some level he was. But he also felt a strange sense of peace settle over him.

"I'm not going to pretend I know what it was like for you to grow up as the world's emotional tampon," Daniel said, "But the past doesn't excuse the present. There are lots of things we can't control in life – too damned many – but there's one thing we can control, and that's the choices we make. You've made your choice, Billy. Now it's time for me to make mine."

Daniel undid his seatbelt, then thumbed a switch on the driver's side door, causing the locks to disengage with muffled *chunks*.

Billy frowned in confusion. "You're going to *give* yourself to them?" He sounded disappointed, as if he felt cheated that Daniel wasn't going to struggle and beg for his life.

"No. I'm going to leave – or at least try to. I have to go work tomorrow, and I've got to mail a check to my ex-wife. You can live in yesterday if you want, but I've been there, and I wouldn't recommend it."

Daniel started to push the driver's door open, and the two shadowmen standing at the window drew back – almost eagerly, he thought – to give him room. He shoved the door the rest of the way open, and stepped out into the cold night. His plan was simple: to start running as fast as he could manage across the muddy field and get as far as he could before whatever happened, happened. It might not have been much of a plan, but that was okay. It was his, and for the first time in months, he felt alive again.

He inhaled deeply and prepared to run as four patches of darkness closed in.

Unwoven

You're staring at your laptop screen, trying to think of the next word to write, when a tiny movement catches your eye. At first you think it's some kind of computer glitch, that some small image is randomly flickering in the upper left corner of the screen. But when you shift your gaze to check it out, you see that a spider has crawled onto your computer. You're startled – you *hate* spiders, so much so that you experience a nauseating twist in your gut, and your skin starts itching all over, as if a million of the spider's relatives are scuttling all over your body.

Without thinking, you grip the top of the screen and slam it shut onto the keyboard, then you yank your hand away from the computer, as if you'd been burned. You sit there for several long seconds, unable to rise from the dining table chair, heart pounding in your ears, breath coming in rapid-nervous dog-pants. Your eyes dart anxiously back and forth, examining the seam where the two halves of the laptop meet, waiting to see where the spider will emerge. But after some time has passed – minutes, hours, it's impossible to say – there's been no sign of the spider and your pulse slows, your breathing eases. You smile with satisfaction.

Gotcha, you little bastard!

Leaving your laptop closed, you stand up and walk out of the dining room – past rows of recessed shelves filled with hardback books, one of the reasons you love to write in here – and head into the kitchen. Your nausea's subdued a bit, and you're starting to feel embarrassed for overreacting. It's a good thing neither the kids nor your husband is home. Sarah would be grossed out and her younger brother Eric would be sad that an innocent spider died. And Mark . . . Well, Mark is Mark. Being overwhelmed by emotion isn't something he understands, let alone sympathizes with.

You realize that Eric would be especially upset over the spider's death. Just yesterday you read a book to him that he'd brought home from the kindergarten library – a book about spiders. Really about one spider, a figure from African folklore called Anansi. You'd never heard of him before, and because he was a spider, you were reluctant to read the book to Eric at first. But you thumbed through the pages – suppressing a shudder – and saw that Anansi was drawn standing upright like a human, and he had a face that resembled that of an African-American male. A *human* face. Kind, if somewhat mischievous, a face that reassured you, and you were able to read the story to Eric without much trouble.

Despite how you feel about spiders, the tale was an interesting one, especially to you, since you're a writer. It told of a time when there were no stories in the world because Sky God hoarded them all for himself. Anansi didn't think this situation was fair, so, through a combination of guile and cleverness, Anansi tricked Sky God into giving *him* the stories, and when the spider returned to Earth, he shared those stories with the entire world. That's why (the book ended) all stories are called Anansi tales.

Eric loved the story – mostly because of the cute illustrations – but you thought it was a good metaphor for how writers find inspiration, and you had to admit that a spider, with its ability to weave separate strands of silk into a web, made an effective patron spirit for storytellers.

Eric, in his child's way, had recognized the metaphor as well.

"Maybe that's where you get your stories, Mommy! Ansani brings them!"

All in all, a cute little book. Not that it could ever change you mind about spiders . . . damned creepy pests . . .

In the kitchen, you tear off a few paper towels from the roll hanging beneath the cupboard next to the sink and head back into the dining room. Now that your fear has dwindled away to almost nothing, you're beginning to think practically again. You have no idea if smooshed spider guts can leak between the keys and get into the electronics underneath, but you figure you'd better clear away the messy remains of Mr. Spider before he takes his final revenge and ruins your brand-new thousand-dollar laptop.

You sit down in front of the closed computer, gripping the paper towels so hard they've become a wadded ball. You take a deep breath, count to three, and with your free hand open the laptop.

You stare for a moment, not quite able to understand what you're seeing – or rather *not* seeing.

There is no squooshed spider – no guts, no blood, no crushed black body with legs curled inward in death. The screen and keyboard are both completely clean.

There's something else weird: the screen is blank. The personal essay you'd been working on – a reminiscence about walking alone outside during a snowy night when you were a child in Oregon – is gone. You were almost finished with it, and it had been turning out great. You enjoy writing fiction, but you've always found nonfiction more satisfying, both artistically and emotionally. As you once told Mark: "All of our lives are stories, aren't they? It's what we're made of, really, one story after another." Of course, he'd had no idea what you were talking about.

Frantically, you put the paper-towel wad aside and open the word processing program's memory files to search for your essay – but it's not there. None of your stories, articles, or essays are there, either. The program's memory has somehow been erased.

Your flashdrive is sitting on the dining table to the right of your laptop. You plug it into the computer's front port to check your back-up files.

Please, please, please . . .

They're gone, too. The flashdrive is empty.

A thought crosses your mind, then. A crazy, awful thought.

That spider . . . what if it had been Anansi, coming to you help you with your essay. Maybe the spider was even *bringing* it to you, like an eight-legged muse. After all, *all* stories are Anasi tales, right?

It's a ludicrous thought, and you try to force a laugh to acknowledge the absurdity, but the only sound that comes out of your throat is a choking gasp.

You've killed Anansi. You've killed all the stories in the world.

You glance over your shoulder at the built-in shelves behind the dining table, and you wish you were surprised to see that, like your laptop and flashdrive, they're empty. The books – the *stories* – are gone.

A detached numbness begins creeping over you as you look at the cursor blinking on the computer screen. You poise trembling fingers over the keyboard and begin to type, but though your fingers depress key after key, no letters appear on the screen. No words.

The numbness grows stronger, and you can't feel your fingers touch the keys, can't feel your body at all anymore. It's almost like what you imagine freezing to death must feel like, expect it's not really cold, it's just sensation of profound nothingness.

Your last thought before you fade into non-existence is to recall one more time what you told Mark.

All of our lives are stories, aren't they?

Several quiet seconds pass in the now-empty house, and then from somewhere within the laptop's casing comes the high-pitched skittery-scratchy sound of laughter.

Skull Cathedral

Pre-Op

You lie naked on cold stainless steel, coils of barbed wire wrapped around your wrists and ankles, the wire bolted to the table, holding you in place. The wire is tight enough for the barbs to dimple flesh but not draw blood. But you know you can't slip out of your restraints, can't so much as shift position without doing serious injury to yourself, and so you lie still. Which is, after all, the point. Ridiculously, you're relieved that the barbed wire is new; less chance of tetanus that way. As if *that* was your biggest fucking worry right now.

Bright light above you, sour yellow, like pus from a boil frozen in the instant of bursting. Warmth radiates from the light, too much warmth, like the fever-heat of a raging infection. Your stomach clenches with nausea, sweat issues from your pores, and despite the heat, you start shivering.

You only see blackness beyond the wash of pus-light, and you can't tell where you are. You have the sense of largeness, as if you're inside an empty warehouse, but the air is stale and still, and for all you know, you could be in a room scarcely bigger than a closet. Doesn't matter, you decide. Big, small . . . wherever the hell you are, it's somewhere you sure as shit don't want to be, and that's a fact.

"You're awake." A pause, as if the speaker is considering this development. "Good," he pronounces at last.

The sudden sound of the voice should startle you, but it doesn't. It seems appropriate somehow, and reassuring. At least you're not alone. And then it occurs to you that whoever owns the voice is probably the same person responsible for you being in your current predicament, and you no longer feel quite so reassured.

You hear the sound of hard-soled shoes scuffling on tiled floor, and though you still can't see the speaker, you know that he's coming closer to the table. (You almost think *operating* table, but you won't allow your mind to go there, not yet, not until there's no choice.)

In reflex, you turn your head in the direction of the sound of approaching footsteps, and your left cheek presses against the table's cold metal.

The speaker – who's close enough now to be a shadowy silhouette – *tssks*. "I see I've neglected to put on the head restraints. Getting forgetful in my old age, I suppose."

A hand emerges from the darkness – gray liver-spotted flesh, finger joints knotted with arthritis, nails dirty and jagged. The fingers grip your chin, their touch dry and lizard-leathery, and the speaker turns your head back so that you're looking directly up at the light again.

"Now you stay like that until I can get the final restraints on. You'll be tempted to wriggle, I'm sure, but the procedure will go far more smoothly – not to mention safely – if your head is held absolutely motionless. And you won't be able to do that on your own." You can't see the man's face, but you can hear the smile in his voice as he adds, "Believe me."

The hand withdraws into shadow, and the speaker moves off. He returns a few moments later, and when the hand emerges from the darkness again, you see that it's now holding a fresh coil of barbed wire. A second hand appears, this one gripping a pair of wire cutters.

You're still screaming after the man's finished wrapping the wire (three times around the forehead, three times around the chin), and then fixing the loose ends to the table somehow, in a way you can't see, but is extremely effective nevertheless, because you can't move your head. Hell, you don't want to even try. You can feel the blood trickling down the sides of your face, pooling beneath your head, against the tops of your shoulders.

A clatter, and you realize the speaker – who you're starting to think of as *the doctor* – has dropped the wire cutters to the floor, discarding them. More foot shuffling, and then the doctor reappears (or at least his silhouette does), the gray hands holding something that looks like a misshapen crustacean shell covered in porcupine quills. A thick clear jelly coats the quills, and a stench like decaying vegetable matter, wet hair, and spilled semen assaults your nostrils.

"I'm sure you're very confused right now, but I assure you, this treatment is your only hope. You . . . think things you shouldn't. Things –" a pause, and you imagine the doctor's mouth (assuming he has one) pursing in distaste. "Well, let us just label them *inappropriate* and leave it at that, shall we? If your thoughts affected only you, that would be one thing. But you have the arrogance to inflict them on others. It's criminal, really. If it were up to me . . . Well, nevermind. I'm doctor, and I took an oath to help others, so let's get to it, shall we? I regret that I'm unable to offer you any anesthetic," he says, sounding not sorry at all. "But for the procedure to be successful, you must remain completely aware the entire time." You hear a grin in the voice. "But on the bright side, there's a decent chance you'll die not long after we begin, in which case you'll be out of your misery soon enough. Now let's begin."

You try to open your mouth to protest, but the instant your jaw starts to move, the barbed wire around your chin bites into your lower lip, and the only sound you manage to make is a hissing intake of air.

The doctor places the shell-device against your forehead and begins to slowly push. The quills pierce the thin flesh of your forehead as if it were half-melted butter, and you feel their sharp points begin to scrape against the bone of your skull.

You scream with your mouth closed, and the procedure begins.

Midnight in Some Flaming Town (Neurocranium)

You huddle in an alley, wet, cold, and shivering. A steady rain falls, but it does nothing to weaken the fires. They've burned too long, grown too large, too strong. You imagine you can hear the hiss of rainwater turning to steam before the drops reach the flames, and maybe you do. You've always had strong hearing.

Your sense of smell is quite keen as well, and you breathe in the scents of charred wood, wet ash, hot metal, and – faint but unmistakable – burning flesh. You imagine you hear skin crackling as it blackens, fat sizzling and popping, blood boiling, cooking veins from the inside out. You think you hear the echo of distant screams followed by agonized moans and final exhalations of breath, but you're sure these sounds must be fantasy, for anyone caught in the fires' flickering embrace would've succumbed to smoke inhalation before beginning to fry.

At least, that's what you hope.

You have no idea how far the flames have spread – do they cover the whole town, the state, the whole goddamned world? Maybe the entire universe is aflame, the heat death of all things occurring in a far different way from how physicists predicted. All you know is that this alley is free from the fire. If you hadn't smelled the smoke (those heightened senses of yours again), hadn't woken up, left your apartment, gone down the fire escape, and found this alley – perhaps the one safe place left in all Existence – you'd be dead now. Like the others.

Another bit of luck: wind accompanies the rain, keeping the worst of the smoke from filtering into the alley, helping to make your little pocket of safety that much safer. If you can manage to stay alive long enough, surely someone will come . . . firefighters, national guard, military . . . to battle the flames. Someone . . .

You hear a noise then, and this time it's not your imagination, though you wish to hell it was. A cross between a bird's raucous squawk and an infant's cry cuts through the night, turning your guts to icewater. It's not the first time you've heard such noises since the flames began, but you've never heard one so close before. It sounds like it came from right outside the alley . . . No, you realize. From *above*.

You don't want to look up, but you can't stop yourself. Though it's night, there's more than enough light from the nearby flames to illuminate the tops of the two buildings that form the boundaries of your fragile sanctuary. You see them on the roofs, dozens of them, leaning over and looking down at you. Eyes wide and staring, mouth-gashes split into hungry grins.

One of them – you can't tell which, not that it matters – speaks in a voice like a cawing crow.

"*Told* you we missed one!"

The creatures . . . naked, hairless . . . stand. They reach down between their legs and take hold of flabby organs that don't resemble penises very much, but it's the only comparison you can think of at the moment. Then, with a chorus of those hideous cries, they began pissing streams of fire down onto you.

You try to scramble to your feet, intending to dash out of the alley and into the street, to take your chances with the flames out there, but the first stream hits you on the shoulder, and you know it's too late. An instant later, you're covered in fiery piss, and as you attempt to scream, the burning liquid flows into your mouth, searing your tongue, running down your throat, flash-frying your vocal chords, and you –

Nothing. It's gone. All of it.

Very good, says the doctor. *Let's move on to stage two, shall we?*

A fresh wave of pressure against your head, and you know the doctor is pushing the quill-shell farther into you. You feel a sickening pop as the quills pierce the inner layer of your skull and keep going, sinker deeper.

Deeper . . .

Dee –

Seas of Wasted Blood (Forebrain)

You're laying face-down on a raft made of human skin, leathery swatches joined together with irregular, jagged stitching. Not your best work, but it was all you had time for before the ship went down. How long ago that was, you're not sure. Days, surely. No more than that, else you would've died of thirst by now, right? A line of poetry drifts through your consciousness. *Water, water everywhere and not a –*

Except the ocean you're bobbing on isn't made of water. It's dark red, thick, and reeks of salt, copper, and sour piss. You instinctively know what it is, but you don't want to admit it to yourself. Can't.

Sunlight – harsh, unforgiving – beats down on you. And *beats* is definitely the right word to describe it, for the shower of photons pounds into you second after second like a series of blows from a white-hot sledge hammer wielded by one royally pissed-off deity. For perhaps the zillionth time since the boat went under, you wish you'd been able to make a sun shield of some sort. But you barely had enough time to flense the skin from the bitches you'd brought with you on your little sea junket and stitch their supple hides together before the boat went under. And you wouldn't have been able to accomplish that much if you hadn't already been planning on killing the women once you were finished making the adult film you'd (supposedly) hired them to shoot. You had the right assortment of knives, and more importantly, you had the experience. You'd like to put your survival down to effective foresight, but if you truly were good at planning, you'd have made sure to buy an emergency life-raft before setting out, maybe paid for someone to inspect the boat to make sure it was seaworthy and wouldn't go down in the middle of the night. Truth is, you're just a homicidal jackass who got lucky, and you know it.

Maybe not alive for very much longer, though. You've already lost your mind, or else you wouldn't think the sea had turned to (*don't think it, don't think it*) blood. You could go any moment. Hell, every time you blink your eyes, you're not sure they're going to open again. It's a miracle your homemade raft hasn't drawn the attention of every shark for a hundred miles. (Can sharks survive in such a sea? you think. How could their gills extract oxygen from blood?) You're dead and you know it. In the end, maybe the women had it good after all. They went fast, if not easy, but your agony just keeps going on and on . . .

Stupid whores.

A thought occurs to you then. You used as much of the women's hides as you could to make your raft. Their breasts have served as head rests and hand holds, especially when the (blood)sea has gotten choppy. You made sure your raft includes another body part, though. One of your favorites, though so far you haven't had a use for it. Four vaginas, arranged in the center of the raft, stitched so closely together that they're nearly touching.

You figure, if you're going to check out, you might as well bust a nut one last time. That's all whores are good for anyway, right? In a way, you'll be allowing the four airheads who fell for your making-a-film bullshit to fulfill their true (and only) purpose one last time. Looked at that way, it's really kind of noble of you.

You know you're weak, but you're surprised by how much trouble you have sitting up and taking off your shirt and pants. (No shoes and socks. Those went down with the ship.) You finally succeed, though you almost pitch over the side of your flesh-raft into the (blood)sea in the process. You toss your clothes overboard.

It's not like you're going to need them again. You position yourself over one of the vaginas – the pubic hair is reddish-brown, so you know which woman it belonged to, though you can't remember her name, if you ever knew it.

A flicker of fear passes through you as you press your organ against the red-head's hole. What if you're too weak to get hard? Wouldn't *that* suck, having four vaginas to play with, wanting to get off one last time, but not being able to get a stiffy? But your penis swells fast, and you're rock-hard within seconds. You remember reading somewhere that men often ejaculate at the moment of death, the body's way of making one last desperate attempt to spread its seed before dying. Evolution might be an unforgiving bitch, but as least she's working in your favor right now.

The hole is dry as sandpaper in the Sahara, and despite how hard you are, you can't force your way inside. You slide over to the edge of the raft and scoop up a handful of the only lube available and smear thick red-black clots over your organ. Then, doing your best to ignore the warm, slimy sensation that's coating your rod, you scoot back over to the red-head's pussy and plunge inside.

And the raft ripples beneath you.

You freeze, fearing that an ocean predator has found you at last, is circling beneath the raft, bumping its smooth, streamlined head into the flesh-raft, testing it, trying to decide whether or not it's good to eat. But after several moments pass without any other disturbance, you decide it was just a wave and you start thrusting in and out.

The raft begins to ripple again, now in time with your thrusts.

You stop, the raft stops. You start again, so does the raft. It's almost like the raft is, is . . .*alive*, and getting off on what you're doing.

A raspy bark of a laugh escapes your throat. You've gone completely around the bend now, no doubt. You decide to go with it, though. You're already insane, so what does it matter?

Pump-pump-pump, and the raft writhes and wriggles beneath you as ecstasy builds. You figure, why should the other three whore-holes miss out on the fun, and you jam your fingers inside and begin moving them in circular motions. Slowly at first, then with increasing speed.

The flesh-raft remains silent – you didn't include any mouths when you put it together – but you can tell it's enjoying itself by the way it bucks beneath you, and you're glad you decided to finger the other three holes because they give you something to hold on to. You feel your own climax building, testicles expanding like tiny balloons, coming closer and closer to exploding. And just when you're almost there – right on the verge, man – you recognize the stink wafting off the red-black ocean. It's blood, all right, but not just any blood: it's menstrual blood. You understand then what this sea is . . . all the menstrual blood that's flowed from the holes of every woman who's ever lived. A whole ocean of it.

The red-head's vagina clamps tight on your penis, and the other three clench down on your fingers. You can't move, and the flesh-raft ripples in a new way, undulating, kind of dolphin-like, you think. And as the raft begins its descent into the ocean, you think how unnecessary and convoluted this revenge is. It's not like you have anywhere to go, even if you could escape. It's overkill, quite literally. You let out a burbling sigh as the blood-sea rises over you.

Just like a woman, you think, as the darkness closes in.

That's it, the doctor murmurs as the blood-sea evaporates. *Let it go, let it all go . . .*

He presses the quill-shell further into the soft, gelatinous mass that passes for your brain, and you know by now that there's no point in screaming, so you don't even try.

The Infinite Sadness of the Anus-Eyed Man (Midbrain)

"Organic bananas taste better than regular ones."

"I believe in having multiple men around the house: a kitchen bitch, a house boy, and a bed boy."

"It's a luck fetish made of buffalo horn. I bought it when I was trying to get pregnant. You're supposed to wear it . . . you know, *inside*. But I was too intimidated to use it. It's old and the ivory is cracked, and I thought it might, you know, *hurt*."

"Is this Clark's brother Roy? Is it? Omigod, Clark was supposed to give me James' number, not yours! This *is* Roy, right? Clark's brother Roy? *Roy!* R-O-Y . . ."

You're sitting at a table in a twenty-four hour coffee shop. It's late in the evening, not yet midnight, but close. A grande coffee sits in front of you, but you haven't touched it yet. You like your coffee warm, not volcanically hot, and it needs to cool off a lot more before you can drink it. You're wearing an expensive charcoal-gray suit – immaculately tailored – and equally expensive Italian shoes. Your tie is Bill Blass, and you could buy a lot of coffee for what it cost. Your glossy black hair is just beginning to show hints of gray at the temples, but your facial skin is still supple and smooth. You keep your fingernails well manicured, getting them done once a week, sometimes twice.

And you have a pair of assholes where your eyes should be.

"I think we're supposed to turn in a portfolio at the end of the semester, but I couldn't find anything about it on the syllabus so I –"

"What time do you want to meet? One-thirty? Two?"

"Like, seventy-one. Is that considered short?"

" – butt plug shaped like a American Eagle . . ."

You sigh, your eye-anuses puckering in disappointment. Here you sit, a bonafide miracle in a dull-as-dishwater world – I mean, c'mon, your eyes are *assholes*, for godssakes – and no one has paused in their inane chatter to notice, let alone gape open-mouthed and say in a too-loud voice, Omigod, *look* at that guy! Are those what I *think* they are?

These people have no time to acknowledge the dark wonders around them. They're too busy carrying on meaningless cell phone conversations, texting banalities to one another, logging onto the Internet to get the latest celebrity gossip. Pathetic.

A heavy melancholy settles deep within your soul, and you stand, still leaving your coffee untouched on the table. You draw in a deep breath and then speak in a loud, clear voice.

"You know the old joke that goes, If I want any shit out of you, I'll squeeze your head?"

You scowl, scrunching your facial muscles as tight as you can, so tight your head trembles as if it might explode. Your eye-anuses pulse, quiver, and then release. Twin streams of liquid brown shit blast out of your optic orifices, and *now* the mindless morons take notice of you. They scream, knock over chairs and each other as they try to flee, bend over and vomit violently, their rank gut-acid blending with the ripe tang of wet fecal matter that continues to gush from your head as if you had two high-pressure hoses connected to a bottomless septic tank surgically implanted in your skull.

Soon the screams turn to gurgling moans, and you hear splashing as people try to stand, sit up, raise their heads above the rising shit-tide that engulfs them. A few moments after that, and you don't hear anything except the splatter of fresh eye-shit arcing through the air and adding to the thick brown morass. You figure that's enough, and you squeeze your eyes shut and cut off the shit-streams.

The shit is almost up to your waist, and you're not pleased. You doubt you'll be able to salvage the paints, let alone the shoes. Still, you're determined to look on the bright side. It'll give you an excuse to go shopping again.

You slog through the horrid muck you've created, reach the front door, and push it open. You hold the handle tight to steady yourself as shit floods out onto the sidewalk. A body bumps into the back of your legs, but you ignore it. When the flood subsides, you step out onto the sidewalk and head off to grace others with the sinister miracle of your existence. Whoever you find, you hope they will be perceptive enough to notice you. They'd better be.

The night breeze is pleasantly cool on the soft sore flesh where your eyes should be, and despite how things worked out at the coffee house, you find yourself feeling a small spark of hope. Maybe this time, you think, will be different. Whistling a jaunty tune, you head off to –

Just a little farther . . .

You concentrate, resisting the voice intruding on your thoughts.

Whistling-a-jaunty-tune-you

Stop resisting. I'm almost through . . .

JAUNTY-GODDAMNED-TUNE-YOU-HEAD-OFF-TO

A soft pop and the Anus-Eyed Man is no more. There's only you, naked and shivering, lying on the steel table, held down by barbed wire, a faceless doctor holding a rough, craggy shell pressed against you, its quills embedded in your skull.

"Your resistance is understandable," the doctor says, "but you're only going to hurt yourself if you keep it up. Things will go easier if you submit. Not as much fun perhaps –" a grin in the voice – "but easier."

The doctor presses the quill-shell tighter against your head and you

The Methods of Cannibals (Hindbrain)

Warm blood dribbles down your chin as you chew on a mouthful of toddler thigh. The meat is tougher than you expect, and you think about Inuit people gnawing on whale blubber. The flavor is a bit gamey for your taste as well. All in all, you think, your first excursion into cannibalism isn't turning out quite the way you expected.

You pick up a cloth napkin from the table and wipe your chin, white linen turning wet crimson. You force yourself to swallow the raw meat, and it slides down your throat like an oyster. You fight to keep from grimacing as you turn to your host.

"I don't mean to criticize, and I'm the first to admit that I've never had long pig before, but why serve the child raw? I would think that cooking would bring out the meat's full flavor." *Not to mention making the horrid stuff easier to chew*, you add mentally.

The two of you are sitting at a polished oak dining table, with fine china tableware, gleaming silver service, and wine glasses filled with a dark merlot. A sparkling crystal chandelier hangs above the table, its gentle warm light shining down upon the platter containing your meal. Or rather, what's left of it.

Your host, whose own face could use a good napkin wipe, gives you a smile that's just this side of smug. His teeth are flecked with blood, the spaces between clogged with bits of meat and skin. You're both naked. You thought this was to keep your clothes clean, but when you asked your host if this was true, he chuckled and said, *No, dear, it's to preserve the primality of the experience.* You're pretty sure *primality* is not a real word, but you didn't call him on it, figuring that would be rude. After all, you *are* the guest here.

"Cooking is *absolutely* the wrong choice for preparing long pig. It ruins the natural flavor of the meat, making it taste like beef with a hint of chicken." Your host gives a little theatrical shudder, as if he's unable to imagine anything worse. "But more importantly, cooking burns out the emotional resonance within the meat."

Your stomach gurgles and you fear it's considering rejecting the bit of toddler you fed it. Trying to look as casually as possible, you place a hand on your stomach and push gently. The gurgling subsides and you hope that's the end of it. The last thing you want to do, after receiving the honor of a private invitation to your host's table, is to vomit up the food he's served you.

"I'm afraid I don't understand," you say.

Your host plucks a bit of meat from his teeth, examines it for a moment, and then pops it in his mouth and swallows. He chases the morsel with a sip of wine.

"The proper way to prepare long pig is to slaughter it alive. All animals are capable of experiencing fear on some level, but only humans are fully aware of the horror of what's happening to them as they feel the cold kiss of the knife's edge on their throat. That surge of fear rushes throughout their system like a high-voltage electric jolt, flavoring the meat in a way that no mere spice could ever possibly do. Cooking destroys this flavor. My people have an old saying: *the taste is in the terror.* It's our most important culinary secret."

You nod your appreciation for this bit of gastronomic wisdom your host has deigned to pass along to you. Your stomach gurgles again, and you press your hand harder against it. You open your mouth to speak, but a rush of hot bile floods the back of your throat, and you snap your mouth closed. You try to swallow, but your stomach clenches, sending more acid surging upward. You fear there's nothing you can do to avoid committing an unforgivable faux paus, and you hope that, despite rumors to the contrary, cannibals are a forgiving sort.

Bile rises into your mouth, splashes against the backs of your teeth. You clamp your jaw tight, and –

You feel a sharp piercing pain deep within your head, and you cry out in agony, vomit blasting out of your mouth. You turn your head to keep from covering your host with stomach acid, surprised to discover you still have the presence of mind to pull off such a maneuver. Unfortunately, you turned toward the table and projectile vomit all over the evening's entrée. Your host shrieks as if someone has slathered his testicles with honey and served them to a horde of fire ants for dessert.

Obviously, puke isn't a sauce approved of in cannibal haute cuisine.

"I'm so sorry!" Your throat is raw from vomiting, and your words come out as a raspy croak. Like an idiot, you start mopping up the long pig with your blood-stained napkin, but all you succeed in doing is further smearing barf around on what's left of the child's smooth, pink skin. "Nothing like this has ever happened to me before, I swear! I –"

The pain within your skull worsens, and light flares bright behind your eyes as your overloaded nerves struggle to process the unbelievably intense agony that suffuses your entire being. You reach up to grab hold of a phantom pair of hands that aren't there, but which you sense nevertheless exist, hands that you know are somehow responsible for the soul-searing pain that threatens to consume you far more completely than any cannibal could ever hope to.

Stop struggling. Your wrists are bound by barbed wire, remember? All you're doing is injuring yourself. We're almost there . . . just a few millimeters more . . .

Your host gazes upon the mess you've made of his gourmet meal, his eyes filled with tears.

"My god, if you didn't like it, all you had to do was *say* so!"

You try to reply, but a sudden intense pressure builds within your head, and for an instant you fear you skull is going to explode and add a coating of brains to the ruined long pig. But then, just as fast as it came, the pressure ends, and the pain ends with it.

Post-Op

Sometime later, your eyes open.

"At the risk of sounding like a cliché, how are you feeling?"

The room is lit by gentle sunlight filtering in from a window. You're lying in a hospital bed, IV in your arm, blanket drawn up to your chin. The man standing before you has the doctor's voice, but his skin is no longer gray. He's a nondescript middle-aged man with jowly cheeks and a receding hairline.

You reach up and touch the layers of gauze wrapped around your head. "Better," you say, and it's true.

The doctor smiles and nods. "Excellent! I'm happy to tell you that the procedure was a complete success. From the things you said while I was operating, it sounded like you were having a rough time of it. Your hallucinations were quite . . . vivid." The doctor chuckles. "But you won't have to worry about that sort of thing any more. I managed to locate the region of your brain responsible for the unsettling ideas and images that have plagued you – not to mention those who've been subjected to them in the so-called art you've produced throughout your life. From now on you'll think like the rest of us. You'll be –" the doctor's smile widens. "Normal."

You consider the doctor's prognosis, then ask "And that's a good thing?"

"Of *course* it is! Why anyone would want such *filth* in their mind is beyond me, let alone why you would feel compel to inflict it on the rest of us."

Now it's your turn to smile. "There's a reason why people like me think the things we do."

"*Thought*," the doctor corrects. "And not that it matters anymore, but what reason would that be?"

You open your mouth, and a tiny shriveled corpse climbs over your tongue, grabs hold of your teeth, and pulls itself out. It falls onto the blanket covering your chest and lies there for a moment: naked and pale, its body riddled with puncture wounds that weep blood. Just when it appears the homunculus will never move again, it rises to its miniature feet and gazes up at the doctor with red wet hollows where its eyes once were.

The doctor takes a step back, but before he can do anything more, the homunculus lets out a hissing cry and leaps into the air. The doctor starts to shout “No!” but his voice is cut off as the homunculus dives into his open mouth and wriggles down his throat, the blood from its wounds acting as a very efficient lubricant.

The doctor screams and falls to the floor as the homunculus goes to work inside him. You gaze down at the thrashing physician and, though you doubt he can hear you, you answer his final question.

“It’s quite simple, doctor: people like *you*. *That’s* the reason.”

The doctor’s screams degenerate into liquid gurgles and your smile becomes a satisfied grin.

Do No Harm

The Doctor stood in the middle of a street littered with wrecked and abandoned cars, gazing upon the twisted, bloodied bodies of her people lying motionless on the asphalt. A half dozen in all, an even mix of male and female, ranging in ages from late teens to early seventies, empty metal buckets scattered around them. Several of the Searchers had limbs missing, and those limbs that remained attached had been broken in numerous places. Their flesh was crisscrossed by ragged wounds, some injuries inflicted by knives, but just as many made by teeth. There was blood everywhere – thick and sticky in their hair, soaked dark into their clothes, pooled crimson on the blacktop around them. The Doctor wasn't worried that her people were dead, though. For one thing, she didn't experience emotions such as worry anymore, couldn't remember a time when she did, no longer possessed the capacity to even understand the basic concept. But the main reason she didn't fear her people were dead was that these days death no longer meant what it used to.

She turned to her right and looked at the Lifter. No words passed between them, but none were necessary. The Lifter gazed back at her for a moment, eyes unblinking, and then he shuffled toward the bodies. He was a tall male in his late thirties, broad-shouldered, with black hair and facial stubble that would never grow again. He gave no signal, but three other Cold Ones followed him, all males, all big like him, though none of them as strong as they once were. While the four had possessed individual names Before, they no longer did, and the Doctor saw no reason to give them any. She simply thought of them, inasmuch as she could think at all, as Lifters.

The Lifters were thinner than they used to be, limbs lean, faces narrow, but they were still strong enough to get the job done. The Doctor watched the four males pick up the broken Searchers and put them into the gray wooden wagon they'd pulled all the way from Oakview Street. Once it had been a farmer's wagon, drawn by horses, but the Doctor recalled nothing of such things. She understood the big wheels turned, and that the flat surface the wheels supported was good for putting things onto, and that by pulling the wagon things could be transported from one place to another, and that was the extent of her knowledge on the subject. Still, she was the only one in the Hive with such understanding, which is one of things that made her Queen.

As the Lifters worked, the Doctor kept watch. She turned her head back and forth as the Lifters piled the wounded into the cart, as much to keep scenting the air as to conduct visual surveillance. Heightened senses were one of the small ones' gifts, and if any of Bolt's people approached, she'd smell them before seeing them. It was a warm afternoon in late April, a gentle breeze blowing, birds singing, and pollen thick in the air. The Doctor had suffered from seasonal allergies when she'd been a Warm One, but she breathed without discomfort now. The small ones inside her provided many benefits, immunity to allergens being among the least of them. The town of River's Edge was located in southwestern Ohio, and while the Doctor remembered neither the town's name nor its location, she retained a dim recollection of spring, and she felt a slight stirring deep within, an echoing ghost of something that once might've been joy. But that feeling, faint as it was, was quickly superseded by a sense of wariness. Glenmont Street lay on the edge of Bolt's territory, and she understood instinctively that it had been members of his Hive who'd attacked and injured the Searchers as they'd been out scavenging for meat. It certainly hadn't been the Warm Ones' doing. They committed their violence cleanly – a single bullet to the brain or a swift decapitation. Bolt was a savage creature, and thus his followers were savage too. The Doctor looked up and down the deserted suburban street, and while she saw no sign that Bolt's people remained nearby – or better yet, *smelled* no sign – she knew better than to relax her guard.

She carried no weapon, though they were easy enough to come by these days. As a rule, the Cold Ones didn't use guns. They could fire them well enough, though their aim was awful, but they didn't possess the fine motor skills necessary to reload, and the concept of firearm maintenance was well beyond their limited mental capacity. Simple hand weapons such as knives and clubs were easier for them to handle, but when she'd been a Warm One, the Doctor had taken an oath to hurt no one, and while she no longer had any memory of making that vow, it was such a deep part of her that she continued to live by that oath today. And since she would carry no weapon, no member of her Hive would either. It was the way of things now.

A scent of dried blood and old filth drifted to her on the wind, and she knew that one or more of Bolt's people were returning. They needed to leave before the others arrived. Even malnourished, her Lifters were stronger than she, but there were only four of them, and without weapons – and more to the point, without the savagery that drove Bolt's people – they would stand little chance against their attackers. In the wordless way of the Queen, she urged the Lifters to work faster, and they responded, moving stiffly but more rapidly, and within moments the last of the wounded was loaded onto the wagon. She'd gathered the Searchers' buckets while the Lifters worked and dropped them in the wagon too. When everything was ready, the Lifters took up their positions, two on either side of the wagon's shaft, grabbed hold of it, lifted, and began pulling. They were no longer as strong as they once were, and it took some effort to get the laden wagon moving, but finally the wheels turned and the wagon began rolling slowly down the street. The Doctor walked alongside the wagon, senses alive and alert for danger. Though the wounded in the wagon displayed no signs of life, she could sense their pain, and on a level so deep she was scarcely aware of it, she wished she still could speak so that she might offer them words of comfort. But she had no voice, not to mention no capacity for language, and so she walked in silence.

The most direct route to the Hive's home was to take McKinley to Main, and then continue on Main to Oakview. The Doctor recalled none of these names, didn't recognize the street signs for what they were, and even if she had, she wouldn't have understood the tiny marks on the signs were letters, let alone been able to read them. But she was able to find her way around River's Edge through instinct, and it was that same instinct which told her that the most direct route home was also the most risky. For McKinley Street was where the high school was located, and while she didn't remember what the group of buildings was called or its original purpose, she understood its current function quite clearly: it served as the Warm Ones' nest. And a good nest it was, too. The ground floor entrances and windows had been barricaded to keep intruders out, and the Warm Ones were able to fire upon any attackers from the second floor windows or the roof. The Warm Ones were most active during the day, and while they tended to stick close to their home territory, it didn't pay for any Cold One to roam too close to their nest, especially during the daylight hours. The wounded Searchers in the back of the wagon needed to be returned to the Hive's nest as soon as possible so the Doctor could treat them, so she was willing to travel along the outskirts of the Warm Ones' territory, but she knew better than to go too deeply into it. She wanted to repair the Searchers as soon as possible, but to do that she and the Lifters needed to survive to reach the Hive.

So they would take a more roundabout way: McKinley to Robertson to Hyacinth and *then* to Oakview, approaching the Hive's home from the opposite direction. It would take longer –

nearly forty-five minutes longer, though the Doctor no longer reckoned time by the ticks of a clock – but it would have to do.

The Doctor and the Lifters continued toward home, moving in the slow, plodding way of their kind.

* * * * *

There were many things the Doctor no longer remembered, her human name chief among them. She'd once been Jennifer Carducci, MD, a general practitioner, in her early forties, married to an architect named Jim (they were so close people often referred to them as JJ, as if they were one person), and mother of two children, Arlene 12, and Robbie, 8. She'd worked at HealthCore Physicians, Inc., a joint practice with two other doctors. Not the biggest practice in River's Edge, but large enough, and she'd been happy. Sure, there were student loans to repay, and the malpractice insurance payments were a bitch, and dealing with the red tape of insurance providers and the endless visits of pharmaceutical reps were persistent pains in her ass, but she loved being a doctor – almost as much as she loved being a wife and mother – and she wouldn't have traded her life for anything.

And her life would have continued along that path – and everyone else's in the world would've continued trundling along theirs – if some insanely bright and well-intentioned corporate scientist hadn't invented the vergrandi (from the Latin *vergrandis*, meaning small). A quantum leap in nanotechnology, the vergrandi were of special concern to the medical community, for they were designed to constantly renew the body's cellular structure, repairing injuries, protecting against disease, and combating aging. In short, they would do for humanity what physicians had been struggling to accomplish for thousands of years: make the practice of medicine obsolete. Jennifer had been skeptical when the first announcements of the vergrandi's existence hit the news, but as the months passed and more information was released, she became cautiously optimistic. Yes, if the vergrandi worked as advertised, her profession would become a thing of the past, but as far as she was concerned the benefits for the human race far outweighed any personal inconvenience to herself and her fellow medical practitioners.

But when it was revealed that the vergrandi were, in a sense, alive and could reproduce, Jennifer's optimism began to wane, and when it was discovered that the nano-devices mimicked life to the point where they could mutate and evolve, her optimism gave way to fear. She was hardly alone in her misgivings. Many of the world's top scientists sounded increasingly strident notes of caution, but the company that held the patent on the vergrandi assured everyone that the nano-devices were being tested under conditions of strictest safety, and there was nothing to worry about. And then the damned things learned how to move from one body to another like a virus and escaped their "tightly controlled" environment.

The nano-devices spread across the globe like a plague of good health, infecting the human race with almost unimaginable rapidity. Within three months, every man, woman, and child on the planet had millions of vergrandi floating in their bloodstreams, keeping them healthy and strong. At first it seemed like the only people to suffer would be the stockholders of the company who'd accidentally given the vergrandi to the world free of charge. But then things began to change.

A small segment of the population became resistant to the vergrandi, and their bodies rejected the nano-devices, returning the hosts to their previous state of unassisted health. A much larger segment of the population dropped dead, all within the course of a few weeks. No one was sure whether their bodies rebelled against the presence of the vergrandi or whether the nano-devices had somehow malfunctioned and killed their human hosts. A last segment of the population – larger than those who no longer possessed vergrandi, but smaller than those who'd died – transformed. They continued to enjoy the health benefits of their artificially created passengers, but their higher brain functions deteriorated. Why, no one knew. Some malfunction in the vergrandi's programming, perhaps, or a result of mutation. Some believed the vergrandi purposely damaged their hosts' brains, in order to keep them from being smart enough to discover a way to neutralize the nano-devices. Whatever the reason, the body temperatures of those afflicted dropped significantly, their skin becoming ice-blue and cold to the touch. And the vergrandi inside them, who'd once drawn nourishment from the food their hosts ate, no longer were able to fuel themselves on Twinkies, fast-food hamburgers, and other staples of the human diet. Now they could only metabolize one fuel source: human flesh – and not just any humans; only those without active vergrandi in their blood. The vergrandi weren't cannibals, after all. They wouldn't eat others of their own kind.

The Cold Ones' seriously diminished brain functions – which also resulted in their becoming slow-moving and uncoordinated – should've given the Warm Ones the advantage, making it easy for them to reclaim the planet. But the vergrandi gave their surviving children some new attributes to compensate for what they'd taken away. The Cold Ones began to group in Hives centered around a King or Queen, one of their kind who possessed a higher degree of mental functionality than the rest. In truth, the difference in brain power wasn't all that great, but in the kingdom of the mindless, the slightly more intelligent ruled. Once a Hive formed, the vergrandi linked together in a network that provided the Hive members with a low-level degree of wordless communication that functioned like a form of telepathy, with the King or Queen in control.

Jennifer remembered none of this. She didn't remember her husband and children dying when the vergrandi in their bodies turned sour for whatever unknown reason, and she didn't remember the three days it took for her to lose most of her mind as the nano-devices inside her – instead of killing her, which she would've much rather preferred – transformed her into a Cold One. And not just any Cold One, but a Queen.

Thus Jennifer – who thought of herself as the Doctor, when she thought of herself at all – found herself living in a new world, a mostly empty one, with only a handful of Cold Ones and Warm Ones scattered across the globe, contending with one another as they fought for survival.

Not exactly better living through technology.

* * * * *

The Doctor looked down at the motionless Searcher lying upon the examining table. There was no light in the room, but that didn't matter. Thanks to the small ones, her eyes could see in the dark as well as they could in full daylight, which – since there was no electricity to power the lights in the building – was useful. In her previous life as a physician, she would've examined the middle-aged woman, checked for symptoms, listened to her chest and lungs with a stethoscope, and then drawn on her training and experience to make a diagnosis and develop a treatment plan. But her mind didn't work that way anymore. Step-by-step logic was beyond her capabilities. But diminished as they were, she wasn't entirely without mental resources to draw on. The woman – who'd been an accountant named Phyllis Basner once, and a patient of the Doctor's, as were most of the members of her Hive – had lost her left leg below the knee and her right arm up to the shoulder, along with a good portion of her face, all thanks to Bolt's people. Her left arm and right leg were still attached, but the bones had been broken numerous places in both limbs. The small ones had stopped the bleeding, but they'd done nothing to seal the wounds or knit the broken bones, let alone begin regrowing the missing limbs. The small ones could work miracles, it was true, but they couldn't do it on their own. They needed help. They needed meat.

The Doctor bent down and reached into a metal bucket one of the Lifters had brought in. Inside were pieces of a dead Warm One Bolt's people had killed several days ago: bits of skin, muscle, fat, and organs they'd left behind when they were done feasting. The Doctor's Searchers had discovered the remains at the edge of their Hive's territory – not far from where they'd been attacked today – and they'd brought back everything they could scavenge off the mostly picked-clean corpse. It hadn't been much, not even two buckets full, but it was more food than the Hive had seen in a week. The Doctor had been in contact with the Searchers when they'd made their discovery, and she'd felt how tempted they were to devour the meat, little as it was, but she'd made them resist. They hadn't liked it, but they'd done as she commanded – they had no choice – and brought the meat back to the HealthCore building, where the Doctor had once practiced medicine and which now served as the nest for her Hive.

The Doctor had divided the meat equally between two buckets. She'd then fed the contents of one bucket to the weakest among her Hive – those who could barely move – and she'd saved the second bucket for medical emergencies. Like today. It wasn't fresh, but there was no electricity to power a refrigerator to keep it in, not that the Doctor would've remembered how to use one even if the building had still possessed electricity. But the meat hadn't yet rotted to the point where the small ones couldn't draw at least some nourishment from it, so it would do

Though the Searcher on the table appeared dead, the Doctor could sense that the small ones inside her were still alive, just weak from lack of fuel. She pulled a gobbet of flesh out of the bucket – the mostly empty bucket, for this was the last of the six Searchers she had treated today, and the meat was almost gone. She then straightened and placed the grisly morsel inside the woman's mouth. The woman didn't respond at first, but the Doctor waited patiently, standing statue-still and unblinking. Eventually, the woman's jaw muscles twitched once, twice and then she began to chew. The Doctor could no longer understand that the vergrandi didn't need to wait for the woman to swallow the meat, that even now they were flooding into her mouth, carried by saliva, and beginning to break down the meat into fuel for themselves. She only knew that meat would help, and that it wouldn't take long.

The small ones went to work rapidly.

First they closed the most serious of the woman's wounds – the leg and arm stumps chief among them – so they wouldn't begin bleeding again. They then set about repairing the broken bones in her two remaining limbs. The Doctor watched as the limbs shifted and writhed like serpents, the bones inside making soft rustling sounds as they set themselves and began to fuse. But while the bones did rejoin, the limbs didn't straighten completely, and when the small ones finished their work, the woman's arm and leg had healed crooked. The woman began to show signs of life once more, moving her head so that she could gaze down at the bucket, hunger in her dull gaze, mouth moving as if she were imagining chewing on what meat remained within the bucket.

The Doctor had a basic understanding of what had happened. The morsel she'd fed the woman hadn't provided enough fuel for the small ones to repair her fully. They had done the best they could with what they'd been given. The same thing had happened to the five Searchers the Doctor had treated before this one, and all had turned out the same: functional, but crippled.

The Doctor sent out a wordless summons, and a moment later a Lifter came into the examining room. He picked up the Searcher and carried her out. Before the door closed behind them, the woman cast a last longing look at the bucket, and then they were gone.

The Doctor knew the woman could no longer do the work of a Searcher, not with only one leg. And of the others she'd attempted to heal, only two of them would be able to go out into the streets and search for meat again. The other three were just as crippled as the woman and just as unable to fulfill their role in the Hive. The Doctor knew that she should've ordered the Lifters to destroy the wounded Searchers, or better yet, never gone out to retrieve them in the first place. They had taken meat that others needed to survive, and for what? They were useless now, and they would still require meat to survive – meat they could no longer help procure. But the Doctor had been unable to go against her nature. She'd had no choice but to bring the injured Searchers back and heal them as best she could, imperfect as the results had been. Perhaps they could be put to work as Watchers now. The Hive already had ten Watchers posted in various places surrounding the HealthCore building – on the first floor of houses, atop roofs, standing in alleys – keeping an eye out for Warm Ones and Bolt's people. Having four more pairs of eyes out there wouldn't hurt.

But what the Hive *really* needed was meat, and a lot more than what few scraps they could scavenge from Bolt's leftovers. The Doctor's understanding of things might have been quite limited these days, but she understood *that* all too clearly. Without meat, the small ones had no fuel to burn, and without fuel, they couldn't keep the Cold Ones strong and healthy. Without meat, the Doctor's Hive would wither and eventually die. But the Doctor would hurt no one – *could* hurt no one – including Warm Ones. She had no problem with her people eating the Warm One's meat, just as long as they did not kill the Warm Ones to get it. But with every passing day it was becoming more difficult to find meat to scavenge. In the first few weeks after the Hive had formed, meat had been plentiful enough. There were more Warm Ones around back then, and because meat had been relatively easy to come by, when Bolt's people killed, they'd done so with savage abandon, eating their fill and leaving the rest behind. The Doctor wasn't sure Bolt's Hive had Searchers, Lifters, or Watchers. As far as she knew, he had only Hunters, and they were sloppy and wasteful, attributes that did nothing to make their Hive stronger, but which were a benefit to hers. In addition, sometimes the Warm Ones would fight among themselves, and a death would result. The body might be buried, necessitating some digging, but more often it was left to lie where it fell, making retrieval a simple process for her Searchers – as long as the body was outside the human's nest, of course.

But there were fewer Warm Ones on the streets these days. They'd either learned to avoid the Cold Ones more effectively, or they'd joined with the other Warm Ones in their nest. And with the scarcity of Warm Ones, Bolt's people had stopped being wasteful and started stripping the meat from their kills and taking it back to the rest of their Hive. They were still somewhat sloppy when it came to stripping a carcass, but nothing like they had been. Overall, pickings were mighty slim for the Doctor's Hive these days, and while they were managing to survive – barely – they were hardly thriving.

And this presented the Doctor with a dilemma that she instinctively grasped, though she wasn't capable of fully articulating it to herself. She could not cause harm to others, but by not allowing her Hive to actively hunt and kill Warm Ones, she was causing harm her Hive. But she could not choose to permit her Hive to hunt. They were bound to her, and thus behaved as she did, and there was nothing that could be done about that.

Could there?

The Doctor struggled to think, but it was so difficult, and she was physically weak from lack of meat. She hadn't eaten in days, denying herself so that others in the Hive might have food, but she knew she couldn't keep that up. She was Queen. Her strength was the strength of the Hive. There was still a bit of meat in the bucket, and the Doctor picked it up and put it in her mouth. She felt a faint, distant hint of an emotion that might have been guilt that she was seeing to her needs ahead of others', but that didn't stop her from chewing and swallowing.

She felt a familiar, welcome warmth spread through her body as the small ones swiftly broke down the meat, absorbed its nutrients, transformed them into energy, and delivered that energy to key systems in her body. In particular, she felt her link to the Hive –which had grown somewhat tenuous over the last few days – strengthen once more, and she sensed a Watcher's mind reaching for hers. She'd been distantly aware that someone had been trying to get her attention for the last several minutes, but now she could "hear" the Watcher's mental call more clearly. This Watcher was stationed at a ten-minute oil change garage just down the street from the HealthCore building, and he was crouched inside, doing his best to remain hidden while looking out the front window. The link between them was so strong now that the Doctor could see what the Watcher saw just as if she were crouching beside him. Though it was dusk outside, the Watcher's eyes were as sharp as any member of the Hive, and he had no trouble seeing a group of Cold Ones stealthily making their way through the alleys on the other side of the street. He knew they were Cold Ones because of the stiff, jerky way they moved, and he knew they weren't members of his Hive because he would've felt a connection to them if they were. Bolt's people then, closer to the HealthCore building than they'd ever come before.

The Doctor wondered what they were doing. Hunting? The last of the Warm Ones had abandoned this part of town weeks ago, and there was no meat to find here. Perhaps Bolt's people were having trouble finding meat, despite their more aggressive nature, and they were forced to hunt outside their territory. But a thought whispered from deep inside the Doctor's mind, perhaps a remnant of the woman she'd once been or perhaps simply a realization delivered by the vergrandi. Whichever the case, the thought went as such: Bolt and his people were hunting, all right, but they weren't hunting Warm Ones. They were hunting the location of the Doctor's Hive. The attack on the Searchers earlier hadn't been the result of an accidental encounter. It had been planned. Bolt knew she would come to retrieve her wounded people, and when she had, one of Bolt's Cold Ones – or perhaps even Bolt himself – had followed the Doctor and her Lifters back to the HealthCore building, and once he had the location of their nest pinpointed, he had summoned the rest of his people. Now they were massed together and moving toward the building, intending to attack and . . . and . . . Her mind struggled to put the pieces together, and the vergrandi gave her brain a small boost to allow her to do so.

Bolt was coming because he wanted to destroy the Doctor's Hive. With them eliminated, his Hive would be the only one remaining in town, and there would be no more competition for meat.

She was amazed that Bolt had been able to conceive of such a complex plan, let alone carry it out – even with the vergrandi's help, she could barely understand the concept of *plan* right now. But perhaps that was the answer: the small ones, in order to protect their hosts, and directed Bolt in what to do, just as her small ones were guiding her now. The small ones had only two purposes: to survive and reproduce. They had already made great changes in their hosts to transform them into Cold Ones, and it seemed they could make even further changes in order to safeguard their existence, if necessary. The Doctor felt these things subconsciously more than understood them on a cognitive level, but she didn't need much in the way of brain power to know what to do next. Enemies were coming; the Hive had to flee.

She sent the command to her people even as she left the examining room. She told them to scatter throughout their territory, find a place to hide, and then remain there until she summoned them. She felt no fear, experienced no panic, only the urgency to depart the building with swift efficiency. Once in the hall, she bumped into members of her Hive who were leaving the examining rooms where they'd been standing motionless, conserving their energy, waiting until such time as their Queen had a task for them to perform. Now they moved silently, faces expressionless, eyes empty of all thought and emotion, half of them heading for the front entrance, half for the rear, walking calmly, as if they were still Warm Ones engaging in nothing more important than a routine fire drill. But there was nothing routine about what was happening.

The Doctor headed for the front of the building, for no reason other than it was the closest exit for her. But when she reached the lobby, she found it jammed shoulder to shoulder with her followers, all jostling one another as they attempted to reach the door. Those who were too weak or crippled to walk on their own were carried by Lifters, but given how malnourished the entire Hive was, the Lifters looked as if they might drop their passengers at any moment. With the Doctor's arrival, her Cold Ones began to move aside to make room for her. She hadn't requested them to do so, but she was their Queen, and instinct prompted them to get out of her way. They could only manage to create a narrow aisle for her, but it was enough. She started toward the glass door that served as the entrance to the building, but before she was halfway across the lobby, she saw a group of Cold Ones approaching from outside, a male leading the way, a tire iron clutched tight in his hand.

He was in his mid-thirties, medium height, stout, with shaggy blond hair, thick arms and legs and a round belly. He wore a red T-shirt with a yellow lightning bolt emblazoned on it, along with jeans and running shoes. His clothes were torn and encrusted with dried bloodstains, rendering the lightning bolt almost invisible. The Doctor hadn't known Bolt in life. He hadn't been one of her patients, and their paths had never crossed before the vergrandi had come and changed the world forever. She'd only seen him once before, from a distance while she'd been out helping her Searchers, but she had instinctively recognized him as a Hive King, and she'd felt an instant, instinctive antipathy toward him. He obviously felt the same way about her, for his fleshy, blue-tinged features twisted into a mask of hate – lips drawn back from his teeth in a feral grin, eyes blazing with rage – and he started toward her.

The members of her Hive needed no prompting from her to act. She was their Queen and they would do whatever was necessary to protect her. They closed ranks before Bolt, blocking him from reaching the Doctor, and the male snarled, raised his tire iron, and brought it down on the head of one of the Hive in front, an elderly male who was so thin from malnourishment that he looked like a skin-draped skeleton. Bolt was much better fed than the Doctor's people, and he was able to put a decent amount of muscle behind his strike. The tire iron crunched into the old man's head, denting the top of his skull, and he collapsed as if he were a machine whose off switch had just been flipped. Normally, the small ones inside him would've been able to compensate for the injury, healing it instantly, but they had few reserves to draw on. The man wasn't dead – the Doctor would've sensed that – but he wasn't going to be getting up any time soon.

More of Bolt's people were filing into the building, men and woman, adults and children, young and old, all of them armed with knives, bats, hammers, broken bottles . . . simple weapons, but deadly in the right hands. Especially when their opponents couldn't lift a finger to fight back. Bolt's eyes locked onto hers and he grinned savagely. He was a King, his mind stronger than the average Cold One, and though she couldn't literally hear his thoughts, she had no trouble understanding the message implicit in that awful smile.

You're mine . . .

At a wordless command from Bolt, the members of his Hive started forward, wielding their weapons with crude efficiency. The Doctor's people stood their ground, taking blows and strikes with detached passivity, doing nothing to defend themselves. One by one, they bled and they fell, and the Doctor could do nothing but watch and know it was her fault. If only they would *fight* . . . but she could not cause harm, and therefore neither could they. All they could do was stand there and allow the members of the rival Hive to ravage their flesh in defense of a Queen who could do nothing to save them.

Her instincts kicked in then, warning her that she couldn't afford to stand there any longer, not if she didn't want Bolt – who was swinging his tire iron in deadly arcs, the metal coated with blood, brain matter, and bits of sodden hair – to kill her. So she turned and began to walk down the hallway as rapidly as her stiff-legged gait would permit her, heading for the back door, Bolt's shout of frustration following her. He might have been cunning enough to draw her out into the open and follow her back to the Hive's home, but he was still a Cold One, and he wasn't smart enough to send some of his people to attack from the rear, and the Doctor stepped out of the HealthCore building and into an empty alley. She turned right and kept walking at a good clip, and as she fled, she sent a message to her Hive, telling them to flee the building and hide themselves. She would summon them later, when it was safe. Assuming it ever would be again.

She walked on, keeping to the shadows, feeling the pain of those left behind as they surrendered to the violence of their attackers, Bolt and his people doing their savage best to make sure their enemies would never rise again.

* * * * *

A half moon hung high overhead and the cool night air was still. The Doctor stood next to a large oak tree, keeping close to the trunk so that she might seem to be part of it should anyone glance in her direction. The tree was one of several dotting their grounds of the high school, and the Doctor had stood here for three hours, gazing upon the dark buildings where the Warm Ones lived. She'd seen few signs of life during the time she'd been here. The Warm Ones rarely ventured out at night – though they had sentries posted, and the Doctor remained concealed to avoid offering them target practice – and they kept their windows barricaded and little light leaked through. But sometimes she'd see a flickering shadow pass by a window, perhaps caused by a Warm One carrying a candle to light his or her passage through the school's hallways.

The Doctor had come here for two reasons. The first was that her small ones whispered that this was the last place Bolt would look for her, for he wouldn't be any more eager to place himself in the Warm One's gun sights than she was. The second reason was because she wanted to think – or at least come as close to thinking as she was capable of. These buildings were filled with meat, maybe the last meat in River's Edge. Meat her Hive desperately needed if it was to survive. Meat they couldn't claim because she wasn't a hunter, wasn't a killer, and therefore no one in her Hive could be either. She was Queen. She was supposed to lead her Hive, guide them, protect them. But all she was doing was slowly killing them. Something had to be done, but what?

So she stood motionless in the night next to the tree, gazing upon the dark buildings filled with meat, trying to cudgel her dead brain into providing some kind of answer. But she didn't need to think, not when the small ones inside her could do the thinking for her. The Hive needed meat, and since they could no longer scavenge it, they needed a leader who could kill. The small ones had changed the Doctor once, and now – with the Hive's survival at stake – they began to change her again.

The transformation was well underway when she sent the Hive a command to gather at a new location. She then left the shelter of the oak tree and began walking away from the Warm Ones' nest, the small ones inside her hard at work.

* * * * *

The moon was hidden behind clouds by the time the Doctor reached the house. *Her* house, the one she used to share with her husband and children. She hadn't chosen this location for the Hive's rendezvous consciously, and she had only the vaguest sense that this place had once been important to her, but it seemed fitting. A two-story house at the end of a cul-de-sac in a little neighborhood situated on the southern edge of the largest park in River's Edge, with a view of a duck pond from the kitchen window. No cozy glow from the windows, no porch light on and waiting for her. The house was dark, so much so it seemed painted black, and the surrounding yard covered with tar. Strange how dark it was; normally she could see so much better at night.

As she walked up the driveway, she realized her sight wasn't the only sense that had diminished. Her hearing wasn't as sharp as it used to be, and her sense of smell was dulled. And she felt warmer than usual, warmer even than she felt after eating meat. Almost as warm as when she'd been . . . been . . .

She tried to reach out to the Hive, to touch their minds through the link they shared, to confirm they had gathered in the house as she'd commanded, to check to see how many of them had survived Bolt's attack. But she felt nothing. The link was gone.

She stepped onto the front porch and reached for the doorknob, but she hesitated before gripping it. She wasn't sure why, but she was experiencing an emotion she hadn't felt in a long time, one that only a short time ago she wouldn't have been able to put a name to. But she could name it now: fear. Foolish. She was Queen; she had no reason to fear her Hive.

She opened the door – it wasn't locked and the knob turned easily – and entered.

It was dark inside, and she walked slowly through the foyer, trailing her fingers along one of the walls to guide her. When she reached the hall, she right turned and kept going until she reached the great room. They were waiting for her there. She couldn't see them, but she could hear their soft breathing, and even with an unenhanced sense of smell, their odor – like overcooked meat stored in the refrigerator too long – was unmistakable.

She wanted to communicate to them through the link, reassure them everything would be all right, but instead for the first time since the small ones had taken up residence in her body, she opened her mouth and spoke.

"I'm home," she said.

The surviving members of her Hive fell upon her eagerly, and as their teeth tore into her now warm flesh, she understood what the small ones had done to her, and she approved. The Hive would have meat tonight. True, they would be without a Queen, but without her reluctance to harm others holding them back, they would be free to hunt – and free to find another Hive. Perhaps Bolt would claim them. He would be a good King for them, for he was far more suited to survive in this world than she was.

Yes, her people were free. And now, through the grace of the small ones, so was she.

Country Roads

Eric glanced at the digital clock on the dashboard, and saw it was 3:38 a.m. He'd been driving all over Cabell County for almost three hours now, and so far the most interesting thing he'd seen was a raccoon. The animal had sat frozen in a ditch, staring at Eric's Altima as he drove by, eyes wide and shining bright as the light from the car's headlights washed over it. That was all: no deer, no coyotes, no other vehicles out cruising the back roads . . . and certainly not what Eric was searching for.

He reached for the thermos sitting in the cup holder, picked it up, and raised it to his mouth. The coffee inside had long ago gone cold, but it was strong and bitter, and full of caffeine, which was all that mattered. Eric was down to the dregs now, only a few swallows left at most. That, more than the length of time he'd been driving, made him consider giving up for the night and heading home.

And that's when he saw her.

She stood at the side of the road, draped in a sheer white outfit that might have been a dress, but might just as easily have been a nightgown. Her hair was long, black, and straight, and though it was windy tonight, both her gown and her hair remained still.

Eric eased his foot off the gas and slowly pressed down on the brake. In his rearview mirror, he saw the red glow of brake lights color the road behind his car, and he couldn't help thinking how eerie the light looked, like his Altima was wounded and trailing blood.

The woman's chalk-white complexion made her age difficult to determine – Eric guessed late twenties, early thirties, but she could've been anywhere from fifteen to forty-five. She stared straight ahead, expressionless and unblinking, like a life-sized porcelain doll. Just as he remembered her.

His heart pounded in his chest, and he felt a cold surge of fear at the base of his sternum. He clasped the steering wheel so tight his knuckles throbbed, and it took every ounce of self-control he possessed not to lift his foot off the brake, tromp down on the gas, and get the hell out of there. But he'd been searching for this women for hours, and now that he'd found her, he wasn't about to flee, no matter how much he wanted to.

The Altima slowed to a stop next to the woman, and Eric put the car in park. He put his finger on the control to lower the driver's-side window, hesitated for a couple seconds, and then pressed it. The window receded into the door with an electronic hum.

The woman gave no sign that she was aware of him – she didn't lower her gaze to look at him, didn't move, didn't even appear to be breathing. Cool spring air wafted in from outside, bearing with it the sounds of insects and nightbirds. The noises seemed out of place, far too normal given the circumstances. It should be deathly silent, the air chill, and there should be a faint unpleasant odor like graveyard mold and bone dust. But Eric didn't smell anything other than the coffee on his own breath.

Now that he was here, now that he'd actually found her, he wasn't sure what to do . . . wasn't sure what he *wanted* to do.

"Uh . . . Hi. My name's Eric. Eric Montrose. I grew up around here, over in Huntington. I . . . I've seen you before. It was twenty years ago. Well, twenty-two, to be exact."

The woman continued starting straight ahead. No reaction at all.

"I had a friend, Joe Weidner. He and I used to drive around a lot on the weekends when we were in high school. We were both kind of shy, so neither one of us dated much, and there wasn't a lot to do except drive around and drink beer. There were no computer games back then, no satellite TV, no Internet . . . nothing else to do but drive, drink, and talk. We saw a lot of weird stuff out here late at night. Once we drove by a pasture, and a big animal was standing at the fence watching us. I thought it looked like a horse with a skull head, but Joe said it didn't look like anything he'd ever seen before. One thing we did agree on, though. As we drove past, the thing *smiled* at us."

Eric shivered and forced out a laugh as if to dispel the memory, but it just made him shiver harder.

The woman's catatonic expression didn't change, but Eric had the sense that she was listening to him. Or maybe that was just what he wanted to believe.

"Another time we saw a tree that was filled with dead animals – possums, rabbits, weasels, foxes . . . Someone had skinned them and lodged them in the crooks of branches. The trunk of the tree was covered with strange symbols that had been carved into the bark. They looked like letters from a foreign language, but it wasn't one that Joe or I recognized. 'Course, it wasn't like either of us was exactly a genius in that department. We were both barely passing Spanish."

The woman still didn't lower her gaze to look at him, but Eric thought he saw a glimmer of reaction, a slight narrowing of her eyes, but he knew it could be his imagination.

"One Saturday night – prom night, as it turned out – we saw *you*. Neither Joe or I had dates. I'd been going out off and on with this one girl, Becky Schlosser, but it was one of our off times, and she went to prom with someone else. Joe and I talked about going stag, but we decided it would be too depressing, so we decided to just do our usual thing and go cruising. A lot of times when we went driving, we'd sit and listen to whatever song was on the radio, sip beer, and think our private thoughts. But other times we'd talk about stuff . . . which teachers bugged us, dumb things our parents or siblings did, girls we wished would look at us, let alone talk to us . . . A lot of times we wouldn't pay attention to where we were going, and we'd end up lost. That was part of the fun, not knowing where we were and trying to find out way back to town. Anyway, it was prom night when we drove down this road and saw you.

"It had rained earlier, and the roads were still shiny wet. We were both kind of depressed about missing prom – though we'd never have admitted it to each other – and we'd been drinking more than usual. I was driving that night, and I was concentrating extra hard on driving, you know, the way drunks do, and so Joe saw you first. 'Check it out, man!' he shouted. 'It's a girl!' At first I thought he was messing with me. We used to try to spook each other like that all the time. But sure enough, there you were, looking just like you do now, and I slowed down. I was driving on old beater Nova in those days, and the engine coughed and rattled like it was going to fall apart any minute. But despite all the noise my car made, you didn't pay any attention to us as we got closer.

"'Look at the way she's staring,' Joe said. 'You think she's crazy or something?' I told him that you might've been hurt or had suffered some kind of emotional trauma. I wanted to stop to see if you needed any help. But when I told Joe, he said, '*You're* the one who's crazy! I mean, look at her! She looks like some kind of ghost or vampire! And even if she is just a crazy person, what if she's got a knife or something and tries to kill once when we stop? Just keep going! We can call the police later!' And he grabbed hold of my right leg just above the knee and shoved my foot down on the accelerator.

"Nowadays, if I saw someone I thought needed help standing alongside the road, I'd call 911 on my cell, but nobody had cell phones back then. The only options we had were to either find a pay phone – and there sure as hell weren't any out here – or stop at a farmer's house, pound on the door until he woke up, and ask to use his phone. Either way, it would be some time before any help could get out here, and by then it might be too late. I knew that, and I'm sure Joe did too, but we both felt a horrible sense of *wrongness* about you . . . though it had rained, you were dry, and though it was windy out – like tonight – your hair and gown didn't move in the breeze. You didn't look like you were blinking or even breathing. So it didn't take much for Joe to convince me to keep on driving. As we roared past, I checked the rearview mirror, half-expecting not to see your reflection, but there you were, still standing there, still not looking at us.

"We kept driving for about a half hour after that. Seeing you instantly sobered us up, but it took that much time for us to calm down. I convinced Joe that we should come back and look for you, just to make sure you weren't hurt, but we hadn't paid attention to what road we'd been on or how many turns we'd taken as we'd kept driving, and we couldn't find the right road again. We drove all night and we didn't give up until close to dawn, and even then it was only because we were almost out of gas. We both got in big trouble when he got home. Both of our parents were sure we'd been out screwing around with a couple girls, and we let them think that. We knew they wouldn't have believed us if we'd told the truth.

"After that, whenever we talked about seeing you, we referred to you as our prom date. We asked around to see if any other kids had seen you, but no one had. I did some research in the town library on ghost legends and discovered that sightings of women in white have been common throughout history. Since I'd never heard of women in white before, that convinced me you were real. Joe wasn't so sure. He figured you might have just been someone who *had* heard of the legend, slipped on an old nightgown, and stood alongside the road to freak people out. I asked him why anyone would bother standing out in the country in the middle of the night when no one ever drove by. Joe said, 'We did, didn't we?' and that was the end of that."

Eric paused to drink the last of his tepid coffee. For a moment, he felt as if he should offer the woman in white a sip and the thought almost made him smile.

"I got a call from Joe's wife last week. He moved to San Antonio about ten years ago to work for a computer company there. He'd had a massive heart attack and died in his sleep. I live in Ohio now – I'm the manager of a Barnes and Noble there. I've got two teen-age daughters, an ex-wife, and more bills than I want to think about and, truth to tell, not much else. Joe and I kind of lost touch after high school, but once I learned he'd died, I started thinking about all those nights we used to drive these roads . . . all the things we talked about and all the things we saw. And I realized it had been a long time since I'd been home, and an even longer time since I'd been young."

He looked at the woman in white. He couldn't be sure, but he thought her head was angled slightly downward now, though her gaze still didn't meet his.

"I've been driving around out here all night looking for you. I'm not sure why. I just wanted to see you again, I suppose. Wanted to make sure you were real. Wanted to make sure that those nights twenty years ago were real. I guess memories are ghosts, too. But they don't haunt us with images of what used to be – they haunt us with reminders of the way things aren't anymore and can never be again."

The woman was looking at him now, though her eyes remained glassy and staring. He thought her bloodless lips twitched, as if she were about to say something, but she remained silent.

"Well, I guess I'd better get going." Eric pressed down on the brake and put the Altima in gear, but he didn't drive off right away. "This is probably going to sound weird, but . . . thanks. Thanks for giving me something to be scared of, to wonder about, for giving me hope that the world is more than just going to work, paying bills, and marking time until I die. Thanks for being a mystery." Eric smiled. "And for being my prom date."

As he raised the window, he wondered if the woman might tap on the glass to get his attention, maybe open the door, reach in and grab him, or perhaps just materialize in the passenger seat next to him, morphing from woman in white to phantom hitchhiker. But she did none of those things, just continued standing there, and Eric pressed down on the gas pedal and slowly pulled away. He tried to resist the urge to gaze in his rearview mirror, but he couldn't. When he looked, he saw the woman in white bathed in the red wash of his tail lights, patiently waiting for the next driver to come by who needed something to believe in . . . something to help carry him a little further down the road.

Darker than Winter

PANEL ONE

A cartoon of a man hunched over a drawing table, sketching a picture of a man hunched over a drawing table sketching a picture of a man hunched over a drawing table sketching a picture of man hunched over a drawing table sketching a picture of a man . . .

* * * * *

Patrick stabbed the butcher knife into his victim's chest with a satisfying *chuk!* The blade slid in easily, almost as if it belonged there and was being welcomed home. Patrick let go of the knife handle and stepped back to admire his handiwork. His victim lay prone on snow-covered ground, knife handle pointing straight up to the sky.

Looks too posed, Patrick thought.

He pulled the knife free and slid it in again, this time at a slight angle. He nodded. Much better. Now for some blood. After all, what was a murder without a little gore?

He removed a small plastic bottle of strawberry-flavored syrup from his coat pocket, flipped open the lid, took aim, and squeezed. A thick dark-red stream jetted forth from the bottle's opening and splattered onto the victim's chest, soaking the area around the knife blade a bright crimson.

Patrick stopped, considered for a moment, and then sprayed some more syrup. *To hell with a* little *gore,* he decided. *Let's go for a lot.*

He'd emptied half the bottle before he was satisfied, and the smell of strawberries hung heavy and sweet in the crisp winter air. He flipped the lid closed, tucked the syrup bottle back into his pocket, and then reached into his other pocket and took out a camera. He stepped back once more and observed the scene of carnage that he had created through the camera's viewfinder. He grinned. Perfect.

He took a half dozen pictures, each from a different angle, before running out of film. He would've liked to take a few more, but he hadn't brought a fresh roll with him. He supposed the shots he'd gotten were good enough. He put the camera back inside his coat pocket and crunched through the snow to his victim's side.

He regarded the prone figure for another moment – the copious blood, the angle of the murder instrument – before reaching for the knife handle and pulling it free.

"Looks like I'm rightwise born King of England," he said, sorry that there was no one else in the park to hear him. That was a good one. He'd have to remember to jot it down once he got back to his apartment.

He turned to go, eager to get to the drugstore and drop off his film to be developed, but he paused. The park was a small one, only a block away from where he lived. In fact, he could see it from his bedroom window, which was how he'd first spotted the snowman that had fallen over. At least, he'd assumed it had fallen. He supposed it was possible someone might build a snowman in a lying-down position, but he couldn't imagine why.

And that's when he'd gotten the idea to grab the knife and strawberry syrup from his kitchen, come out here, and stage a bloody snowman murder. It was a funny idea, and it would make for an even funnier picture, he was certain. Hopefully, good enough to be the photo on the front of a humorous greeting card, with an inside gag line that said, "God, I *hate* winter," or maybe "Beware – spring is coming." Something like that.

But though there wasn't much to the park – an acre or so of land, some trees, a couple picnic tables, a swingset and a green metal climber – the kids in the neighborhood still used it. After all, hadn't one or more of them built the snowman, pressed rocks into its head for eyes and a mouth, then stuck branches into its sides for arms? There was a second snowman, too, a much smaller one that someone, maybe the same kids who'd built the toppled snowman, had placed on one of the picnic tables. The snow munchkin resembled its larger twin – rocks for features, twigs for arms – save that it was still upright, and not covered with strawberry-syrup blood, of course.

And it was the blood that was the problem. Patrick wasn't sure how he felt about the possibility of kids coming to the park and seeing the bloody mess he'd made of the fallen snowman. In the right context, like on a greeting card accompanied by a good gag, the image of a bloody snowman was funny. But lying on the ground, surrounded by a bunch of confused and frightened children . . .

He decided not to worry about it. There really wasn't much he could do. He could hardly carry the snowman away, and if he stomped it flat, the strawberry smear would remain, and it would look even more like something had been injured or killed here. Besides, this was a late season snow, and the weather was supposed to warm up over the next couple days. Frosty the Snow-Corpse would be gone soon enough. And anyway, if he'd discovered a bloody snowman when he'd been a kid, he'd have thought it was pretty damn cool. Who's to say the neighborhood kids wouldn't react the same way?

Rationalization firmly in place, Patrick walked away from the snowman, careful to conceal his butcher knife by holding it backwards, blade parallel to his forearm. The last thing he wanted to do was explain to a police officer that he'd brought the knife to the park to stab a snowman.

As he walked, he had the feeling that someone was watching him, but when he turned back to check, he saw no one. No one, that is, except the mini-snowman standing atop the picnic table.

"Yeah, right," Patrick said, and then laughed as he turned around and headed home.

* * * * *

After dropping off his film at the drugstore on the corner (one-hour developing, guaranteed!), Patrick trudged back to his apartment complex. Though it was barely below freezing, his toes were numb at the tips and his sinuses were raw from breathing cold air. He was looking forward to getting back inside, brewing some coffee and getting to work.

He stopped at the row of mailboxes outside the building and hesitated before the one marked 32-B. He knew from experience that it was smarter to get the mail toward the end of the day, after he'd gotten some work done. But he took his keys out of his pocket and opened his mailbox anyway, against his better judgment.

He quickly flipped through the mail. Most of it was bills, as usual. There was a card from his older brother in Cincinnati, no doubt a late birthday card. Mark was always busy, and he tended to forget birthdays, anniversaries, and the like. Last was an envelope from *Ferret Lovers Magazine.*

Don't open it, don't open it, don't open it, he told himself.

He opened it.

> Thanks for submitting your cartoons to *Ferret Lovers.* We receive many submissions each month, but unfortunately we can publish only a few in each issue. Keep trying us and better luck next time.
>
> Regards,
> The Editorial Staff
> *Ferret Lovers Magazine*

At the bottom of the form letter, scratched out in red pen, was this addendum: *Your ferrets look like furry worms with feet.*

"Screw you," Patrick muttered and tromped up the stairs to his apartment.

Once inside, he tossed the mail onto the kitchen table, then put the knife back in the butcher block and the strawberry syrup in the fridge. He took off his coat and slung it over one of the two kitchen chairs he owned (both of which came from Goodwill) then sat down and tried not to think about the rejection from *Ferret Lovers,* especially the nasty little handwritten note, as he opened his brother's birthday card.

On the cover was the cartoon face of a man wearing a comically exaggerated expression of shock. The word balloon above his head contained the dialogue: "Goddamn! You're really, really, *really* old!" Inside was another drawing of the man, only now his facial expression was one of relief. Inside the world balloon: "Oh, you're only forty? Well, in that case, you're only really, really old."

Below the drawing, in handwritten letters: *Happy B-day, Bro! I was going to get you a mid-life crisis for your birthday, but I figured you already had one! Love, Mark.*

Patrick looked at the card and tried to smile. It was handmade, drawn and written by his brother, who taught design at Cincinnati Technical Institute and had his own freelance commercial art business on the side. The card, which was of professional-level quality and could easily be sold to a greeting card publisher, was funny as hell. It was also ten times better than anything Patrick had ever done.

"Fuck." He closed the card and started to tear it in two, but then he stopped, sighed, and set it upright on the table. He sat there and looked at it, all thought of coffee and doing his own work forgotten.

PANEL TWO

The cartoonist is sitting up straight now and regarding the picture that he's drawn with a thoughtful expression. All the cartoonists in the series of infinite regressions are sitting straight as well. There's a thought bubble floating over the cartoonist's head, and inside it is another thought bubble, and inside that one, another, and in *that* one another, and . . .

* * * * *

Patrick didn't feel like working anymore, so he plopped down on the couch he'd salvaged from a dumpster six months ago and which still had a musty-sour odor. The only thing in the one-bedroom apartment that he'd bought brand-new was the drawing table that stood over in the corner. But after getting the rejection from *Ferret Lover's*, he might've tossed the goddamned thing out the window . . . if he could've worked up the energy.

He was about to turn on the TV – which was a hand-me-down from his brother, discarded after he'd gotten a new plasma screen television – when the phone rang. The receiver rested on the arm of the couch, and he reached over, picked it up, and answered.

"Hello?"

"Hi, baby."

He smiled. It was Liz. Maybe talking to her would cheer him up. "Hi yourself. What's up? I thought you were working today." Liz ran a small sign-making company called Sign Wave, and Patrick sometimes did a little freelancing for her to help make ends meet. It was a business relationship that worked out well, especially considering that she was also his girlfriend.

"I am, but Andy from Bigtime Cinema just called. He wants someone to come paint a reproduction of a movie poster in the window of his theater."

Patrick stifled a groan. By "someone," he knew that Liz meant him. He hated doing jobs like that. Not that they were hard work, but because they were boring.

As if reading his thoughts, she said,"C'mon, Pat. Take the job. I know you can use the money. My birthday's coming up, and you're going to need some serious cash to buy the kind of present a fine lady such as myself deserves."

Patrick laughed. "All right, I'll do it. Okay if I go out there tomorrow? I've been working here, and I'm kind of on a roll." Sure, it was a lie, but he didn't feel like doing anything today, especially hackwork.

"No problem. The movie Andy wants to advertise doesn't start until next week." A pause. "So . . . what are you working on?"

Patrick sighed. Liz wasn't exactly a nag, but she made it no secret that she thought he could, as she put it, "apply himself more," as if he were some sort of epoxy or rash ointment.

"I was out walking by the park today – you know, the little one near my house? – and I came up with a great idea. A pretty original one, I think," he said with a touch of pride, and then he told her about staging the snowman murder and his idea for using the picture as a greeting card.

"That *is* a good idea," Liz said when he was finished. "I did something like that during a skiing trip in college. Though my friends and I used a ski pole and ketchup for blood. It was a lot of fun."

Patrick grimaced. "Yeah. Sounds like it." So much for his *original* idea.

They chatted for a couple more minutes, but his heart wasn't in the conversation, and they soon ended the call. He then picked up the remote, turned on the TV, and pretended to watch a boring reality show while trying not to think about how much cooler a ski pole was than a butcher knife.

But just as he was starting to settle into a decent funk, there was a knocking at the door. The sound was crisp, businesslike, insistent. *Rap-rap-rap-rap-rap-rap-rap!*

Patrick turned off the TV, hauled his depressed ass off the couch, and walked to the door. He looked out the peephole and saw a fishbowl-lens view of a man wearing a blue suit. The man's facial features weren't all that clear through the peephole glass, but it was no one Patrick recognized.

"Who is it?" he said, loud enough to be heard through the door.

"Police, Mr. Bragg. I need to ask you a few questions."

The man's tone was calm, his voice coolly professional.

Patrick pulled his face away from the peephole, but he didn't immediately reach to unlock the door. Just because the man said he was a police officer didn't make it true. Patrick considered going into the kitchen and grabbing the butcher knife he'd used to stab the snowman. But if the man at the door really *was* a cop, and Patrick answered the door holding onto a knife . . .

Rap-rap-rap-rap-rap!

"Mr. Bragg? My name is Detective _____, and I must insist on speaking to you."

The man's voice was so soft that Patrick didn't catch his name, just his rank.

"Um, can you show me some ID? Just hold it up to the peephole." As soon as he'd said it, Patrick felt like a paranoid idiot, one of those people who hid behind their doors, terrified that everyone and everything in the world was out to get them.

But the detective reached into the inner pocket of his suit jacket and removed a black wallet. He held it up to the peephole and flipped it open to reveal a metal badge with a design engraved on it that resembled an asterisk. At least, Patrick thought that's what it looked like. The peephole had become cloudy, as if covered with a thin coating of frost, and it was hard to see.

The detective flipped his wallet closed and tucked it back into his jacket pocket. Patrick was tempted to ask the man to display his ID once more, and keep it out longer this time, but he didn't want to risk angering the man if he really was a cop. Besides, he didn't want to come off as more of a frightened wimp than he already was.

"Just a minute." Patrick undid the chain lock and turned the deadbolt. When he opened the door a gust of cold wind was sucked into the apartment. Dressed only in a *Doonesbury* T-shirt and a ragged pair of jeans, Patrick shivered. Despite what the long-range forecast had predicted, it seemed that the temperature had dropped several degrees once he'd set up his little photo shoot at the park.

"You are Patrick Bragg, correct?"

Now that Patrick looked at the man without the peephole's interference, he could see that the detective was in his forties or fifties, completely bald, and almost cadaverously thin. His eyes were ice-blue and his skin was so pale that it verged on chalk-white.

"Yes, that's me."

Patrick waited for the detective to identify himself again so he could catch his full name, but instead the bald man said, "We're investigating an *incident*, Mr. Bragg." His upper lip curled slightly as he stressed the word *incident*. "One that occurred in the park earlier today. The park that your building overlooks. We're checking to see if anyone saw anything . . . *untoward*." That lip curl again, more pronounced this time.

The detective's sentences were even and measured, his gaze direct, almost but not quite a stare. Patrick knew it was ridiculous, but he could've sworn the man didn't blink.

"Untoward?" Patrick glanced up and down the walkway in front of the neighboring apartments on this floor, but he saw no other officers, no *we* of which the man spoke.

"I'm not at liberty to divulge the exact details as our investigation is in its early stages. You understand." Still no blinking.

"Yeah. Sure, I understand." Patrick was starting to get nervous. Had someone witnessed his staging of the snowman's murder, or perhaps seen him entering or leaving the park carrying the butcher knife?

He was about to tell the officer what he'd done and why he'd done it – as awkward and embarrassing as such an explanation would be – when the detective said, "I can tell you that it's a serious matter, one that involves the highest of crimes."

Patrick's words died his mouth. He couldn't believe what he was hearing. Serious matter? Highest of crimes? For an instant, he thought this was some kind of joke, maybe something his brother had set up as a late birthday prank. But the man's demeanor was so reserved, so businesslike, that Patrick believed he was sincere. Besides, there was no way Mark or anyone else could've observed what he'd done in the park, and even if they had, they wouldn't have had enough time to arrange a gag like this.

"As I said, your building overlooks the park. Did you happen to glance out a window and see anything strange there today?"

"Strange?" Patrick felt stupid parroting the man's words, but he was stalling for time, hoping the detective would eventually say enough to give him some idea what was going on.

"Strange," the detective repeated. "Out of the ordinary. Not run of the mill. Unusual. Atypical. Out of place. Odd."

If it hadn't been for the man's calm, emotionless tone, Patrick would've thought the detective was making fun of him.

"No, I can't say that I did."

The detective stared at Patrick for a long time, still without blinking. Finally, he gave a perfunctory nod. "Very well. If I have any further questions, I shall return." The man then walked away, moving with a liquid grace that was at odds with his otherwise bland and colorless persona. It was almost as if he didn't so much walk as glide.

Patrick stood in the doorway and watched the man descend the steps to the ground and continue across the parking lot in his strange, graceful way. Not once did the detective look back. Nor did he stop and knock on any other doors to question any other residents. And neither was he joined by anyone else to form the *we* as in *we're* investigating.

When the man was out of sight, Patrick closed and locked his door, then hurried to his bedroom, to the window that faced the park.

PANEL THREE

The cartoonist is looking up at the thought balloons within thought balloons. He's scowling and gripping his pencil – a *sharpened* pencil – tight in his hand.

* * * * *

An emergency vehicle sat in the park, lights flashing blue. It was white with a red emblem on its side that looked like the asterisk on the Detective Blue-Suit's badge. Two police cruisers – also white, also with blue lights flashing, also with asterisks – were present, as was an unmarked blue Ford that Patrick assumed belonged to the man who had questioned him.

He watched as Blue-Suit came into view, glide-walking toward the park. A pair of men in white uniforms carried plastic buckets full of snow – some of it stained red with strawberry syrup.The detective stopped the paramedics (if that's what they were) and spoke to them for a moment. Then the three of them turned to look in the direction of Patrick's building.

Though he doubted they could see him at this distance, especially with the glare of sunlight on the window, Patrick nevertheless took several steps back and had to fight an urge to close the blinds and draw the curtains.

They can't see me, he told himself. And even if they could, it wasn't as if he'd really done anything. It was just a prank . . . a stupid joke he was thinking about turning into a greeting card, for chrissakes! And even if he had done something wrong – which he most definitely had *not* – there was no way they could prove it. There were no witnesses to his "crime," and no evidence.

Oh, yeah? a voice inside him said. *What about the footprints you left at the scene? What about the knife in your butcher block? Not to mention the photos you dropped off at the drugstore. One-hour developing, guaranteed!*

The photos . . .

Patrick stepped closer to the window. The detective and the two paramedics were no longer looking his way. The cop had moved off and was now standing next to the picnic table where the small snowman sat. He faced the little snowman, and though Patrick couldn't tell because the man's back was to him, he had the impression that the detective was saying something, almost as if he were *talking* to the little snowman.

No, not *talking. Questioning.*

Patrick turned his attention to the paramedics. They were loading the snow-filled buckets into their emergency vehicle, alongside a half dozen others.

This was insane! They were collecting the snow as if it were bodily remains. And the detective was interrogating the little snowman as if it were a witness to a crime. And not just any crime: a *murder.*

But the snowman was already lying on its back when I got there!

It was just a snowman. Not alive, *never* alive. You couldn't kill something that had never lived . . .

Whatever was going on in the park, no matter how strange, he told himself that it had nothing to with him. He turned away from the window with every intention of going back to the couch and vegging out for the rest of the day. But then he remembered once more: the photos.

Don't do it, he told himself. *Don't.*

But a moment later he was heading for the kitchen table to get his coat.

* * * * *

Mark and Remark. That's what everyone called them, like Pete and Repeat. Whatever Patrick's big brother did, wherever he went, however he dressed, whatever he said, Patrick copied him.

When Mark would complain to their mother about Patrick – which he did several times a day – she would say, "He only copies you because he loves you. He looks up to you and wants to be like you. You should be flattered."

Patrick, who was always nearby listening, heard their mother's words. The only time Mark could get away from him was when he went to the bathroom, and even then Patrick would stand in the hallway outside the door and wait until his big brother was finished.

Patrick liked his mother's explanation. He *did* love his big brother, and he *did* look up to him, and it made him feel good that his mother recognized this and approved, even if her words only seemed to irritate Mark even more. But deep down, he didn't think that was the reason he copied his brother. The real reason (which Patrick had a hard time admitting to himself) was that he didn't have any ideas of his own.

Whenever his mother asked Patrick what he wanted for a snack, he always shrugged and said, "Idonno." When kids on the school playground asked him what he wanted to play, he did the same thing. Shrug. "Idonno." It wasn't that he wasn't hungry or didn't want to play, and it wasn't, as many adults supposed, that he simply was shy. He just couldn't come up with any ideas. At least, not any good ones.

But Mark was an endless wellspring of ideas, and they were all great. He made up songs as he played, and never sang the same one twice. He could spend hours constructing elaborate objects – both mundane and abstract – from Legos. On the playground, he was always a leader of the other children because he was the one who came up with the idea of playing space pirates or jungle safari. And he drew . . . god, how he drew! Mark filled page after page with animals, spaceships, dinosaurs, and creatures that existed only within his own imagination.

Patrick followed Mark around and copied him not only because he loved him, and not only because it was fun, but because Mark had something Patrick so desperately wanted – an imagination – and he hoped like hell that by being a copycat some of it would rub off on him.

* * * * *

At precisely fifty-eight minutes and thirteen seconds after he'd dropped off his film, Patrick was standing at the drugstore photo counter, ready to pick up his pictures.

The girl behind the counter – who couldn't have been more than seventeen, eighteen, tops – smiled as she handed him the package containing his photos.

"There must be something special in there," she said.

Patrick experienced a tiny surge of panic. "No, nothing special at all. Why do you ask?" He tried to keep his voice normal, but it was strained, and he couldn't stop himself from talking too fast.

The girl's smiled faded as she gave him a wary look, as if she'd just changed her mental classification of him from "ordinary customer" to "crazy fuck."

"It's just that you came back an hour later on the dot. Most people who choose one-hour developing come back a couple hours later, and sometimes they don't come back until the next day."

"Really. That's . . . interesting."

Patrick paid for his pictures and headed for the exit, but he slowed as he drew near the sliding glass door. He'd taken a four-block detour to get here so that Detective Blue-Suit wouldn't see him, and he didn't want to step out onto the sidewalk without checking first to see if the proverbial coast was clear.

He walked up to the door close enough to activate the electric eye, but instead of stepping through the open doorway, he leaned his head out and looked in the direction of the park. The paramedics' vehicle was pulling out of the park with lights flashing, but no sirens blaring. Patrick wasn't worried about the bucket-toting paramedics, though. It was Blue-Suit that he was looking out for.

He didn't see the man's Ford, which hopefully meant that the detective had left while Patrick was waiting to get his pictures. The park was empty now, at least as far as Patrick could tell from this vantage point. There were some trees in the way, and –

"Mister, are you going to just stand there all day?"

Patrick turned to see the teenage clerk glaring at him, though no matter how hard she might be trying to hide it, there was fear in her eyes.

Patrick gave her a smile that he hoped was reassuring. "Sorry. Guess I'm kind of in a mental fog today."

The girl held her ground, but the fear in her gaze intensified. "Just go, okay?"

Patrick wanted to explain to her that she had nothing to worry about, that he was just waiting to make sure that the nameless detective that suspected him of murdering a snowman was gone, that's all. What could be more simple or ordinary? About a trillion other things, that's what.

"Sure. Sorry." He turned away from the girl and stepped onto the sidewalk –

– and saw a dark blue Ford parked alongside the curb halfway down the block.

He didn't stop, didn't hesitate. He turned and began walking in the opposite direction, careful to keep his pace as normal as possible. He felt awkward, like a drunk forced to walk a straight line during a sobriety test. Even if you were only a little drunk, you were so nervous that you walked like someone suffering from both massive brain damage and severe arthritis.

The Ford might not be the one that Blue-Suit drove, he told himself. And even if it was, just because it was sitting at the curb didn't mean that the detective was waiting for him, was even now watching as he walked away. After all, Patrick lived in this neighborhood. It was only natural that he would patronize businesses around here. Nothing suspicious about that.

Just the same, he tucked the photos into the inner pocket of his coat and then pulled the zipper up all the way to the base of his neck. Behind him, he heard the sound of a car engine turning over. He didn't have to turn and look to know that the driver of the Ford had started his car.

If Patrick took the direct way back to his apartment, he would only have a block and a half to go until he was safe. But if he went straight home, wouldn't that make him seem all the more guilty? Maybe it would be better to keep walking, pretend that he had some more errands to run. That way, Blue-Suit wouldn't –

Patrick stopped himself in mid-thought. It didn't matter what it looked like it he went straight home because *he-hadn't-done-anything!* Like a driver who suddenly becomes paranoid whenever a police car follows behind for a while, Patrick was acting as if he were guilty solely because Detective Blue-Suit, odd as the man was, had asked him a couple questions. So fucking what? That was no reason to act as if he were under surveillance or anything. He was a goddamned U.S. citizen, and if he wanted to stab a snowman for a gag, take some pictures, and then have them developed, he could, and to hell with the Unblinking Detective and his Bucket Brigrade.

Patrick walked to the end of the block, waited for the light to change, and then crossed the street.

When he had almost reached the other side, he couldn't keep himself from glancing in the direction of the Ford. It had pulled up to the intersection, and Blue-Suit was indeed sitting at the wheel, head turned and looking at Patrick with his cold stare. But now he was grinning, thin lips pulled back from teeth white as ice chips.

PANEL FOUR

The cartoonist, an irritated expression on his face, jams his sharpened pencil into the thought balloon filled only with an ever-diminishing progression of thought balloons. The main thought balloon is eclipsed by a jagged flash indicating an explosion, inside of which written in big capital letters is the word POP!

* * * * *

As soon as Patrick entered his apartment, he slammed the door shut and ran to the kitchen sick. He unzipped his coat, yanked the packet of pictures out of his pocket and ripped it open. Without pausing to even look at the photos, he crammed them into the disposal, turned on the water, and threw the switch. The disposal made a horrible groaning-churning noise as it struggled to reduce the pictures and their negatives to pieces small enough to pass through its drain.

Patrick turned the faucet to full strength, and after several moments during which it sounded as if the disposal might tear itself free from its berth under the sink and fling itself onto the kitchen floor, the noise became less harsh, until it finally smoothed out to a gentle whirring sound. Patrick let the water run for several more minutes before he finally shut down the disposal and turned the water off.

Now there was no evidence to link him to the "incident" in the park. He started to walk away from the sink, but then his gaze fell on the butcher block – and on the handle of the knife he'd used to stab the snowman.

He yanked the knife out of the block, squirted dish soap onto the blade, and then began to scrub it with an old sponge that he kept on the counter. He didn't just clean the blade; he also scoured the wooden handle to get rid of any fingerprints. After he rinsed the knife, he dried it carefully, making sure to hold onto the handle with the dish towel so that he wouldn't leave new fingerprints to replace the ones he'd gotten rid of. He then very carefully returned the clean, dry knife to its slot in the butcher block.

Now maybe he could . . .

Are you kidding? Do you really think that knife can ever be clean enough? The first thing Blue-Suit's going to do when he gets hold of it is hand it off to some geek in the crime lab who'll stick it under a microscope, press a couple buttons, and ding! Out'll pop a card with the name Patrick Bragg printed on it in bold, easy-to-read letters.

He looked at the knife resting innocently in the butcher block.

Get rid of it.

Patrick grabbed the knife handle and slid the blade out of the block.

And don't forget the strawberry syrup, dumbass.

* * * * *

The knife, wrapped in a dish towel bound with duct tape, sat on the passenger seat next to Patrick. The bottle of strawberry syrup, covered by an old plastic grocery bag, was also wrapped in tape.

He drove down Route 105 in his ancient Firebird, leaving a blue-white trail of exhaust behind him. The engine shook and muttered in protest as the car moved down the road well below the speed limit. Patrick normally took the bus to save money, and it had been a long time since he'd brought the Firebird in for a tune-up.

Patrick was outside of town and driving through the country – farmers' fields covered with snow, gray-black trees that were all branches and no leaves. He was relieved to be away from his apartment . . . and especially away from the park, and now that he was, he felt as if he were slowly returning to his senses. Out here, away from flashing blue lights, snow-filled buckets, and no-name detectives that never seemed to blink, Patrick could admit how truly and profoundly idiotic he'd been. He'd not merely let his imagination run away with him: he'd let it strap a rocket pack to his ass and light the fuse.

He wasn't even sure why he'd driven out this way, other than to put some distance between himself and Detective Blue-Suit. There were no rivers or lakes around here to toss his "evidence" into. The best he could do was throw the objects into a snow-filled ditch, where they'd be discovered sooner or later. More likely sooner given that winter was drawing to a close.

But none of that mattered any more, did it? He'd taken a little mental vacation from reality, but that was over now. He'd drive for a few more minutes – assuming his Firebird didn't shake itself apart first – and then he'd turn around and head home. Maybe he'd give Liz a call and see if he could convince her to knock off work early today. There was a new Charlie Kauffman movie out that he'd been wanting to see. Of course, Liz would have to treat, but she was used to –

A sudden flash of movement drew his gaze to the rearview mirror. There, through the haze of exhaust, was the dark blue Ford. Framed by the windshield, the grinning detective motioned for Patrick to pull over.

He gripped the steering wheel tight as he debated what to do. His first impulse was to jam his foot down on the gas and make a run for it, but he knew his old junker couldn't outrun a kid on a ten-speed, let alone Blue-Suit's Ford.

He sighed, took his foot off the accelerator, and activated his hazard lights.

* * * * *

Patrick sat alone at a metal table in a small, featureless room. It resembled every stereotypical police interrogation room that he'd seen in countless movies and TV shows, with one exception: it was cold as hell in here. So cold that his breath curled out his mouth as fog-mist, and he couldn't stop shivering, even with his winter coat on and zipped up all the way. The only illumination in the room came from a light bulb that jutted forth from the wall above the closed metal door. He wasn't handcuffed, which was something, he supposed, but he hadn't been allowed to talk to a lawyer yet (not that he had one) or even so much as make a single phone call. In a way, he was grateful for this last denial of his rights. He couldn't imagine telling Liz – or god forbid, his brother – that he'd been arrested on suspicion of murdering a snowman.

The door opened and Detective Blue-Suit walked, a manila file tucked under one arm. Though there was another chair at the table, he remaining standing.

"Mr. Bragg, I'd like to go over a few details of your story again, if you don't mind."

Patrick noticed that the man's breath didn't turn to mist in the frigid air. "It's not a *story*. It's the *truth*."

Blue-Suit smiled in a knowing way, as if he were used to humoring suspects. "Yes, of course. You say that you merely played a prank, that you wished to create a scene you could capture on film and use it to create a greeting card."

"A humorous card, yes. At least one that I hoped would be humorous."

"I fail to see what's so amusing about a dead body, but let's move on. If it was just a prank, then why were you attempting to dispose of evidence when I pulled you over?"

Patrick struggled to come up with a way to phrase his answer, uncertain that he fully understood why himself. "I guess I just let the idea that you might think I was guilty get to me, even though I didn't do anything."

Several seconds passed as Blue-Suit stared at Patrick with his blue-marble eyes. "Is that the same reason you were so nervous when you picked up your photos from the drugstore? Why you attempted to destroy them in your disposal?"

Patrick didn't bother to ask how Blue-Suit knew these things. Maybe he'd spoken with the girl who worked at the drugstore, and maybe he'd searched Patrick's apartment, stuck his hand down the disposal, and found leftover bits of soggy photos. What did it matter how he knew? He did.

Patrick found himself falling back on the same stock answer that he'd used so often as a child. "Idonno."

"Mr. Bragg, I'm going to be direct. Things don't look good for you. Not only do we have all the physical evidence that we need, we also have an eye witness."

"A witness? Who – " And then Patrick realized: the little snowman, the one sitting on top of the picnic table. Who else could it be?

He couldn't help grinning. "All right, I admit it. You caught me. I'm the notorious slayer of snowmen!" He gave Blue-Suit a I'm-in-on-the-joke wink. "But you have to admit, at least it's an original crime."

The detective raised an eyebrow. "Original?" He placed the file folder on the table in front of Patrick. "Take a look."

Patrick hesitated, then with hands that shook only partially due to the temperature, he opened the folder. Inside, along with other papers, were a number of photographs. He spread them out on the table. There were nine in all, and each one showed a snowman lying on the ground in a different position, chest and head covered with crimson.

He looked up at the pale, thin man with the frozen-blue eyes that never closed. "You can't pin these other cases on me!" he protested.

"I don't intend to try, Mr. Bragg. Your crime was committed with less . . . finesse than the others." Blue-Suit grinned, displaying his ice-chip teeth. "What you are, Mr. Bragg, is what we in law enforcement refer to as a copycat killer."

Mark and Remark . . . Your ferrets look like furry worms with feet . . .

Patrick's laughter was shrill, brittle, and very, very cold.

* * * * *

PANEL FIVE

This panel, the last, is empty, save for a pencil lying on the ground . . . a pencil with a broken tip.

Swimming Lessons

The humidity was so thick, you could take a bite out of the air and chew. Scott sat on the hard plastic bleachers in the front row, close to the rec center's pool, trying to ignore the dull ache in his lower back and wishing he had a more comfortable place to sit. *Getting old*, he thought.

Kelsey was at the far end of the pool with the rest of her class, holding onto the edge of the pool for support as she bobbed up and down in unison with the other kids. Scott supposed there was some point to the exercise, but it looked like all they were doing was learning to play Marco Polo.

The pool was filled with children of varying ages, from toddlers to middle-schoolers. At seven, Kesley fell somewhere in between. The kids' parents filled the bleachers, sitting hunched over, probably feeling the same ache in their lower backs as Scott did, their faces covered with slick sheens of sweat. Some talked listlessly on cell phones, some stared at open books with expressions of mild disinterest, and others chatted without energy or enthusiasm. They all looked as tired as Scott felt.

He was here alone. Carley had to work this morning, even though it was a Saturday. She scheduled all their daughter's activities and chauffeured Lindsey to them, often alone – something of a sore point between them. One of many these days.

Scott wiped sweat from his forehead and watched his daughter swim. The kids in her class were now lying on their backs in the water, holding onto yellow foam boards and kicking their legs with froglike motions as they swam backward.

He sighed, and the sound was echoed by the parents around him. Sweat was dripping off of them now as if it were the height of August instead of early March.

Scott wondered for perhaps the twentieth time that morning why Carley had felt it necessary to go into the office today. Sure, they had an ever-growing mountain of bills to pay, but things weren't *that* desperate. She'd gone in last Saturday, too. He wondered if she were having an affair, wondered if he really cared. He wished he were having an affair, wished he were having *something.*

He let out a deeper sigh this time, this one echoed just as deeply by the other bleacher-parents.

Lindsey laughed as she finally reached the other side of the pool, and her teacher praised her determination.

Scott wished he felt as carefree, that a simple word or two of praise could delight him so easily. Had it ever? he wondered. He couldn't remember.

Sweat ran down his chest and back, soaking his clothes. Rivulets trickled down his legs, past his ankles, began pooling around his shoes. The acrid smell of chlorine seared his nasal passages, and he told himself that it was the pool water he smelled, nothing else. More puddles formed at the feet of the other parents and chlorine-scented sweat ran down the bleaching in widening streams.

So many worries . . . unsatisfying marriages, soul-grinding jobs, perpetual bills, noncommittal lovers, inadequacies both real and imagined, unfulfilled dreams, diminished expectations . . .

Scott glanced at the thermometer mounted on the wall. Ninety-two degrees. God, it was stifling in here! The pool water looked so cool, so calm, so inviting . . .

So free.

He heard Lindy's laughter as he reached up to smear away more sweat. His fingers sank into the wet flesh of his forehead, but he felt no pain. As if the action broke the surface tension of his body, Scott's form shuddered and collapsed into water. He felt a surge of a half-remembered emotion that he thought might have been happiness as his liquid substance splashed his seat, flowed onto the floor, and slid toward the edge of the pool. He was joined by the others, and their watery substances merged, flowed into the pool, and together they lost themselves in joyous oblivion.

Their children continued to swim and splash, not noticing that the bleaches were empty, laughing as they slurped in water and spit great mouthfuls of their parents at each other.

Conversations Kill

She became aware of motion first, a steady rhythmic jostling that caused her to sway from side to side. Next the rumble-growl of a hard-running car engine, felt as much as heard. Heated air blowing on her skin, seeping into her flesh, penetrating her bones, until it felt as if her body was filled with warm golden honey. So soothing, so peaceful, so tempting to remain swaddled in darkness, warmth, and comfort. She almost gave in, surrendered herself to the safety of nothingness. Instead, she opened her eyes.

She saw a splash of garish yellow light surrounded by velvet blackness. Her vision cleared a little, and she realized she was looking at headlights illuminating a patch of asphalt. Blackness meant night, asphalt meant a road, headlights meant a car.

"Don't worry. Everything's going to be all right."

A man's voice, familiar. She turned to her left, saw him sitting at the steering wheel. He didn't turn to look at her, kept his gaze on the road ahead. In the soft blue glow of the dashboard lights, she examined his features. Lean face, prominent cheekbones, strong chin. Short straight hair, neatly trimmed beard. There was no way to tell for sure in this light, but she felt certain that his hair and beard were both reddish brown. He wore a brown suede jacket, faded jeans, and ratty running shoes that desperately needed to be replaced. His expression was impassive, almost as if he were wearing a mask, or was perhaps a mannequin someone had buckled into the driver's seat of the car as a bizarre joke. She knew that face, knew it better than she did her own.

"Walter." Half statement, half question.

He didn't answer, but his gaze flicked toward her for a brief instant before returning to the road. In that moment she thought she saw a resigned sadness in his eyes, mingled with a touch of anxiety that bordered on fear.

Why would he be afraid of me, of all people? I'd never . . . The thought trailed away as she realized she couldn't move her arms. Her seat belt was on, but surely she should still be able to move them, at least a little. She looked down at her lap and saw the reason for her immobility: her wrists had been wrapped together with duct tape. She also saw that she wore a sleeveless green dress – a garment she didn't recognize – along with a black belt around the waist, and no shoes. No bra or panties, either. She tried to move her legs and discovered her ankles were also bound with tape. An icicle spear of cold panic lodged in her heart, and her first instinct was to scream at Walter to let her go, to thrash about in an attempt to break free of her bonds. But she forced herself to remain quiet and still. She was a slender woman, not weak by any means, but even though she was in good shape, she knew she couldn't tear the tape apart with sheer strength. In the end, it was confused disbelief that helped her maintain control more than anything else. She simply couldn't conceive of any reason why Walter would tape her wrists and ankles together like this. Walter loved her; he'd never hurt her. This was all too weird, like something out of a nightmare. It couldn't possibly be real.

"You're probably wondering what's going on." He sounded almost apologetic.

She glanced out the windshield. For the last few minutes since she'd wakened, the road had been winding gently uphill, and large pine trees rose on either side, so high that the car's headlights couldn't illuminate them fully, leaving their tops shrouded in darkness. She had the impression that the trees might continue on upward forever without end, that perhaps they were holding the heavens themselves aloft, the stars nothing more than bits of frost clinging to their branches, glittering with reflected light from the nearly full moon.

"I know this area," she said. "It's Krahling Hills. We come up here every summer. We rent a cabin, go hiking, fishing, swimming in the lake . . ."

"That's the thing. We don't. We never have." Walter's tone held a measure of pity now, and for some reason that frightened her more than anything else since she'd awakened.

"How can you say that? I remember – "

"I'm trying to tell you!" he snapped.

The sudden intensity of his words scared her, and without thinking she scooted away from him, closer to the passenger door.

He turned to give her a sheepish smile. "Sorry. It's just . . . this isn't easy for me, you know?"

"No, I *don't. I'm* the one who woke up with duct tape around her ankles and wrists, not you." She was surprised by her own bravado, wasn't sure where it had come from. But the words, and more importantly the attitude behind them, felt right.

"I know. And I'm sorry." Walter turned his attention back to the road but continued to talk. "It's just that I didn't know how you were going to react, and I thought restraining you would make things easier. For both of us."

"What *things?*" Her confusion was quickly becoming replaced by anger. She loved Walter, but his stubborn reluctance to directly answer her questions infuriated her. "I don't remember getting in the car, and I don't understand why I'm dressed like this." She sat only inches from the passenger side window, but she could feel the outside cold seeping in through the glass. She guessed it was late fall, maybe earlier winter, but why couldn't she *remember?* "Where are my shoes? Why don't I have a coat? Why am I your prisoner?"

"You're not. Well . . . not exactly." He took a deep breath and let out a shaky sigh. "This is going to sound weird, but try to hear me out, okay? This is . . . well, it's therapy. For me."

She felt her body pressed back against the car seat as the road's incline grew steeper. *We're getting closer,* she thought. But closer to what, she didn't know.

"Therapy." The word came out flat, toneless. Nothing more than a nudge to keep him talking, like the single swift hand motion of a juggler trying to prevent a spinning plate from falling off the stick.

A nervous laugh, pitched high, an almost feminine sound. "This is probably going to sound weird . . . hell, forget *probably* – " another laugh – "but I've been seeing a psychologist for a while now. Her name is Dr. Naislund, and she's been working with me on, as she puts it, my 'issues' with the opposite sex."

She frowned. She didn't remember any Dr. Naislund, but she decided to keep quiet. Now that she'd gotten him talking, she didn't want to interrupt.

"Dr. Naislund thinks that my problems stem from my inability to relate on a fully mature level with the women in my life." He paused, shook his head. "I sound like a parrot mindlessly repeating psychological terminology, don't I?" He glanced at her, gave an apologetic shrug. "What do I know? I'm just a heating and cooling technician, barely a step or two up from a Mr. Fix-It. Dumb as a box of rocks."

The bitterness in his voice as he said this last bit didn't surprise her, though it did make her heart ache. Walter had always suffered from low self-esteem. It was what had kept him from taking more than a couple quarters' worth of college classes, what kept him from starting his own business instead of working for Builder's Depot.

"Honey, I know things haven't always gone smoothly for us, but I think we get along pretty well." *At least, we did up until the point that you duct-taped my arms and legs together.*

He pursed his lips and wrinkled his nose, actions she recognized as signs of frustration.

"You just don't get it, do you?" His voice was tense, and he gripped the steering wheel so tight that his hands shook. The car edged into the opposite lane for an instant, before he corrected and pulled back.

Sudden anger flared hot and bright within her. "Maybe I'd *get it* if you'd take this goddamned tape off me!" She raised her bound wrists and shook them for emphasis.

He turned to look at her then, and she saw cold hatred in his eyes, so intense that seeing it hit her like a slap to the face. She knew Walter could get angry sometimes, but this . . .

"You're not real."

Of all the things he might've said at that moment – *Fuck off, bitch; shut your damn mouth, cunt* – she hadn't expected Walter to negate her very existence. This whole situation was already way too bizarre, and this last comment of Walter's only served to push it over the edge into total insanity. She couldn't help it; she laughed.

Walter faced forward and kept driving, his hands continuing to grip the steering wheel so hard they trembled.

"What's your name?" he asked softly.

Her laughter died. "What?"

"Tell me your name." He sounded calm now, though his hands still shook on the steering wheel.

"Are you kidding? Have you gone completely – " She was about to say *nuts*, but then a horrible realization struck her. She didn't know her name. She struggled to recall it, wondered if Walter had drugged her in addition to binding her arms and legs. That would explain why she couldn't –

"Joy." The word popped out of her mouth as if of its own accord. "My name is Joy."

Walter half turned to look at her, a small sad smile on his face. "That's my ex-wife's middle name. Kind of a joke on my part, since the women in my life haven't brought me much. Joy, that is. She's the one I used to come up here with, not you."

She felt like a vast chasm had just opened up in the pit of her stomach. "Ex-wife? But you've never been married to anybody but me . . . we met in high school, for godsakes. We got married the August after we graduated."

"That was Laurie Hissong. And I didn't marry her after we graduated. She broke up with me and started going out with Darrin Weidemann. They eventually got married and had four kids. Darrin's the manager of a grocery store now. Doing pretty well for himself, too. Well enough to afford a better car that this old beater Chevy of mine, that's for damn sure."

Laurie . . . Darrin . . . The names meant nothing to her.

"A few years later I met Susan. I was working on the air conditioning at the car parts store where she was a cashier. We got to talking, and she told me she was separated from her husband. We started going out, but it didn't last. She went back to her husband six months later. He was in charge of loans at a bank, made a lot more money than I did. With women, it always comes down to money in the end, doesn't it?" Before she could respond, he shook his head as if to clear away that last thought. "Sorry. Dr. Naislund says I shouldn't generalize about women like that. She says it's a sign of displaced anger."

"I don't understand . . . I used to work at a car-parts store years ago, you know that. But you never told me about any Susan. Are you telling me you had an affair?" Her stomach clenched tight at the thought that Walter could have betrayed her like that.

He went on as if she hadn't spoken. "I met Karen a year or so later. Karen *Joy*. She was a massage therapist. I strained my back on the job, and my doctor sent me to do some rehab at the hospital. Karen helped my back heal, and then when she agreed to be my wife, she healed my heart." His laugh was self-deprecating. "Sounds cheesy, huh? But that's how I felt."

"Walter, honey, I don't know why you're so confused, but *I'm* a massage therapist. Remember? I got tired of being a cashier and went back to school. I've worked at the hospital for almost five years now."

"After Karen left me – for a goddamned radiologist almost twice her age – I got depressed, started drinking pretty heavily, messing up on the job . . . My boss told me if I wanted to keep working for Builders Depot I had to get my act together. So I made an appointment to see Dr. Naislund. This was all *her* idea."

Her hands and feet were starting to go numb. The tape was too tight, cutting off her circulation. "You're not making any sense, Walter. Something's wrong, *really* wrong. Please, stop the car, get this tape off me, and let's go home. In the morning I'll call the hospital and we'll find someone who can help you."

"I'm already seeing a therapist, *Joy*. And what's wrong – really, really wrong – is *you*! In case you haven't guessed by now, that's the whole reason for our little late-night drive!"

The sudden fury in his voice frightened her, but not as much as the expression of sheer hatred that twisted his features.

She fought to keep her tone calm as she spoke, but she couldn't keep a quaver of fear out of her voice. "Walter, sweetheart, whatever it is, we can talk it out. I love you."

"Don't you fucking GET IT? There *is* no YOU!" He practically screamed this, eyes wild, spittle flying from his lips.

Ice water sluiced through her veins as she realized her husband was gone and a madman had taken his place.

They drove on in silence for several minutes after that, Walter taking deep breaths, letting them out slowly. When he spoke again, his tone was even, his words controlled.

"I told you earlier: you're-not-real. There is no Joy. You're . . . I don't know how to put it . . . a combination of the women in my life. The women I have *issues* with. Laurie, Susan, Karen . . . You look a little bit like each of them. You have Laurie's eyes, Susan's figure, Karen's long black hair . . . and you're wearing my favorite outfit of Karen's. She wore that dress when we went to Mexico on our honeymoon. She had no bra or underwear on, either. Said it made her feel sexy to go commando."

She felt dizzy, her chest felt tight, and she thought she might be on the verge of losing consciousness. Maybe it was because of the tape, maybe it was because she was trapped in a car with a lunatic that was wearing her husband's face. Most likely it was both.

"Dr. Naislund says my resentment toward women is the cause of my drinking problem, that I'm turning my anger inward and punishing myself. What I need to do is get my anger out, to release it and let it go once and for all. Dr. Naislund's one of those new-agey types, into all sorts of weird stuff. One of the things she's big on is role-playing. She uses it a lot in therapy sessions. She suggested I . . . what's the word she used? *Personify* my resentment and deal with it in a *symbolic* way. That's what you are: a personification."

Her fear edged a notch closer to outright terror. "You can't be serious! Are you saying that you . . . *imagined* me?"

"Yep. I have a good imagination, Joy. *Really* good. Have ever since I was a kid. I just never did anything with it." A pause. "Before now, that is. To be honest, I'm surprised at how well you turned out. It's almost like you're really here. It's pretty amazing, actually."

She stared at Walter for a long moment. "So if I'm real, I'm just a . . . what? A voice in your head? An image in your mind?"

"That's about it, yeah."

"And you imagined me bound in duct tape?"

He gave her a smile that turned her already chilled blood to ice. "Like I said, I have problems with resentment toward women."

"You're insane." The words slipped out before she could stop them. She doubted it was a wise move to tell a crazy person you knew they were crazy, but it was too late now.

"Am I? Then let me ask you one simple question: what we were doing tonight before we started our little – " he smiled – "*joy* ride?"

"We . . ." She hesitated. She figured they'd probably had dinner, watched a movie on DVD, maybe made love before turning in for the night . . . but she had no specific memory of doing any of these things with Walter tonight. In fact, the memories she did have were hazy, generic ones . . . almost as if they weren't real memories at all, but someone else's, memories that had been told to her but which she'd never actually lived.

It's the after-effects of whatever drug he used to knock you out, she told herself. *That's all.*

"You can't, can you?"

She wanted to smack the smug smile off his face, and she might have too, if her hands hadn't been taped together. "Let me make this clear: I don't believe you, and while I probably should humor you, right now I'm too pissed off to do it. But, assuming that what you're saying is true, why don't you tell me how this little psychodrama of yours is supposed to play out?"

"It's all very symbolic. We're going to drive to Stephens Watch, the place where – "

"You asked me to marry you."

"Where I asked *Karen* to marry me. And then I'm going to do exactly as Dr. Naislund suggested. I'm going to release my anger, every goddamned bit of it, once and for fucking all."

In her mind, she saw Stephens Watch – the most scenic spot in Krahling Hills. The area had been shaped thousands of years ago when the great glaciers moved southward, molding the land during their tortuously slow passage across what was now Ohio. Most people thought of the Midwest as nothing but dull, flat plains, but here in southwest Ohio the countryside consisted of deep, lush valleys and beautiful tree-covered hills that, if not quite mountains, were nevertheless breathtaking in their own right. Stephens Watch was located at the top of the largest hill in the area, the highest point of elevation in southwest Ohio. People came from all over Ohio, Indiana, Kentucky, and even further to park at the observation point, get out of their vehicles, walk over to the safety railing, and gaze upon mile after mile of verdant forestland spread out before them, feeling as if they were gods looking down from the heavens. It was a prime spot for taking photos and video, and she remembered doing that very thing, snapping pictures with her digital camera, when Walter tapped her on the shoulder. She'd turned around, irritated because Walter had caused her to muff her latest shot, but she forgave him instantly when she saw the diamond ring he held out to her. It wasn't a huge diamond by any means, but it glittered in the sunlight like a stone five times the size, and she instantly fell in love with it and, without waiting for Walter to formally ask her to marry him, she'd said, *With all of my heart,* and then leaned forward to kiss him.

But according to Walter, it was someone else's memory, not hers. She wasn't *real.*

She was about to ask him how she could have any memories at all if she wasn't real, how she could possibly feel or think. But before she could speak, a terrible thought occurred to her. She remembered what Walter had said.

I'm going to do exactly as Dr. Naislund suggested. I'm going to release my anger, every goddamned bit of it, once and for fucking all . . . It's all very symbolic.

At Stephens Watch.

She remembered what he'd said about the duct tape around her wrists and ankles.

It's just that I didn't know how you were going to react, and I thought restraining you would make things easier. For both of us.

"You're planning to kill me, aren't you? You're going to park at Stephens Watch and then throw me over the safety railing." She surprised herself by how calm she sounded. There was a damn good reason the state had installed the railing there. Though most of the hills in the area possessed gradual slopes, at Stephens Watch it was a sheer drop straight down to a rocky outcropping below – nearly two hundred feet, according to a helpful information sign the Ohio Park Service had erected at the site.

Walter didn't answer right away, and when he spoke, his tone was apologetic. "It's nothing personal, Joy. I just need to get on with my life, you know? My unresolved feelings about my past relationships are holding me back . . . dragging me down. I can't get anyone to go out on a date with me, and I may lose my job because I'm a fucking drunk. My life is in the toilet, and the only way I can crawl out of it is to . . ." He trailed off.

"Kill me," she finished for him, her voice soft, tone hollow.

"Look, I've already told you, it's just symbolic. I'm role-playing in my imagination, acting out both parts – yours *and* mine. You're not really here, not really real, so there's nothing to worry about. Everything will be okay once it's over. You'll see." A sideways glance, a snorting laugh. "Well, maybe you *won't*, but you get the idea."

The road began to level off, and she knew they were drawing near Stephens Watch.

There was no question in her mind that Walter was insane. That he'd never shown the slightest sign of madness during their entire marriage didn't matter. Maybe he had a brain tumor or something, or maybe he'd just snapped for no reason at all. That happened sometimes, didn't it? How many times did you read it in the newspaper: *He was such a nice man. Quiet, polite . . . You'd never in a million years guess he'd do anything like that.* However it had happened, whatever the cause, Walter had gone 'round the proverbial bend, and she was going to be forced to take a fatal swan dive off Stephens Watch as part of her husband's twisted "therapy" – unless she did something and did it fast.

But what? Lunge across the seat and slam into his shoulder, hopefully causing him to lose control of the car? What good would that do? If they wrecked, she'd be just as likely to get hurt as Walter. And with her hands bound as they were, she wouldn't be able to work the release on the seat belt fast enough to surprise him anyway. He'd know what she was trying to do, and he'd be ready.

Walter eased off the accelerator, and the car slowed. The headlights passed over a metal sign, raised letters spelling out STEPHENS WATCH; behind it, curving along the edge of the hill, the thin green metal bars of the safety railing.

The car had slowed enough that she might be able to jump for it. But even *if* she could undo her seatbelt, *and* unlock and open the door, *and* not break too many bones when she hit the asphalt, her legs would still be bound with duct tape. What could she do? Make a *hop* for it?

Walter pulled the Chevy into the empty gravel parking lot, rocks crunching and pinging beneath the tires. Brakes squealed as he brought the car to a stop, put it in park, and shut off the engine. The beater's ancient motor knocked and sputtered a couple times, the car rocking slightly from side to side before finally falling silent.

Walter sat staring straight ahead for several moments, expression unreadable. He'd left the headlights on, the wash of light making the safety rail's green paint look sour yellow. But though the light continued past the railing, it did nothing to illuminate the darkness beyond.

"Walter, honey, you have to listen to me." She fought to keep the desperation she felt out of her voice. She wanted him to think she was speaking out of love and concern, not simply out of fear for her own life. "Whatever's wrong, we can deal with it together.

I'll do anything to help you, sweetheart. I-I love you." Her voice broke on the word *love*, and she prayed he hadn't noticed.

He turned to her then, his expression cold and dispassionate. "Love? What do *you* know about love? What do *any* of you know about it?" He turned away from her, unlocked the car door, and shoved it open. He got out and walked around the back of the Chevy, shoes crunching gravel, tread fast and determined. Then he was outside the passenger window, grabbing the door handle, yanking the door open, and reaching inside for her.

"C'mon, *Joy*. Our little play has just about reached its climax." He pressed the button to release her seatbelt, then grabbed hold of her bare upper arm. His fingers sank into the soft flesh of her slender arm, and she drew in a hissing breath as he tightened his grip. She imagined she could feel the tips of his fingernails scraping against her bone.

He pulled her out of the car, and she gasped as the cold night air sank icy teeth into her skin, slicing through the sheer fabric of her dress as if it wasn't there. She winced as her bare feet pressed down on sharp gravel. Bound as her ankles were, she couldn't shift her weight to find a more comfortable stance, but sore feet were the least of her problems right now.

Walter half-carried, half-dragged her across the gravel toward the safety rail, muttering beneath his breath the entire way. "Fucking bitches, goddamned cunts, oozy-coozies . . ."

When they reached the railing, he stopped, grabbed her shoulders, and turned her around to face him. They stood in the wash of the Chevy's headlights – a spotlight for the final act in Walter's theatre of insanity – and though she expected his eyes to be dancing with madness, she was startled by how calm they were. No, more than that: how *serene*.

"I'd like to say that this is going to hurt me more than it does you, but you know what? This isn't going to hurt me at all. In fact, if this works like Dr. Naislund says it will, I should be feeling pretty fucking good in the next few moments." His grip on her shoulders tightened, his muscles tensed, and she knew he was preparing to shove her over the railing to tumble down, down onto the jagged rocks far below.

A memory flashed through her mind. Karen . . . no, she – *Joy* – kissing him right here, on this very spot, seconds after he'd asked her to marry him. She remembered the words she (Karen-Joy) had spoken just before the kiss, and she said them now.

"With all of my heart."

A look of confusion passed across his face, and before he could react, she leaned forward, opened her mouth, pressed her lips against his, gently sucked his lower lip between her teeth and bit down as hard as she could.

Walter shrieked and pulled back at the same time he shoved her away. Unable to maintain her balance with her ankles duct-taped together, she fell backward onto her rear, a sizeable chunk of Walter's lip clenched between bloody teeth. She saw Walter stumble backward – blood streaming over his chin, pattering onto his jacket – then he turned as if to run, and lunged forward . . . straight into the waist-high safety rail. Disoriented and in pain, he'd turned the wrong way.

It happened fast. He smacked into the railing, pitched forward and over, and then was lost to darkness. Walter released an inarticulate cry that might have been at attempt to say "Joy" but which could just as easily have been a try at "fuck you, bitch." That sound was followed by several solid-meaty thuds as he bounced on the way down – evidently the drop wasn't quite as steep as the park services sign made it out to be – and then all she could hear was her own ragged breathing.

She turned her head to spit out the bloody piece of lip, and then flopped onto her side, rolled over onto her elbows and knees, and managed to maneuver herself into a standing position. Shivering, and not only from the old, she shuffled cautiously up to the railing and peered over.

The blue-white glow of the almost-full moon illuminated the bottom of Stephens Watch sufficiently for her to make out Walter's body. He was lying facedown, head at an unnatural angle, arms and legs twisted out of shape like the soft boneless limbs of a rag doll. He wasn't alone, though. The bodies of a dozen women lay scattered around him, all in various states of decomposition, all slender, all wearing green dresses and nothing else, all possessing long black hair.

You have Laurie's eyes, Susan's figure, Karen's long black hair . . . and you're wearing my favorite outfit of Karen's. She wore that dress when we went to Mexico on our honeymoon. She had no bra or underwear on, either. Said it made her feel sexy to go commando.

Laurie, Susan, Karen . . . Karen *Joy*.

She knew she wasn't looking at a dozen different women, women Walter had selected to kill because they fit a certain image out of his fantasies. She was looking at the *same* woman a dozen times over. Looking at herself.

Evidently Walter's special therapy hadn't worked the first time, or even the twelfth.

"At least you were persistent," she said. "I'll give you that."

As the women at the bottom of Stephens Watch began to fade into the moonlight, as Joy looked down and realized she could see the Chevy's headlights shining through her chest and stomach, she had the satisfaction of knowing that, if this play was finally over, at least one of her had been able to rewrite the ending.

Long Way Home

Lauren felt the first raindrop on the back of her left hand. Without thinking, she called out, "C'mon, Alex! Time to go!" Before she was finished speaking, another drop landed on the back of her neck. On some level, she was already starting to become suspicious – the drops were warm, and they didn't feel right on her skin, were too thick, too globby – but none of that registered on her conscious mind, not yet. She was too concerned with getting her son to listen to her.

"Alex?"

He was on the spider climber with three other kids, all of them about the same age, all arms and legs and mussed hair and crackling energy. They circled the top of the climber, playing a game of tag, shouting and laughing.

Another drop, this one striking the back of her right wrist. She didn't look at it.

Lauren took her hands away from the paperback thriller she had been reading, allowed the book to flip shut. She left it lay on the surface of the wooden table where she had been sitting, a surface that was now speckled with tiny red dots that she almost but didn't quite take note of. She stood and began walking toward the climber, toward Alex and his playmates, none of whom he'd met before this afternoon. She forced herself to walk at a measured pace and did her best to ignore the fluttery, crawly feeling growing in the pit of her stomach.

He won't fall, he's too old to fall, and even if he did, the ground beneath him is covered with cedar chips to cushion the impact. He couldn't get hurt if he tried.

The thoughts didn't help; if anything, they only increased her nervousness. It had taken quite an effort for her to sit and read while Alex played with the other children. This was a large playground, with swings, climbers, balance beams, and a large wooden structure built to resemble a castle. It half-circled the play area with stairs to climb up and corridors to run along, tunnels to crawl through, and poles to slide down. There was no way to keep a close eye on your children here, not unless you followed on their heels as they played. Lauren knew, because they had come here before, and she had shadowed Alex every time, never more than a few feet away, never taking her eyes off him, making certain he was okay.

But on the way here today Alex had asked if she would sit at one of the tables near the play area instead. She'd almost asked why, but she didn't because she knew the answer. Alex was seven; he didn't need, didn't *want* Mommy hovering over him while he played. Especially not if he hoped to hook up with some other kids and maybe make a few new friends.

And so she'd agreed and sat and pretended to read James Patterson, glancing at her watch every five minutes and trying to ignore the whoops and shouts of the children as they played, telling herself they were just having fun, that no one had fallen and gotten hurt. She'd managed to leave Alex alone for almost forty-five minutes, but she couldn't take it any longer, and the rain – though little more than a sprinkle so far – had given her a pretext to call off the fun and take him home.

"C'mon, Alex, it's starting to rain." She was almost to the climber now, and she felt more drops (more *warm* drops, *sticky* drops) plap against her skin. She noticed none of the other parents – mostly moms, but there were a few dads as well – weren't coming to get their kids. They stood around in clumps of two and three, chatting, ignoring their children, probably glad not to have to worry about them for a while. Lauren envied those parents. She couldn't stop worrying, no matter what.

She reached the climber and had to resist the urge to reach up and grab Alex by the arm to get his attention. She knew he'd resent her doing so, especially in front of the other kids.

"It's time we were going, Alex."

He kept circling the climber, pursuing and being pursued in turn. But he acknowledged her approach with a sullen glance. "Aw, Mom, just a few more minutes. Please?"

It was a warm Sunday afternoon in early May, and Alex's red hair was sweaty at the ends, his normally fair skin flushed from his exertions. He needed to rest, needed a drink of water. He did *not* need to keep playing.

Lauren felt a warm drop strike her throat, and she reached up and ran her fingers over the puckered flesh of a scar that peeked out from beneath the collar of her blouse. It was an old habit, something she often did when she was nervous.

"You've played long enough. I have to get home and get dinner started, and you have some homework you need to finish up before tomorrow." She used her Mommy Means It voice, and added a frown to reinforce her words.

It worked. Alex groaned, but he leapt down from the climber and landed with a soft thunk! on the cedar chips.

"I gotta go, guys."

This elicited a couple *Aw man's* and *No ways* from the other boys, but a second later they returned to their game of tag as if Alex didn't exist. He started walking toward Lauren, dragging his feet through the cedar chips, and she almost held out her hand to him the way she had when he was a toddler, but she restrained herself. He was a big boy now, she reminded herself. Too big to hold Mommy's hand in the park – especially in front of other kids.

Alex wore a white t-shirt with a picture of SpongeBob Squarepants on the front, khaki shorts, and running shoes. His shirt was dotted with dark spots which Lauren at first took to be daubs of mud, though the ground was dry – or at least it had been before it started to rain. But as she watched another spot appeared, then another, and she realized they were caused by raindrops hitting her son. But why were they so dark?

Then a drop struck his cheek, just below his left eye, and she saw why they were so dark. It wasn't a drop of water; it was a drop of blood.

"Hold up for a second, sweetie." Her voice sounded too high and quavery, despite her efforts to remain calm. Alex stopped obediently in front of her, and she reached out to touch the drop on his cheek. But before her fingers could reach his flesh, another drop splattered against the back of her hand, and she brought it to her face. The substance was thick, colored a darkish red that was almost black, and it gave off a sour, coppery tang.

Blood.

Her stomach dropped and a cold shiver ran along the length of her spine. *Impossible,* she told herself, her rational mind rising to counter her burgeoning fear. Blood simply did *not* fall from the sky. It was probably just a trick of the light; the sky was starting to cloud over, the air taking on a purplish here-comes-a-storm tint. Dark enough to make water look like blood. Or maybe the rain had been discolored by some sort of pollutant. There were a number of factories on the edge of town, smokestacks pumping out white plumes of toxic chemical cocktails into the atmosphere.

Whatever the hell this dark rain was, Lauren knew that she wanted to get her son out of it as quickly as possible. So despite her earlier restraint, she grabbed Alex's hand and began dragging him toward the parking lot. He made a squawk of protest and tried to pull free of her grip, but he came and that was all that mattered right now. They passed the table where she'd been sitting, and she saw her book sitting there, but she didn't want to take the time to get it. Instinct told her that she needed to get her son out of this rain *now*, and to hell with James Patterson.

Lauren had on a white blouse and light blue shorts, and as she towed Alex across the grass, reddish-black drops spattered on her bare legs and arms, warm and sticky. A wave of revulsion washed through her, and she almost stopped to smear the gook off her flesh, but she resisted. She could worry about cleaning the stuff off of her and Alex when they were both safe inside the van.

As they drew near their Ford Aerostar, Lauren fished the keys out of her shorts pocket and thumbed the remote. The van's locks snicked open, and she pulled Alex toward the side door.

"Mom, what *is* this stuff? It's all ookey!"

"Nevermind that right now. Let's just get inside."

The Aerostar was dotted red-black, almost as if it were bleeding from dozens of pinprick wounds. The handle of the side door was slick with the stuff, and Lauren had to force herself to touch it. The metal was slippery, but she was able to slide the door open without too much trouble.

Alex hopped inside without being told, and Lauren saw that his hair was matted in places, and rivulets of (not)blood ran down his face and neck. His arms and legs were slick with the awful stuff, and his clothes were covered with dark, wet spots. From the way his eyes widened as he stared at her, she knew she looked just as bad.

"It'll be okay, honey. Don't worry." The words were automatic, like the pre-recorded phrases programmed into a child's talking doll. She wasn't sure she believed them, but she was a mom, and those were the sorts of things moms said, even when they weren't sure they were true. *Especially* when.

She gave Alex what she hoped was a reassuring smile, then slid the side door shut with a solid chunk! She turned and headed around the front of the van, half-running, and her left foot struck a slick patch on the asphalt and nearly slid out from under her. She managed to keep herself from falling, but a jolt of fiery pain lanced through her thigh. A pulled muscle, nothing to be concerned about. She continued more slowly, limping toward the driver's side.

She glanced toward the playground and saw the other parents gathering their children and beginning to head for their cars. The sky was almost night-dark now, and the rain – if it could be called that – was beginning to come down more heavily. She lowered her head and squinted her eyes to keep the muck from getting in them, and kept her lips clamped shut to prevent any of it from getting in her mouth. Whatever the hell this shit was, she knew she didn't want any of it inside her.

She reached the driver's door, tried to open it, but her fingers slid off the slick handle once, twice. Finally, she wrapped her fingers in the fabric of her t-shirt and was able to get enough of a grip to open the door. She climbed inside and slammed the door shut behind her. The place on her shirt where she'd touched the door handle was a large red-wet smear.

She sat in the seat, breathing heavily, heart pounding in her ears. They'd made it.

The windshield was spattered with dark-red globs, but Lauren could still see the other parents struggling to reach the parking lot, trying not to slip on wet grass that was becoming slicker by the moment, keeping hold of their children's hands as best they could, given the thick, red substance that was rapidly coating all of their flesh like a second grisly skin.

Lauren felt a pang of guilt. She should get out of the car, go to them, try to help. But she squashed the feeling. Her first - her *only* - responsibility was to Alex.

She inserted the key into the ignition and started the engine. Without thinking, she activated the wipers. After all, it *was* raining, right? The blades moved across the windshield, rubber edges leaving behind viscous red smears.

"Fuck!" She hardly ever swore, and never in front of Alex, but she figured if ever there was a time to curse, this was it. What was happening was insane. Blood – and it *was* blood and not some imaginary industrial waste product, let's face it – didn't just fucking fall from the fucking sky. But it was.

She thumbed the button on the end of the windshield wiper arm and twin jets of blue washer fluid splashed onto the red muck. She kept her thumb on the button as the blades moved back and forth, back and forth, doing their best to clear the blood away. She managed to clean enough of the windshield to see the other parents had made progress toward their cars, but not much. She stopped the washer fluid and turned off the wipers. Better to wait until the windshield was too gooked-up to see again to use the blades.

"Mommy?" Alex's voice was soft, and sounded like that of a much younger child. "Is everything okay?"

His question made her heart ache, and she felt tears threatening. She knew he didn't really want an answer, certainly not a true one; he wanted her to reassure him, to tell him everything was all right, and if it wasn't, to make it that way. That's what mommys were supposed to do.

She turned around and gave her son what she hoped was a convincing simulation of a reassuring smile. "Don't worry, honey. We're going home now."

Alex worked to return her smile, but it didn't last long. His eyes were wide, his face - his poor, blood-streaked face - was pale, and she wondered if he were in danger of going into shock. Hell, she wondered if *she* was.

She turned back around, her fingers reaching up to trace the line of scar tissue on her neck, and she heard the distant, faint sounds of a dog growling. Heard her mother say, *I'm sorry, baby. I'm so sorry.*

Her scar began to throb, but she knew it was just her imagination.

She glanced at the rearview mirror and caught Alex's gaze. "Time to go." She threw the van into reverse and, mindful of the slick asphalt beneath their tires, gently pressed the gas. The Aerostar began to back up and she had to resist the urge to jam the pedal to the floor. The last thing she needed right now was to get into a wreck. Out of the corner of her eye, she saw that some of the other parents had reached their vehicles, were frantically shoving their children inside, starting car engines. In moments, the parking lot would become a demolition derby of frightened parents, all desperate to get their kids the hell out of there. Lauren and Alex had a head start, though. All she had to do was keep cool and they'd be on the street in a matter of seconds.

She braked, put the van into forward gear, pressed the gas. *Easy does it,* she told herself. *Easy-peasy,* Alex might have said. It had become one of his favorite phrases of late, and she found it ringing in her mind now, echoing in Alex's delighted little boy voice.

Easy-peasy, easy-peasy, easy-peasy!

And that's when the bodies began to fall.

The rain was coming down hard enough now that the world seemed cloaked in crimson mist. The bodies were nothing but dark shapes at first, plummeting from the sky, striking grass and asphalt, bouncing once, twice before finally becoming still. Not many: a half dozen or so that Lauren could see through the blood sliding down her windshield. She sat and stared, van in gear, foot on the brake, as the nearest of the shapes shuddered and started to pull itself up.

Sweet Christ, what now?

"Mommy, it's a monster!"

Her first instinct was to tell Alex that there weren't any such things as monsters, but the words died in her throat as she watched the creature closest to them stagger to its feet not more than ten yards away. She hit the washer fluid and wipers again, cleared enough of a spot to get a decent look at the thing. Whatever the hell it was, it had been damaged by its fall – *fall from where?* part of her wondered; there was nothing above the park but empty sky. Empty, that is, before the red rain. Stick arms and legs, all (she did a quick count) nine of them, were broken in several places, and the lopsided head hung to one side as if the neck were broken too. Its chest had burst open, and glistening organs spilled forth: purplish loops that resembled intestines, large pink things that might have been lungs, and other tumorous hunks of meat that she couldn't identify. She couldn't classify the damned thing; it looked like a hybrid of insect and lizard, but that description was a poor approximation at best. It was like nothing she had ever seen before – outside of a nightmare, that is.

She supposed Alex had named it best: *monster.* No other word fit better.

Despite its hideous injuries, the creature lurched forward as best it could on its broken limbs, each step making its exposed organs jiggle and flop about. Laura had the impression that the thing's glistening black eyes were fixed on hers, and she knew it was coming toward them.

"Mommy, I want to go home now! I want to see Daddy!" Alex was seven, but he sounded more like two. Lauren didn't blame him, though; she knew exactly how he felt. But she had to keep it together, for both of them.

Throughout the park, other creatures – all broken and wounded – began to rise and walk, even as more continued to fall around them. If one of the things was too badly hurt from landing, it would pull or push itself forward with whatever functional limbs it still possessed.

"Momm-MEEE!"

Alex ended the word in a shriek that brought Lauren back to herself. She removed her foot from the brake, pressed the accelerator (still resisting the urge to jam down on the pedal, and

Jesus, it was the hardest thing she'd ever done), and the Aerostar began rolling toward the street.

A loud *crunch!* and Lauren jerked forward in her seat. She heard Alex cry out, wanted to turn around and comfort him, but the van was beginning to slide sideways on the slick asphalt, and she needed to hold onto the steering wheel, keep them from slipping into the grass where they might get stuck.

The Aerostar came to rest at an angle to the park's entrance, blocking it. She put the van in park and was relieved to realize the engine was still running. Thank God Daniel had taken it in for a tune-up last month.

Alex was sobbing, breath hitching in his throat. Rain pattered on the roof, louder now; it was coming down harder.

She turned around, smiled gently. "It's okay, honey. Someone just bumped into us from behind. We're fine." As she said these words, she realized she was a fool for stopping. So what if someone had rear-ended them? This was hardly a time to worry about exchanging insurance information and wait for the police to arrive to fill out an accident report. No doubt about it; she was in shock.

Horns sounded behind them, parents desperate to leave the park, to get their children away from the awful broken things that had fallen from the blood-red sky. How many seconds before they began trying to drive around the van – or worse – ram their way through?

Lauren faced forward again and gripped the gear shift. She thought she'd be able to get the Aerostar onto the street without having to back up. The passenger-side tires might have to go over the curb, but they could manage it. She hoped.

Alex still sobbing, rain still pattering, and then a loud pounding on her window. Lauren jumped, almost didn't turn to look. But she did, half-expecting to see glistening black eyes set in a chitinous-scaly face staring at her. What she saw was almost as bad: a crimson mask of anger, eyes filled with fury, mouth open and yelling, white teeth dotted with blood.

Then she realized what she was looking at – a man covered by red rain, presumably the driver of the vehicle that had rear-ended her. Between Alex's sobbing, the rumble of the Aerostar's engine, and the drumming of the rain on the roof, she could barely make out what he was saying, but it sounded something like, "What the hell kind of driving was that, you dumbass bitch?"

Lauren almost burst into laughter. The belly of the sky had split open and was gushing blood on the world, expelling monstrous, twisted things in the process, and this guy was pissed about tapping bumpers. Maybe he was in shock, too. Had to be, else why would he be stupid enough to get out of his car with those creatures –

Claws reached over the top of Mr. Road Rage's head and black talons sank into the skin just above his eyes. The man screamed, and Lauren saw that the creature's fingers were long and multi-jointed, like a spider's legs. The thing jerked the man's head back, and Lauren expected the creature to rip it clean off the neck, but it didn't. Instead, another hand reached around with spider-leg fingers and pried open the man's mouth. Red rain poured down his throat as he struggled to break free of the demonic thing that held him, but the creature was too strong.

Alex's sobs had degenerated into a high-pitched keening. Lauren was distantly aware of it, but she couldn't take her eyes off what was happening outside her window. Mr. Road Rage's skin was erupting in greenish-black patches, and his eyes were clouding over, becoming shiny black.

The rain he had swallowed was making him into one of *them*.

Lauren felt suddenly nauseated. The rain was on her, still wet and sticky, on *Alex*, for godsakes! Neither of them had swallowed any, but what if it could be absorbed through the skin? It might take a little longer to work that way, but in the end it still would –

Something smacked into the passenger-side window. She turned to a green-black palm pressed against the glass, multi-jointed fingers ending in black talons. Another one, and this one wanted to get in, to get at Lauren and Alex, make them *drink*.

"Fuck this shit," Lauren breathed. She put the van into drive and jammed her foot onto the gas, not caring if they slid on wet asphalt, not caring if they wrecked, not thinking about anything except the overwhelming need to get the hell of there right-fucking-now!

The Aerostar fishtailed, slid across grass, juddered as it went over the curb, and then they were in the street, Alex clapping, cheering, "Go, Mommy, go!" Lauren felt a little like cheering herself, but she kept her concentration focused on driving. Their house was only a couple miles from the park, but she knew the drive home was going to be a hell of a lot longer than the drive here. She turned on the wipers, activated the washer fluid, and eased her foot off the gas. *Easy-peasy*, she told herself, and drove forward at a blistering five miles an hour.

* * * * *

When Lauren was five, her mother took her into the backyard to play while she weeded the flower beds. Lauren's mother was the type of person who could only concentrate on one thing at a time, so while she was busily yanking grass from between azaleas, she didn't see her young daughter walk up to the chain link fence, open the gate, and go through.

To Lauren, it was a fine joke to play on her mommy – a game of hide-and-seek with a little adventure tossed in for good measure. She'd never gone through the gate by herself before, wasn't allowed to be in the front yard without a grown-up watching her. But the forbidden nature of what she was doing only made it all the more fun. She knew not to go *very* far of course, but she thought it would okay if she walked down the driveway to the sidewalk, maybe sat there and looked around the neighborhood, see who was out playing, watch cars go by, or just listen to the birds singing and feel the breeze move gently across her skin.

But she never made it to the sidewalk. Halfway there, a neighbor's dog – a big white boxer with brown patches on its flanks – came trotting toward her. Lauren had seen the doggy before, running around the neighbors' backyard, sometimes sitting on the porch with one of its owners nearby. But Lauren had always been in the company of an adult before, and the dog had never seemed to take any special notice of her. But not so today. Today no one was around: not the dog's owners, not her parents. It was just Lauren and the doggy. She wondered how the doggy had gotten loose, wondered if maybe it was doing the same thing she was, having a little adventure and playing a joke on its owners in the process.

As it came toward her, she smiled, and said, "Hi, doggy!"

The boxer picked up speed, starting running toward her, growling low in its throat. Instinct welled up inside Lauren, and she screamed and turned to run. She'd only managed to take three steps before the dog was on her, sinking its teeth into her shoulder and shaking her like she was its favorite chew toy.

She screamed and screamed, tried to pull free, rolled over and tried to hit the dog with her fists and make it let her go. But the animal held her down with its forelegs and bit her hands, teeth shredding flesh and grinding against bone. Blood gushed from the wounds, fell downward onto Lauren's face, got in her eyes and blinded her.

She was distantly aware of her mother yelling something, but Lauren couldn't make out the words, couldn't even tell where they were coming from, near or far. All she was aware of was fur and claws, fangs and lolling tongue, rumbling growls and hot smelly breath.

Then she felt fire erupt on the left side of her neck, and a shriek tore free from her throat that just as much that of an animal as any noise the dog had made. The burning pain was swiftly followed by in-rushing darkness, and Lauren had only a second to wonder if she was dying before she knew nothing more.

She woke in the hospital – white sheets, uncomfortably stiff bed, tubes running out of her arms. Her mother, eyes and nose red, sodden tissue clutched in her hand, sitting next to the bed. Lauren was sore all over, but the left side of her neck hurt most of all. She tried to move her right hand, but the tubes restricted her motion, so she used her left hand to reach up and feel the bandage taped to her neck.

"I'm sorry, baby. I'm so sorry." Mother's voice was so soft she could barely hear it. "I tried . . . I wanted . . . I was so scared, all I could do was stand there . . . If Mr. Dupree from next door hadn't come . . ." Tears rolled down her cheeks and Mother brought the crumpled wet tissue to her face.

Lauren watched her mother cry for a few minutes, and as she realized what had happened, something hardened inside the girl. She had been in trouble, her mommy had come to help her, but then her mommy *hadn't* helped her. Her mommy had just stood there while the dog chewed her up. Just . . . stood . . . there.

Lauren didn't make a vow then, at least not consciously, but from that moment when she realized how truly weak her mother was, a grim determination began to grow inside her. If Lauren ever had children, she would do whatever it took to protect them, no matter what.

* * * * *

It seemed as if the entire world was covered with blood. Streets, sidewalks, buildings, trees . . . everything dripped crimson. Lauren remembered something she'd learned in school, a mnemonic device to recall the color spectrum: Roy G. Biv. Red, orange, green, blue, indigo, violet. It looked as if the other colors had somehow been removed, and only the R remained.

And still the rain fell – and with it, the creatures.

They made driving even more difficult, as if the blood-slick roads weren't bad enough. The damn things lurched across yards, along sidewalks, through the streets . . . They were so slow that Lauren normally wouldn't have had much trouble driving around them, but the slippery roadways made any maneuver other than driving in a straight line tricky. She nearly lost control of the van a number of times as she detoured around one of the broken-limbed gut-hangers. Worse, the damn things kept falling. Several landed right in front of their van, necessitating a last-minute course correction, and one had even struck their roof, causing a dent that came down almost to the top of Alex's head. Luckily, Lauren had managed to keep control of the vehicle, and she watched the creature roll off into the street in her sideview mirror. But she kept driving, no matter what, all the while mentally repeating to herself: *Easy-peasy, easy-peasy . . .*

The blood and the creatures weren't the only hazards. The other drivers on the road were just as bad, if not worse. No one seemed to be paying any attention to traffic laws – they drove wherever they wanted, however they wanted. She'd witnessed a half dozen wrecks and drove past the aftermath of at least a half dozen more. So far, she'd managed to keep them from getting into an accident, though there'd been a couple near misses.

They'd been driving for a half hour, and she estimated they'd made it three quarters of the way home.

Alex still cried on and off, though his tears came silently now. She occasionally made comforting sounds, told him everything would be all right, that it wouldn't be much longer, not paying attention to her own words, letting them come out automatically. But as she drove and continued to comfort her son, one part of her mind watched the creatures, trying to learn what it could, to detect some pattern to this madness.

So far, she had come to these conclusions. One: wherever the blood rain was coming from, that's also where the creatures were coming from. Two: the fall to earth damaged the creatures, but not so much that they couldn't function, at least for a while. Three: the blood rain could transform humans into the creatures, and the creatures wanted to hasten this process. Since she'd witnessed one creature forcing the man at the park to drink the red rain, she'd seen variations on the same scene over and over.

Four: the farther she drove, the more unhurt creatures she saw – no broken limbs, no protruding organs. She took these to be transformed humans who, since they hadn't fallen from the sky, were not damaged. Five: after a time (and presumably "reproducing" by forcing people to drink red rain) the wounded creatures succumbed to their injuries and died. She'd seen hundreds of the dead creatures lying about, had even accidentally driven over a few. It reminded her somewhat of the way cicadas would leave behind the shells of the early stage – the one where they resembled giant fleas – as they changed into their winged incarnation.

Six: while the creatures that fell from the sky seemed interested only in transforming humans, the "new" creatures demonstrated a slightly wider range of behavior. She saw some that forced unchanged humans to drink sky-blood, but she saw others that dug talons and teeth into soft, pink flesh and began tearing it to shreds. Wherever she saw this happening, she ordered Alex to close his eyes and tried to ignore the canine growling that rumbled in her ears.

She drove for what seemed hours more before finally seeing a street sign through her blood-smeared windshield. The sign was splattered with red, but enough of the letters were visible for her to make it out: Stafford Avenue. Their street.

"We're almost home, honey." Absurdly, Lauren hit her right turn signal as she pulled onto Stafford. She actually began to feel somewhat cheered. She'd gotten Alex through chicken pox, a broken collar bone, and having his tonsils and adenoids removed. She was going to get him through this, too. Damned if she wasn't.

You're not dealing with a simple childhood disease here, a voice whispered in her mind. *This isn't something antibiotics, hugs, or encouraging words will fix. The whole goddamned world has gone bugfuck. You can't protect Alex . . . not this time.*

She did her best to ignore the voice and kept driving.

Her neighborhood had become an awful parody of wintertime, with blood-red replacing snow-white. Trees, lawns, driveways, and houses were covered in crimson, and more was falling all the time. Sky-blood gushed from rain gutters, streamed down both sides of the street toward sewer grates. She wondered how long it would be before the sewers backed up and small lakes of blood began to form. Would the rain keep coming until, like a hellish version of the biblical flood, it covered the entire world? Or would it cease once some critical mass of infestation had occurred, when there were enough transformed humans to take over the job of turning the rest?

Most of the cars on Stafford Street were parked in driveways or along the curb, but there were a couple wrecks – a Geo Metro wrapped around an oak tree in someone's front yard; an SUV overturned in the middle of the road, its windows shattered. In both cases, the vehicles were empty, their drivers nowhere to be seen. Transformed, or maybe killed. Either way, they were gone.

Front doors were shut and presumably locked tight, though a few stood open, barely hanging on their hinges. It was obvious what had happened in those cases: one of *them* had gotten in.

Daniel.

Ever since the rain had begun to fall, she'd been so focused on protecting Alex and getting him home that she hadn't thought much about her husband. Normally, she would have called him on her cell phone in an emergency, but it hadn't occurred to her. Maybe it was the shock of dealing with the nightmare the world had become, or maybe she had needed her total concentration to get this far, but it was almost as if she'd completely forgotten Daniel.

She took her cell phone out of the glove compartment, turned it on, and pressed the number that automatically called their home phone. One ring . . . two . . . three . . . four . . and the machine picked up.

Hi, you have reached the home of Daniel, Lauren, and Alex. We can't come to the phone right now, but please leave a message after the beep. Thank you for calling.

The promised beep came, and Lauren said her husband's name several times, but he didn't pick up.

She disconnected, but she left the phone on, just in case he should call.

Had Daniel been out puttering in the yard when the rain began to fall? Had he gotten in his Camry, intending to drive to the park and help them? She hadn't seen his car on the way home, but visibility had been so poor, she could have easily missed it.

Or had something else happened to him? Something bad?

She didn't want to think about that. *A few more minutes and you'll be home. Daniel will be there, worried sick, but happy to see you're both safe. The three of you will sit down to watch the news, and the reporters will explain not only what the fuck is going on, but what's being done to stop it. And just like that, everything will be okay, or at least on its way to becoming okay. Easy-peasy.*

She turned around, smiled at Alex – at pale, trembling, wild-eyed Alex.

"Almost there, sweetie. Just hold on another couple minutes." Her voice nearly broke on the last word, and she fought back tears. She couldn't afford to let them come, not yet.

Alex didn't acknowledge her, didn't even look in her direction. He just continued staring forward.

Lauren turned back around. *He'll be okay once he's home. I'll* make *him okay.* She pressed the washer-fluid button to clean off the windshield again, but nothing came out. She pressed the button several more times, each more violently than the last, but still nothing. She'd used up the fluid.

She took her foot off the gas, but she didn't press the brake, not yet. She tried the wipers by themselves, but they hadn't worked before on their own, and they didn't work now. There was no hope for it: she'd have to roll down her window and stick her head out to see. She'd probably be okay if she kept her mouth closed. She and Alex had gotten plenty of sky-blood on them at the park, but they hadn't changed. And while she would be leaving herself vulnerable to attack by one of the creatures, she'd only seen a handful prowling the neighborhood so far. She supposed one could always fall from the sky and crash down on her head – and wouldn't that be an absurdly Loony Tunes way to die? – but she decided to risk it.

She started to roll the window down, but then her head snapped forward and the seatbelt dug painfully into her chest. She sat for moment, confused, hands gripping the steering wheel white-knuckle tight before she realized the van had come to a stop. The engine sputtered once, twice, then died.

"No." She tried the ignition, but the engine refused to turn over.

You hit one of the cars parked on the street. You couldn't see through the windshield anymore, and you took too long trying to decide what to do about it. Now here you are, less than a block from your house, and you killed you van. Smooth move.

She turned to check on Alex. He sat still, lower lip trembling.

"Are we home yet, Mommy?" They were the first words he'd spoken in what seemed like hours.

"Almost, baby. Just a little more to go." *Don't cry. Whatever you do, don't start crying, because if you do, you'll never stop.*

She unbuckled her seatbelt, then reached into the back to do the same for Alex. She didn't even consider the possibility that they might stay in the van and wait for someone to come help them. Even if there were police officers or EMT's still alive – or still *human* – out there somewhere, there were hundreds of other people in town who needed help. It could take hours, hell, maybe *days* before anyone could get around to helping them. And how long would it be before one or more of the creatures came scuttling down the street, searching for humans to change – or to kill?

They didn't have any choice. They had to walk in the rain.

"Alex, listen to me carefully. We're very close to our house, but our van is broken. If we want to get home, we're going to have to walk. We're going to have to go outside."

Alex's eyes grew even wider and he began shaking his head.

"No. They're out there, Mom."

She didn't need to ask who he meant by *They*. "We have to, sweetie. It'll only be for a few minutes. We'll be okay."

He looked at her then, his gaze clear. "Promise?"

How could she? How could she not?

She smiled. "Of course. Now you sit there and wait. I'm going to open my door and go outside, then I'll open your door. After that, we'll walk the rest of the way home together, all right?"

A flicker of a smile, a nod.

"One more thing, Alex. When we're outside, we'll need to keep our mouths shut tight. The rain . . . it's bad, sweetie. It won't hurt us if we just get it on our skin, but we have to keep from swallowing it. Understand?"

Another nod, more definite this time.

"Good." She patted his blood-caked cheek. "Let's go."

She took a deep breath and prayed to whatever deity might still be listening (if any) that one of the creatures wasn't waiting outside. She opened the door, but the only thing she saw was rain. She didn't allow herself to feel relief; she knew their luck could change any moment.

She stepped into the rain. She'd forgotten how warm and sticky it was, and she shuddered with revulsion. She experienced a surge of panic: what if she were wrong about how the blood-rain was absorbed? What if it just took longer to change you if it got on your skin?

She froze, unable to lift her hand to the van's side-door handle. Then she heard her mother's voice, soft, ashamed.

I'm sorry, baby. I'm so sorry. I tried . . . I wanted . . . I was so scared, all I could do was stand there.

The scar on Lauren's neck throbbed with a dull ache, echoing pain over two decades old but never forgotten. She wrapped her hand in her t-shirt, got a grip on the bloody side-door handle, and slid the door open. She then held out a hand to her son, the fingers crimson-slick.

He hesitated, and she hoped she wouldn't have to say anything to encourage him, didn't want to risk opening her mouth, but she would if she had to. But it didn't come to that. Alex took her hand and allowed her to guide him out of the van and into the rain.

Holding tight onto her son, Lauren began walking down the street toward their house, careful to detour around the scaly carapaces of those creatures that had dropped dead in the street, like salmon dying soon after spawning. And if she saw other dark shapes in the crimson haze of the falling rain, *moving* shapes, she told herself they were too far away to worry about, and she kept moving.

* * * * *

The front door of their Cape Cod was open. Only a crack, but a crack was more than enough. Worse, the porch – which should have been protected by the metal awning above them – was covered with bloody patches that looked far too much like footprints for Lauren's comfort. She looked closely at them, trying to determine if they'd been made by human feet or –

"What's wrong, Mommy?"

Lauren looked up from the footprints. "Try not to talk. Until the –" *blood* "– rain dries."

She tried to think, but her brain felt sluggish, as if were on the brink of shutting down. But she couldn't afford to let that happen, not yet, and she forced herself to concentrate. If Daniel had been outside working on the yard when the rain began to fall, he might've rushed inside (leaving crimson footprints on the porch), failing to close the door behind him. He wasn't normally one to forget a detail like that – he was a T-crosser and an I-dotter if ever there was one – but there was nothing normal about today, was there? Even Daniel might forget to close a door on a day like this.

And maybe those footprints were left by something else, something that got inside. Maybe Daniel's nothing more than a pile of shredded meat and splintered bone lying on the carpet. Or worse – maybe Daniel wasn't Daniel anymore. Maybe he was –

She stopped that particularly nasty train of thought before it could go any further. There was no sign the door had been forced. No scratch marks on the wood or the knob. It was just . . . open.

"Mom?" His voice was higher-pitched now; he was getting worried.

"Hush now. Let me think."

"Mom, there's something in the street. It's . . it's coming this way."

No time left to think. She pushed the door open and pulled Alex inside. She slammed the door shut behind them, engaged the deadbolt and latched the chain. She doubted the locks would keep one of those things out if it wanted in badly enough, but she still had to try. Maybe with the door closed, the things would ignore the house, keep searching for someone still out in the rain.

And how long will it be before they start going door to door, killing or changing whoever they find?

Another thought to ignore. She put a hand on Alex's shoulder and steered him away from the door and down the front hall.

"Mom, why is there blood on the floor?"

She looked down, saw bloody patches on the tile similar to those on the porch. "Your father probably tracked it in." *I hope.* "Try not to step in it." What a laugh; as if they weren't dripping the goddamned stuff everywhere.

As soon as she said the word *father*, a hopeful look came into Alex's eyes. "Daddy?" he called, then louder, edged with panic. "Dad-deeeeee!"

Nothing.

She tried. "Daniel! Daniel, are you here?" She listened for a reply, but again, there was none.

Tears began to roll down Alex's cheeks, leaving flesh-colored trails on his bloody face.

"Shhhh. It's okay."

It's not okay, you lying bitch! The town's fucked, maybe the whole goddamned world for all you know! Don't tell him everything's going to be okay when you damn well know it isn't!

She continued steering Alex into the living room. The carpet was stained with more blood, a violation in the place where they watched TV, played video games, listened to CD's, read books. This, more than anywhere else in the house, was the place where she, Daniel, and Alex came together as a family. It was bad enough when the blood-rain and the monsters and the insanity they represented were out there, but for the madness to be in *here*, in their *home* . . . it was almost more than she could bear.

She forced herself to look at the footprints, to try and detect a pattern in them, as if she were a hunter examining animal tracks in the snow. She couldn't tell a thing, though, other than whoever (or whatever) had made them had walked all over the carpet, as if determined to stain as much of it as possible, or perhaps simply mark its territory.

Alex shrugged off her hand and turned to look at her. “Where’s Daddy?” Demanding now, his tone saying she better have a damn good answer.

“Once the rain began falling, maybe he got worried and decided to go to the park and get us.” She knew this wasn’t true; Daniel’s Camry was still in the driveway. She hoped Alex had been too afraid of walking in the rain – and what else had been walking out there – to notice.

“You mean he’s . . . outside?”

Wrong thing to say. “Wherever he’s at, he’ll be home soon. Let’s get ourselves cleaned up, and I bet your father will be home by the time we’re finished.”

Alex frowned, and for a horrible instant she feared he knew she was feeding him a line of pure and utter bullshit, and that he was finally going to call her on it. But in the end he just nodded, wearily this time, she thought.

She looked at the TV sitting in its place of honor on the entertainment center, screen black and empty except for two small curved reflections of mother and son. She was torn; they needed to get this damn gunk off before it infected them, but at the same time she was desperate for some news – *any* news – that might explain why all this was happening and what was being done about it. She debated a second more, then walked over to the TV, adding her own bloody footprints to those already smearing the carpet, and pushed the ON button.

The screen flared to life, high-pitched electronic tone and white letters against a blue background: EMERGENCY BROADCAST SYSTEM. STAY TUNED FOR FURTHER DETAILS. She and Alex stood before the TV for a minute, then another, but despite the screen’s promise, no further information was forthcoming.

Lauren tried flipping to other channels, but the same message appeared on them all.

She decided to leave the TV on, just in case, though she had a sinking feeling that it would be some time, if ever, before anyone came on with an explanation. Worse yet, maybe there *was* no explanation. The blood-rain was falling and the demon-things were coming down with it and reproducing simply because they were. End of story.

End of the goddamned world, you mean.

Lauren had been getting quite good at pushing away thoughts in the short time since the crimson rain had begun to fall, and she had no trouble getting rid of this one either.

"C'mon, let's go get this stuff washed off."

They left the living room and walked through the dining room. They had to pass the kitchen entrance to reach the master bathroom where the shower was, and Lauren saw the kitchen floor was, like the rest of the house, covered with bloody footprints. She also saw that the back door was wide open.

"Stay here. I'm going to go shut the door."

Alex gripped her hand tight, obviously not wanting her to go. She smiled and gently but firmly pulled free and walked into the kitchen, stepping carefully to avoid slipping on blood-slick tile. But as she reached for the door knob, a dark shape lurched onto the back porch. It was covered with blood-rain, but patches of greenish-black hide were still visible. Glistening obsidian eyes, multi-jointed talons, nine limbs – arms, legs, and some which she couldn't put a name to – all unbroken. This creature hadn't fallen from the sky; it was a newborn.

It's Daniel, she thought. *Who else would it be? He's been waiting for us to come home.*

There was no way to tell if this thing had been her husband – no scraps of his clothing clung to the beast, and there was nothing recognizably human left in its eyes – but in the end, it didn't matter who the creature had once been, did it? It could've been Daniel, a neighbor, or a complete stranger. Whoever it had been, it was a monster now, and it was coming for them.

She turned away from the door, started back toward Alex, slipping and sliding on the slick floor. She grabbed the counters to steady herself and shouted, "Go to the basement! Now!"

For a moment, she thought Alex was going to freeze with terror, but he turned and ran to the basement door. He threw it opened and pounded down the stairs, from the sound of it taking them two and three and a time.

Lauren kept making her way across the kitchen floor, trying at once to hurry and go slow so she wouldn't slip and fall. She knew that if she lost her footing, it would be all over for her. And if anything happened to her, there wouldn't be anyone left to protect Alex.

She heard the creature enter the house behind her. Moist, raspy breathing; clawed feet plapping on blood-covered tile. She prayed it couldn't move any faster than she could on the wet floor, that its arms weren't long enough to reach out and snag her before she made it back to the dining room. Did she feel air move behind her, as if clawed fingers sliced downward, almost but not quite connecting with their prey? Maybe.

She reached the dining room and the traction its carpet offered. She ran for the basement doorway, made it through, and slammed the door shut behind her. She locked it, if you could call the tiny switch on the knob that she turned a lock. She wished there was a chain, a deadbolt, a fucking crossbar, for christsakes, but who had those things on the inside of a basement door? Who ever thought the day would come when you would need to barricade yourself inside because there was a monster in your kitchen?

Something heavy slammed into the door, and Lauren started, nearly losing her balance. She grabbed onto the hand railing and managed to keep her balance, if barely. Another slam, this time accompanied by the soft sound of wood beginning to splinter. She turned and saw the basement below was dark. It was a wonder Alex hadn't broken his neck going down the stairs so fast without being able to see. She debated whether to turn on the light or not. Would they be safer hiding in the dark, or would it be better to see in case she had to fight the creature?

In the end, she flipped the light switch on. If there was even a chance the light would help them, she had to take it.

Another slam, the sound of wood cracking louder this time.

She hurried down the stairs, keeping hold of the railing so she wouldn't fall. Alex waited at the foot of the stairs, shivering as if he were outside in the dead of winter.

Slam!

"Let's go into the laundry room." She took Alex's hand and led him through the finished part of the basement – pool table, mini bar, dart board on the wall,– and through an open doorway into the unfinished part where the washer and dryer were, as well as Daniel's workbench. A pile of dirty clothes lay in a clump before the washer, and past the workbench were haphazard stacks of empty cardboard boxes saved from when they'd moved here almost five years ago. Keeping the boxes had seemed to make sense at the time, but now Lauren wondered what the hell they'd been thinking.

Wood splintered like a shotgun blast, and she knew the thing had broken through.

Lauren steered Alex to Daniel's workbench as she desperately tried to think of what to do next. Have the boy hide in the dryer? No, he was too big. Under the workbench? No, the thing would see him easily. She scanned the tools lying on the bench, hanging on hooks on corkboard. Hammers, screwdrivers, saws . . . could she use any of them to try to fight the creature off? She knew they could die; she'd seen plenty of their bodies during the drive home. But she also knew they were tough as hell: the original ones that fell from the sky had survived their horrible injuries long enough to reproduce. Even if she could hurt the monster thudding down the stairs, she doubted she could do enough damage to prevent it doing what it would to them.

And there was no way to know what that would be. It was a newborn, and sometimes newborn creatures changed humans, sometimes they killed them.

Alex was breathing rapidly, and she was afraid he might hyperventilate. She found herself looking around the basement for a bag that he could breathe into, and when she realized what she was doing, she almost laughed. What did it matter if he hyperventilated now?

She strained to hear over the sound of her son's breathing. She thought the creature was close to the bottom of the stairs.

In her mind, she heard the faint echoes of a dog barking, saw the apologetic, shame-filled eyes of her mother looking at her daughter lying in a hospital bed.

I'm so sorry . . .

And she understood then how her mother must have felt upon witnessing her young daughter being savaged by a dog. Seeing her girl's blood spraying in the air, hearing her shrill screams of pain. No matter how much you worried, how close an eye you kept on your children, there were some things in life you couldn't protect them from. In the end, all parents are helpless, and it was the realization of that horror which had frozen her mother into inaction that day twenty years ago, and it was this same realization that Lauren was faced with now.

She reached up and touched the scar on her neck, and her fingers came away coated with sticky blood. For an instant, she thought the old wound had reopened, but then she realized it wasn't *her* blood on her fingers: it was sky-blood.

The creature that might or might not have once been Daniel lurched into view on the other side of the doorway. It hesitated only a moment before starting toward them.

Lauren knew she had only seconds left, but thanks to the blood on her fingers, she also knew that she wasn't helpless. Not completely.

She ran her hand through her wet hair, got as much blood as she could on her fingers. She looked down at Alex, smiled, said, "I love you, sweetie," and jammed her fingers into his mouth, pushed them back as far into his throat as she could.

The last sound she heard was the boy gagging; the last sight she saw were greenish-black patches erupting on his skin; the last thought she had was *He's safe now.* Then she felt talons grabbing her hair, yanking her away from Alex, but it didn't matter what happened to her anymore. She'd done what she had to do, what any good mother would've have done given the circumstances.

She had prepared her child to make his way in the world. Not the world as she might wish it to be, but the world as it was. A world that from now on, Alex would call home.

She tried to tell her son she was sorry, but she couldn't get the words out before the monster that might have once been her husband did as it pleased with her.

Sleepless Eyes

It's 1:38 a.m. on a Thursday night, and you're sitting at a small round table tucked into a dim corner of an all-night coffee shop. A steaming mug of hot liquid sits before you, and you know it'll be at least another fifteen minutes before it cools enough for you to drink. To pass the time you glance around at your fellow late-night caffeine addicts. One of the main reasons you came – besides suffering from insomnia – is that this place, especially at this time of night, is usually a prime spot for people-watching.

The barista at the counter, a raven-haired woman in her early twenties, asks a customer, "Would you like aqueous fluid drizzled on top of your whipped pus?"

The customer nods the middle of his three scaled heads, and the barista leans over his drink and squeezes her right eyeball as if it were a large ocular pimple. Clear fluid spurts out of a fissure in the organ and splatters onto the yellow-white mass floating atop the customer's drink.

You turn to look at the fireplace in the corner opposite from where you're sitting. One of the employees has recently added fresh fuel to the fire, and the severed arms and legs – the small, delicate limbs of children – sizzle and pop as the fat beneath the blackening skin cooks. Sitting in a cushy chair next to the fire, an obscenely fat man – naked, completely bereft of body hair – methodically inserts long sharp needles into his testicles, one after the other, as if his balls are fleshy pin cushions. As he works, he chats with a woman whose entire body, including her face, is covered by tight black leather. Only her mouth is visible through an unzipped slit, and you can see she has no teeth in her swollen, bleeding gums.

Over by the window, a pair of exotically beautiful conjoined twins – Asian, high cheek bones, straight black hair down to the middle of their backs, jade-green mini-dresses sans panties – are masturbating each other with dildos fashioned from metal rods wrapped in steel wool. As the women moan in ecstasy, blood runs down their well-toned legs and pools on the tiled floor beneath their table. An old woman that reminds you a lot of your grandmother, except for the pulsating lesions covering her skin, kneels next to the twins, her head lowered to the floor as she furiously laps up the twins' blood-cum with a tongue encrusted with fat, happy tics.

You turn to look in the direction of the restrooms, your attention drawn by the screams coming from behind the door to the men's room. The screams stop, and a few seconds later a man in his thirties walks out. He's wearing a white turtleneck and jeans, and he looks okay, if you don't count his ashen skin and uncomprehending expression of stark terror on his face. He manages to take three steps before bloodstains begin to show through his turtleneck. Pieces of his body begin to fall off and hit the floor with meaty-wet plaps. Just a few at first – an ear, a nose, a lip – but then more and more, until there's a veritable rain of flesh, blood, and bone, and the core of the man's body collapses into a heap. A cheer goes up from the crowd and everyone – the barista, the three-headed man, Pincushion-Balls, Leather-Girl, the Steel-Wool Twins, Grandma Tic-Tongue, and all the others in the coffee shop – race toward the grisly mound and fall upon it, grabbing slick handfuls of viscera and jamming them into their mouths.

"Now that's good eatin'!" Grandma Tic-Tongue exclaims around a mouthful of kidney. Her fellow gourmands grunt their agreement.

But you haven't joined in the feast. Instead you slither over to the counter and wrap one of your smaller facial tentacles around a to-go cup. You grab a plastic lid with another tentacle then return to your table, leaving a glistening trail of slime in your wake. You pour your still-hot spinal fluid into the cardboard cup, fasten the lid on, and then put the empty mug on the counter for the barista to collect later. You then lift your coat off the back of your chair – a coat made from the stomach linings of a dozen syphilitic nuns – and head for the exit while the bloody revelers continue gorging themselves behind you.

As you stride out into the night, disappointed, you think to yourself that you need to find a new late-night hangout. This place is getting too predictable.

The Faces That We Meet

"Hi, Daddy!"

Gordon Markley could barely hear his daughter's words over the roar of the lawnmower, but she mouthed them in exaggerated fashion, added a wave of her hand, and he knew well enough what she was saying. He nodded, for he needed both hands to steer the mower, and smiled. Sarah was walking down the street with two of her friends, girls he recognized by sight but whose names he could never remember. They were three of a kind: twelve going on thirteen, t-shirts displaying images of Hello Kitty or Britney Spears, far-too-expensive jeans, coltishly thin arms and legs, and bubbly, giggly girl energy. Energy that was already fueling the beginnings of puberty.

He suddenly felt old, too conscious of the roll of flab pushing over the top of his belt, his receding hairline, the gray at his temples that had seemed to spring up overnight, like silver-white weeds. More than old, he felt foolish. He imagined how the girls saw him – a paunchy man in his forties in a white t-shirt, tan shorts, running shoes, and white socks that nearly came up to his knees – sweating and breathing hard as he pushed a lawnmower around his postage-stamp sized front yard on a Sunday afternoon. A ludicrous, clownish figure that inspired giggles, sideways glances, and behind-the-hand whispers.

Cut it out. Sarah's a good kid. Her old man may not measure up to the pretty boys on the cover of Non-Threatening Teen Heart-Throb *magazine, but that doesn't mean she thinks any the less of you for it.* But that wasn't the question, was it? The question was, did *he* think any the less of himself?

The girls continued on up the driveway, heading for the backyard. Gordon almost stopped the mower so he could call out to Sarah and ask where she'd been. He hadn't even been aware that she was outside, had thought she was still in the house watching TV or listening to music. But he didn't want to cramp her style and embarrass her in front of her friends, so he just waved back.

Sarah grinned, showing off white, even teeth that until just a few weeks ago had been in braces, and waved one more time as she passed around the side of the house.

And that's when Gordon noticed the blood on her fingers.

* * * * *

"Did you tell Sarah that she could play outside?"

Gordon stood in the kitchen before the sink, half empty glass of ice water in his hand. His sweat-soaked shirt clung to his skin, feeling cold and clammy here in the air-conditioned house.

Kathy sat at the dining table, her back to him, laptop open and turned on, checkbook and bank statements near to hand as she worked to update Quicken.

"For god's sakes, Gord, she's almost a teenager. She doesn't *play* anymore." Kathy sounded amused.

He took another drink of water, but the cool liquid did nothing to soothe his scratchy throat. He should've taken a decongestant before going outside. He'd probably end up with a throbbing sinus headache before too long.

"You know what I mean. She came walking down the street with those two girls she always hangs around with. You know the ones – "

"Abbie and Melissa." She tapped on the keyboard, kept her attention focused on the screen as she spoke. "So what? She's at the age where she'd rather run around with her friends than be stuck at home with her boring old Mom and Dad. It's perfectly natural." She looked over her shoulder, gave him a smile. "What's wrong? Feeling a bit obsolete?"

That was exactly what he was feeling, but it wasn't all. There was something else, something deeper, darker, but he wasn't sure he could articulate it, even to himself. He saw Sarah wave, saw the reddish-brown stains on her fingers once more.

"I'm just . . . concerned. This is a safe enough neighborhood and all, but it's not like when you and I were kids. Back then, we could run around outside all day long, from sunrise to well after sunset, and no one worried about us because they didn't have to. Most of the moms stayed home and they all kept an eye on each other's kids. But now . . ." He paused to take another sip of water and gather his thoughts. "Well, look at what's been going on the last couple weeks."

Kathy had turned back to her laptop and continued to input data, fingers click-click-clicking on the keys. "You mean the dogs?"

"Yes." His throat felt more dry than ever, as if it were plastered with sandpaper, and the word came out as a raspy croak. Over the last month, three dogs had been killed in the neighborhood, all horribly mutilated – throats cut, intestines pulled out, eyes and tongues removed, limbs torn from sockets . . . The assumption was that teenage boys (who else?) were responsible, though the local paper, probably in a bid to drive up circulation, hinted that a serial killer with a doggie fixation was on the loose.

"Sarah's not a dog, Gord." That tone of amusement again. "I think she'll be fine."

"That's not it." He thought a moment. "Well, maybe it is, a little. I mean, that's how it starts, right? A sicko begins with dogs and then works his way up to people. Kind of a like an artist doing sketches in preparation of beginning a painting."

"I'm not sure I agree, but I have to give you style points for the comparison."

Gordon grimaced. Kathy had always had a sharp tongue; it was the quality he liked least about her, especially because he could never think of a good comeback.

He walked to the back door and looked through the window. Outside, he saw Sarah and her three friends sitting in the middle of the backyard, near the swing set she was too old to use anymore. They sat in a close circle (since there were only three of them, he supposed a triangle would've been a more accurate description) looking down at something on the ground between them. What, he couldn't tell, for their bodies blocked his view. He wished he could see Sarah's hands, see if they were still stained red-brown, but her back was to him and her hands weren't visible.

He watched for a moment longer before turning away to face his wife once more. "All I'm saying is that maybe we should keep closer tabs on her."

Kathy, her back to him, made an mm-hmm noise as she continued typing. Irritated, Gordon said, "I'm going to take a quick shower." This time, he received no response at all so he drained the rest of his water, set the glass on the counter, and headed for the bathroom.

* * * * *

He had plenty of time to think as he showered, the water washing away his concerns as effectively as it cleansed his body. It hadn't been blood on Sarah's hand. How could it have been? Dirt, maybe, even rust. Despite what Kathy said, Sarah was still a girl and still played, though perhaps not as often as she used to. There were a million ways she could've gotten dirt or rust on her hands: playing on a swing set, exploring a cluttered basement or garage . . . Hell, maybe she'd been over at one of her friends' houses trying on makeup. Sarah was always after Kathy to let her try on lipstick or eye shadow. Maybe she'd been wearing lipstick and when she saw he was out mowing, she quickly wiped it off with her fingers, but forgot to conceal the reddish-brown smear when she waved. There were any number of explanations, all rational, all comforting, all equally likely to be true. He could take his pick.

He turned off the water, stepped out of the shower, and began to towel himself dry.

What had he been worried about anyway? That Sarah and her friends were doing something they shouldn't – like killing a dog? The thought was beyond ridiculous. He *knew* his daughter; she'd never do anything like that. If she found a spider in the house, she'd catch it in a cup and take it outside rather than kill it. Not exactly the sort of kid who went around disemboweling animals.

And yet . . .

* * * * *

"What's on your mind, Gord?"

Gordon looked up as Jerry entered the small room that served as a lounge for their practice. It wasn't much – a round table, three plastic chairs, a small fridge and a microwave – but it gave them a place to eat their lunch. Gordon wished they could've afforded something a bit more luxurious, but while dentistry paid the bills, it hadn't exactly made either of them rich.

"Nothing."

"My ass. You're wearing your basset hound face. You know, the one you get whenever something's bothering you."

Gordon didn't reply, though he knew Jerry wouldn't give up until he pried the truth out of him. They'd gone to dental school together, been business partners since they graduated. In all that time, Gordon had never been able to keep a secret from him. Gordon picked up his tuna sandwich, took a bite and chewed while Jerry got a Lean Cuisine – pasta Florentine with miniature red potatoes – out of the fridge and popped it in the microwave. While his meal cooked, he sat down across from Gordon, an expectant look on his face.

"Well?"

Gordon swallowed, considered taking another bite to stall, decided against it. "It's Kathy."

"Ah-ha! Trouble on the homefront! Now we're getting somewhere!"

Jerry was the prototypical single man without a care in the world, approaching life as if it were one big party and he the guest of honor. Even though he was in his forties, his face was still boyish and he still had a head full of black curls. His short-sleeved blue dental smock – twin to the one Gordon wore – only reinforced the impression of youthfulness. It wasn't really a uniform, more like a t-shirt or pajama top.

"It's not really that serious. I mean, she's not having an affair or anything like that." Gordon put his sandwich down on the cellophane he'd been using as a makeshift placemat and took a sip of his Diet Sprite. "Kathy took Sarah out shopping for soccer shoes last night. Kathy had been in the process of doing laundry, and she left a basket of clean clothes on our bed. Normally, she'd just put them away after she got home, but I thought I'd surprise her and put them away for her." Kathy only worked part-time, had ever since Sarah came along. Since she was home more than Gordon, she did the lion's (or perhaps that should be *lioness's*) share of the household chores. Maybe that made them an old-fashioned couple, but they were comfortable with their roles.

"So what's the big deal? Sounds like you were just trying to be helpful and maybe score a few points with Kathy in the bargain."

Gordon felt suddenly uncomfortable despite the fact that he and Jerry had been friends for years. There wasn't anything about each other's lives that they didn't know. But this problem was more . . . personal than the ones they usually discussed. At least, more personal than what Gordon brought up. Jerry had no trouble sharing the most intimate details of his life – and in the most graphic detail imaginable yet.

Jerry's eyebrows lifted. "Waitaminnit! I get it! You folded Kathy's undies and started to put them away in one of her dresser drawers when you found something."

Gordon felt his cheeks burn as he blushed. He couldn't meet Jerry's gaze, could only nod once.

"Let me guess: you found what is euphemistically known as a 'woman's best friend.'" The microwave dinged, but Jerry made no move to get up.

"If by that, you mean a vibrator, yes."

Jerry laughed and clapped Gordon on the shoulder. "C'mon, man! That's nothing to be upset about! Hell, it's a good thing."

Now Gordon turned to look at his partner. "Huh?"

"You can add it to your repertoire, if you know what I mean. Wink-wink, nudge-nudge."

Despite himself, Gordon smiled. "Do you ever think about anything besides sex?"

Jerry grinned. "Who's the one who brought the subject up? Seriously, though, why is this bothering you? It's perfectly normally. Every woman I've ever dated has had one. Hell, at least one. I dated this one girl once who had a closet full of sex toys, and I couldn't figure out what most of them did." He shrugged. "It's no different than men masturbating."

"I know. At least, that's what I've been telling myself." Gordon paused. Jerry's shrug had shifted the collar of his smock, revealing an edge of white. It looked like a necklace of some kind. A necklace made of . . .

Jerry frowned, looked down at his collar, and casually reached up and adjusted it, concealing the necklace, or whatever it was, once more. But now that Gordon was aware of it, he could see the outline of the object beneath the smock's blue cloth. It seemed bumpy, kind of like a string of pearls, but the individual pieces were more square than round.

"Then why aren't you believing yourself?"

The question startled Gordon out of his scrutiny. He took his gaze from the necklace and looked Jerry in the eye once more. "What?"

"You said you've been telling yourself it's normal for Kathy to want a little electric assist ever now and then. So why are you still bothered by it?"

"I'm not sure." Actually, he knew exactly why. It wasn't so much the vibrator itself as the *kind* of vibrator it was. Curious – and though he'd never admit to this Jerry because he didn't want to be teased – a little turned on, Gordon had removed the silvery object from the drawer and inspected it.

It was a foot long and shaped more like a giant lipstick than a phallus. The surface was smooth and shiny, and the metal felt cold and hard in his hand. He had a difficult time imagining Kathy, or any woman for that matter, being turned on by having this sterile, unyielding *thing* inside her.

There was a switch on the base of the vibrator. He couldn't resist thumbing it.

The device jerked to life in his hand, emitting a soft *mmmmmmmmmmmm* that reminded him of a cat's purr. This was it? It didn't even have a speed setting. You'd think it would at least –

Snik!

Gordon let out a cry and dropped the vibrator to the carpet. It was now covered with barbed hooks, like some kind of oversized fishing lure. Gordon could only stare at the machine *mmmmmmmmmm*ed, some of the hooks jangling against each other, some catching in the carpet. After a few moments, he knelt down and, careful to avoid the vibrating hooks, touched the switch on the base. The device stopped shivering and tiny panels, their seams invisible a second ago, opened. The hooks that weren't caught in the carpet smoothly withdrew, and the panels slid shut, their edges melding seamlessly into the silver metal once more.

He carefully freed the remaining hooks from the carpet, each one retracting as soon as he did. When the vibrator was back to the way he found it, surface smooth and unblemished, he put it back and closed Kathy's underwear drawer. Then he went out in the kitchen and poured himself a scotch, drank it down, and poured another.

"Afraid you won't measure up to the miracles of modern engineering?" Jerry asked.

Gordon came out of his memory and gave his friend a smile, though he feared it came out more of a grimace. "A bit. But what really bothers me is that Kathy and I have been married for fourteen years. I should know her by now." The woman he'd married, the woman he'd lived with day in and day out for almost a decade and a half, the woman who'd fathered his child, wouldn't get off by putting such a monstrous machine inside her. And how could she use the goddamned thing without shredding her vaginal canal in the process?

"People grow, Gord. They change. But even if they didn't, no one *really* knows anyone else. Not completely." Jerry scratched his chest, just about where the lower curve of the necklace (or whatever it was) hung.

"I'm not sure what you mean."

Jerry finally stood and went to the microwave to get his pasta. When he sat again, he took a forkful of noodles and creamy whitish-green sauce – which was still steaming despite how long it had sat untouched in the microwave – and chewed. "When I was a kid, do you know what my grandmother used to call Halloween masks? False faces. 'Time to go out begging, Jerry. Get your false face on.' I think all of us wear false faces, all the time. We can't always say what we think or what we feel, right? If we did, we'd have a world full of perpetually pissed-off people. So we lie, we conceal, we evade and avoid. We pretend to be something we're not." He took another mouthful of pasta. "It's how we get along."

"My god, I knew you had a cynical streak, but that's the most goddamned bleak thing I've ever heard you say!"

"Not at all. We don't do it just to protect ourselves. We do it to protect the people we love, the people we work with. It's very altruistic, in a way. You have to admit, it's certainly adaptive. We couldn't function as a society any other way."

"So you're saying that last night – "

"You caught a glimpse behind Kathy's mask, that' all. And if you're smart, you won't say anything about her little vibrating friend. Things are good in your marriage, right? Emotionally and physically?"

"Sure." It was true. Gordon and Kathy had their problems, but no more than any other couple. And he couldn't complain about the frequency or the quality of their lovemaking.

"So why rock the proverbial boat? Just keep your mouth shut and go along as if nothing happened. Use *your* mask. Hell, that's what it's for. And if you're still feeling down tonight, when you and Kathy hit the sack, remind her what it's like to have something organic between her legs." He grinned, then took another mouthful of pasta.

Gordon did his best to grin back, but he couldn't get the image of those hooks out of his mind, and he couldn't stop thinking about what Jerry had said, that no one really knew anyone. After all, he hadn't known Jerry wore a necklace. Certainly not one which appeared to have been made out of human teeth.

* * * * *

After getting out of the shower, Gordon went into the bedroom and dressed in yet another t-shirt, pair of too-wide shorts, and nearly knee-high socks, as if it were some sort of springtime uniform for suburban husbands slash fathers. He avoided looking at Kathy's dresser, though he couldn't keep from thinking about the silvery object which lay inside – or from wondering if it were the sole means of self-pleasuring which she had stashed away.

No one really *knows anyone else. Not completely.*

Gordon put on a pair of running shoes – not the same, worn-out, grass-stained shoes he used when mowing the lawn; those were in the gardening shed along with the mower – and went to the kitchen.

Kathy still sat at the dining table, tapping keys on her laptop as she continued to work at balancing the checkbook. Or at least, that was what it *appeared* she was doing. Gordon didn't know much about computers. She could be doing just about anything on the damn machine for all he knew. Composing e-mail to a lover, logging onto an Internet gambling site . . . He was half-tempted to stroll casually past her and glance over her shoulder at the computer screen, but he resisted the impulse. He refused to give in to the seed of paranoia that Jerry had planted within him. Besides, a marriage should be based on trust, right? Even if Kathy did have a secret or two – in his mind, he heard a *snik,* saw hooks lunge forth from smooth metal – they were minor secrets, nothing to get worked up about.

He imagined her lying back on the bed, naked, legs spread apart, vagina glistening as she gripped the base of the vibrator, hooks jangling as it *hmmmmmmmm*ed. Imagined her guiding the machine closer . . . closer . . . eyes closed, breath coming fast and shallow, biting her lower lip as the first of many hooks slid inside her . . .

He gave his head a shake to force the image away. He tried to swallow, but his throat was still dry. Damn allergies. He decided to get another glass of water and, as he sipped slowly, he walked to the back door and looked out the window. Sarah and her friends were still sitting cross-legged on the grass, laughing as they passed something back and forth, as if they were playing a game of hot potato. But no matter how long Gordon watched, he couldn't make out what they were playing with.

Then he noticed the gardening shed: its doors weren't quite closed all the way. The shed was an old, cheap thing that had been here when they bought the house. The doors were thin, flimsy metal and had a tendency to open back up, especially if a strong breeze were blowing. He was always going back outside and shutting the doors to make sure birds or rabbits didn't get inside to nest. He knew he should probably get a chain lock of some sort, or even just use a simple bit of rope to tie the door handles together, but like so many other little chores around the house and yard, he'd never gotten around to it.

But he was grateful for the doors' tendency to open now. It gave him a pretext to go outside, should he wish to use it. He considered for a moment, drained the last of his water, put the empty glass on the counter next to the one he'd used previously, and went out the back door.

The girls looked his way as soon as the door opened, like animals suddenly scenting danger, he thought. He waved – it would look suspicious if he ignored them completely – and walked down the back steps. The May afternoon was warm, warmer even than it had felt when he'd been mowing, and immediately beads of sweats began collecting on his forehead. Perhaps, he thought, the sweat was due to nervousness as much as heat. The air was filled with the smell of freshly cut grass, a smell he used to like, until one day when Kathy pointed out that the smell was due to the chlorophyll released from the grass: the plant equivalent of blood.

He walked across the yard, taking his time without trying to look like he was taking his time. The girls watched him without looking as if they were watching him. Out of the corner of his eye, he tried to see what they'd been playing with, but they kept their hands pressed to the ground, their fingers – and presumably whatever they'd been playing with – hidden by the grass, despite the shortness of its length.

He reached the shed, pulled the doors shut, and then turned around, trying to think of another excuse to remain outside, but he came up empty. The grass was cut, and since he had a mulch mower, there was no need to rake it. It was still too early in the season for the hedges to need trimming, and while there was probably work to do in the flower beds, those were Kathy's department. He hadn't the first notion about what might need doing, and besides, it would look odd to Sarah if her father took a sudden interest in gardening.

He had no choice but to go back inside. Maybe, though, he could swing by the girls, say hello to Sarah's friends, make a friendly show of being a nosy parent and ask what they'd been up to so far today. It wasn't like him – he usually didn't take such a close interest in what Sarah did with her friends – but it wouldn't be as much *un*like him as puttering around in the flower beds would be.

Decided, he started toward the girls.

But before he got more than halfway to them, they stood and started walking away from him. Sarah, he noted, kept her right hand closed in a fist, as if she were trying to hide something from him. And he could see now that there were definite stains on her fingers – reddish-brown stains – and that the other two girls had similar stains on their own hands.

"Where are you going, Sarah?" It sounded like more of a challenge than he would've liked, but he couldn't help it.

She didn't turn around as she answered. "Over to Melissa's. Her brother just got a new video game, and he said we could play it."

He didn't know which of Sarah's two companions was Melissa, but didn't want to let on. He tried to think of a follow-up question that wouldn't sound suspicious, wished he could come out and demand that the girls halt, turn, and hold out their hands for his inspection. But he had no good reason to do so, nothing but vague fears he couldn't put a name to.

"All right. Have a good time, but make sure to be back home in time for dinner."

"I will." Her tone held an adolescent's edge, as if he'd just made the most unreasonable demand in the world, and she had the patience of a saint for deigning to respond to it.

He sighed as she watched the three girls open the wooden gate, go through, then close it. Sarah was growing up fast. Too fast.

His little spy mission had been a bust. Yes, he'd managed to see that the girls had some sort of stains on their hands, but that in and of itself hardly –

And then it hit him. He walked over to where the girls had been sitting, knelt down, and inspected the grass. It looked normal enough, but when he ran his fingers through the blades, they came up coated sticky red. And while he wasn't a medical doctor, he didn't need an MD after his name to tell what the substance was.

*****

"I think I'll go out for a walk."

Kathy looked up from her computer screen, left eyebrow arched. "Oh?"

Gordon felt suddenly self-conscious. He'd never been the active type – something Kathy, who *was*, had teased him about numerous times over the years. "The doctor's always telling me I need to exercise more." He shrugged. "And I don't really have anything else to do."

He waited for Kathy to challenge him, or to at least make a cutting remark or some sort, but all she did was nod once. "Good for you." She turned off her laptop and shut the lid. "It'll give you something to occupy your time while I run to the grocery."

"Again? You just went yesterday." Kathy made three, sometimes four grocery trips in a week. Gordon often joked that they should buy a house next to the grocery to save on gas.

"You know I like fresh food." It was true; Kathy preferred to shop in what she called the "European fashion," buying fresh fruits, vegetables, and meat as needed and preparing them that night. She hated the taste of frozen food, said it was like eating musty ice.

She stood, gathered the bank statements, then came over and gave Gordon a peck on the cheek. "Don't tire yourself out. I may have plans for you later on this evening." She waggled her eyebrows with mock lasciviousness, and Gordon forced a smile.

Ever since discovering her "woman's best friend," he'd had trouble getting excited at the prospect of sex. The thought of putting his penis inside her, inside the same place where she put all those *hooks* . . .

"I'll try to conserve a little energy," he managed to reply.

* * * * *

Kathy went to the bathroom after that, which gave Gordon time to rummage through the junk drawer in the kitchen and find Sarah's address book. Kathy insisted Sarah keep the addresses of girls who attended her birthday parties and the like so she could write thank-you notes. The book, which had a picture of a unicorn on it in bright pastel colors, was small and had only a dozen or so entries in it. It took him no time at all to find Melissa's name, Melissa Syler to be exact. 1707 Kittredge Avenue. Only a few blocks away.

He closed the book and replaced it in the drawer before Kathy finished in the bathroom. He went into the bedroom – again not looking in the direction of her dresser – grabbed his keys off his dresser, called out a quick "see you later" as he passed the bathroom, and headed for the front door.

Outside, he was struck again by the smell of cut grass, only now the scent didn't seem so fresh, so springlike. It was sour and stale, the stink of death and decay. He went down the front steps, cut across the lawn to the driveway, then walked onto the street. Forrester, the street they lived on, had no sidewalks. This was an older part of Oakmont, and most of the homes had been built in the early to mid twentieth century. The yards were small, and there were few garages, and even fewer sidewalks. It was expensive to live here, though not nearly as costly as on the other side of town, which residents referred to as the "Sunny Side." You needed to be a millionaire just to be able to afford to look at houses on Sunny Side, let alone actually purchase one.

But Gordon was happy where he was. The houses and yards were well kept, the neighbors were mostly professional people like himself – doctors, lawyers, college professors – and there was hardly any crime to speak of. Unless you counted dog mutilations, of course. Otherwise, Oakmont was like a refuge from the rest of the world, a suburban bubble where the good life was preserved and protected.

As he walked down the street, he waved to neighbors who were out working on the lawns, some mowing, some landscaping. They smiled and waved back, though he doubted more than half of them knew his name. But that didn't matter; living in Oakmont meant being friendly, even when you didn't know someone. *Especially* when you didn't.

He reached the intersection of Forrester and McKimson, looked both ways, saw no traffic. He turned right. Halfway down the block, he saw a police car parked on the side of the street, its lights flashing silently. He felt a tingling at the base of his skull and his abdominal muscles tightened. Even though the police car wasn't parked in front of Melissa's house – Kittredge Avenue was still a couple of blocks over – his first thought was that something had happened to Sarah, that maybe his fears had come true and the dog mutilator had finally decided to abandon canines in favor of two-legged prey.

He started walking faster, almost but not quite jogging. The air was warm, and by the time he drew near the police car, he was dripping with sweat.

A small crowd had gathered in the street a half dozen yards from the police vehicle, a mix of men and women, some middle-aged like him, others in their sixties and seventies. All were dressed for warm weather – t-shirts, light blouses, shorts, sandals – but none of their clothing was worn or faded. It looked new, as if they had gone shopping this morning to purchase outfits just for this occasion.

As Gordon approached he recognized one of the men as a patient of his, and he struggled to recall his name. Sam? Scott? No, it was Steve.

"Hi, Steve. What's going on?"

Steve (Gordon couldn't recall his last name) turned and frowned at Gordon for moment, obviously not recognizing him. Then his eyes widened and he smiled. "Gordon! How're you doing?" He stuck out his hand and Gordon shook it. Steve was tall, lean, and tan, looking younger and more fit than Gordon, though he was in fact at least a decade older.

"Not bad. Teeth still holding up?"

Steve flashed Gordon a smile, displaying white, even teeth. "That whitening treatment sure did the trick. My smile hasn't looked this good in years."

It'll stay like that for a long time if you'd give up smoking, Gordon thought. The man's breath reeked of tobacco and coffee. Still, Gordon kept smiling. That's what the good, friendly people of Oakmont did. They smiled no matter what.

Gordon nodded to the police car. "Nothing serious, I hope."

Steve's smile dimmed a few watts. "Afraid so. Another dog's been killed. This one in broad daylight, too." His tongue tssked behind those white-white teeth, and he shook his head slowly from side to side, the movement mechanical and unconscious, more ritual than honest reaction.

Gordon turned to look at the house. It was a Cape Cod, red brick, white trim, black shutters. Covered front porch, red-wood fence enclosing the back yard. Lawn was neatly trimmed (of course), and while the flowerbeds were bare, they were cleaned out and mulched, ready to accept whatever plants the owners decided to put there. There was something about the house that Gordon found familiar, but he couldn't quite think what it was. Maybe it was simply that it looked like so many other homes in this part of Oakmont, his own included. But he couldn't shake the feeling that it was more than that.

The gate to the backyard was open, and he could see a police officer in his late twenties, early thirties, speaking with a short, stout women in her forties dressed in a white blouse and light blue shorts. The woman kept wiping her fingers across her cheeks, and Gordon knew she was crying.

"Just like the others," Steve said. "All torn up." He leaned closer, presumably so he wouldn't be overhead by anyone else in the crowd, especially the children. "Seems there are a few pieces missing this time." There was an unmistakable undertone of glee in his voice. Even the good life in such a perfect place as Oakmont could get a little dull from time to time, and the occasional neighborhood scandal helped spice things up a bit.

Gordon experienced a sudden wave of loathing for Steve, and he nearly shoved him away, but he restrained himself. Gordon was a civilized man, and Oakmont was a place dedicated to civilization. One simply didn't shove one's neighbors here, no matter how much they deserved it.

Instead, Gordon gave the expected reply in this upper middle-class call and response. "How awful." He looked into the backyard again, but the officer and the woman were no longer visible. He assumed they'd moved into another part of the yard, perhaps to get a closer view of the dead animal. Gordon wished he could sneak up to the open gate, peek into the yard and see the dead dog for himself. Not out of morbid curiosity (and least, not only) but because if he could see the extant of the animal's injuries, he might . . . might . . .

Might what? he thought. *Get a better idea of who might have done such a thing? Three little girls, for example?*

It was absolutely insane. There was no way Sarah and her two friends could possibly be responsible for this latest dog mutilation, let alone the others.

But that's what's been in the back of your mind, ever since you first saw the blood on Sarah's fingers.

It wasn't blood. It was dirt, rust, anything else. But not blood.

You saw them playing with something in your backyard, tossing it back and forth. They hid it from you, took it with them when they left, but you found blood in the grass where they were playing.

Then there was Steve's nasty little tidbit. *Seems there are a few pieces missing this time.*

Pieces small enough to play hot potato with in the backyard?

"Stop it," he whispered to himself without realizing he spoke.

"Excuse me?" Steve said, frowning.

"Nothing. Just . . . thinking out loud." He gave a small, embarrassed smile. "Bad habit."

Steve looked at him for a moment before finally nodding. "Well, it was good to see you, Gordon." It was time to move on and share his little revelation about missing doggie parts with someone else.

"Same here. Keep taking care of that smile."

"I will."

Steve moved off into the crowd, but Gordon remained where he was, gazing through the open gate and into the backyard, trying to figure out why this house seemed so familiar to him. And then he had it: this was the home of one of Sarah's friends. Not Melissa, but the other one. He struggled to recall a name but came up blank. It didn't matter; he didn't need a name. He remembered stopping here once to pick the girl up when he drove Sarah and a few of her friends to a roller-skating party. He had honked the horn and the girl came running from the backyard. He remembered the gate banging open, the girl running down the driveway, not bothering to close the gate behind her. Remembered wondering if he should tell her to go back and close it or if he should get out of the car and do it himself. In the end, he'd done neither, just driven away once the girl was inside and belted in.

It could be a coincidence, of course. Just because the home – and the dead dog in the backyard – belonged to one of Sarah's friends didn't mean that they'd stopped here before wandering through the neighborhood and eventually ending up in Gordon's backyard. Didn't mean that whatever secret plaything they'd tossed back and forth between them had once been something wrapped inside canine flesh and fur.

Jerry's words came back to him. *No one* really *knows anyone else. Not completely.*

Fuck off, Jerry, Gordon thought. But despite the warmth of the May day and the sweat that coated his body like a second liquid skin, he felt a chill as he moved away from the crowed and continued walking toward Kittredge Avenue.

* * * * *

1707 wasn't hard to find. It was on the corner of Kittredge and Stansbury, another Cape Cod, though this one had an unattached garage off to the side, a two-car one at that. Melissa's parents (assuming they were the ones who'd put the garage in and not the previous owners) had sacrificed a good deal of their backyard in order to make room for the garage, but Gordon thought it was worth it. Less grass to mow, and more to the point, you'd have a place to shelter your car from the elements. No ice to scrape off windshields in the winter, no blazing hot upholstery in the summer. Funny how the little things like garages and roomy backyards seemed like such a luxury here. In a smaller, less pricey town, there'd be garages everywhere and no one would give them a second thought.

Not that Gordon really cared about the garage. He knew he was just trying to distract himself from the real reason he'd come here: to find out what Sarah was up to.

She's not up to anything. Playing with Barbies, listening to a CD of the latest, hottest boy band . . . Normal, everyday girl stuff.

Mutilating another household pet?

Stop it! he told himself. *Just stop it.*

And maybe that wasn't such a bad idea. Now that he was here, standing in the street and looking at the house – closed door, windows rendered opaque by the shadows within – he considered turning around and leaving. He remembered something else Jerry had said.

Why rock the proverbial boat? Just keep your mouth shut and go along as if nothing happened.

Gordon had a good life, the kind everyone sought but didn't always attain. A lucrative career, a nice house in an expensive (but not outrageously so) neighborhood. A good marriage and a great kid. Sarah got straight A's in school, played soccer, belonged to girl scouts, played flute in the school orchestra. She was sweet and well-mannered, everything that parents could hope for in a child. And if there was something. . . more, did he really want to know about it? If his life was the equivalent of a soap bubble – shiny on the surface but all-too-easily burst when pressed – did he truly want to risk destroying it?

He almost walked away, it was *that* close. But in the end, he started up the driveway. He decided against knocking on the front door. What would he say? *Hi, I'm Sarah's dad. I just came to see if my little girl was pulling the intestines out of your dog. Or maybe you have a cat. As far as I know, she hasn't killed any cats yet, but here's always a first time, right?*

Melissa's parents would slam the door shut before he was finished speaking and be on the phone to the police before he stepped off the porch. So what options did that leave him? Sneak around the house and peer through the windows? He could see the headlines in the *Oakmont Daily Call* now: *Local Dentist Turns Peeping Tom.* Scratch that.

The backyard, then. After all, that's where they'd been playing at his house, and the most recent dog mutilation had taken place in a backyard, too. And if Melissa's parents caught him, he could just say he'd come to collect Sarah and thought he'd heard the girls playing out back. A lame excuse – after all this was Oakmont; you knocked on doors first here, no matter what – but at least it was plausible.

He headed for the backyard, listening as he walked. He heard no laughter, no conversation, just the soft rustling of leaves in the mild breeze. The Sylers' backyard was enclosed by a chain-link fence, not wood as was the norm in Oakmont. *They'll probably receive a few pointed comments about that from the zoning board,* Gordon thought. He reached the gate, opened it, stepped through, then walked around the side of the house.

The backyard (what there was of it since the garage took up most of the space) was empty. No gardening shed, but then with a garage, you wouldn't necessarily need one. The grass was neatly trimmed, of course, but there were no flower beds, no hedges, not so much as a single tree.

And no trio of twelve-year-old girls playing keep-away with something small and secret.

Gordon didn't know whether to feel relieved or concerned. Sarah had told him they were coming here, so where – And then he remembered her exact words when he'd asked where she was going.

Over to Melissa's. Her brother just got a new video game, and he said we could play it.

If that was true (if, if, if) then they wouldn't be outside, would they? They'd be inside, sitting cross-legged in front of a TV set, eyes bleary, fingers furiously working game controllers. He glanced at the back door, but decided against knocking on it. It would seem odd to go to the rear door first. He should go back around to the front.

He started toward the gate again, but took less than a half dozen steps when his shoe came down on something moist and yielding.

He stopped and debated far longer than he expected before bending down to pick up the object. There wasn't much left . . . pieces had been chewed off . . . and he was a dentist, not a veterinarian, but he was fairly confident that what he was holding in his hand was the remains of a dog's heart. He looked at it for several long moments, trying to ignore the sweet-sick stink of raw meat that's been out in the sun too long. Finally, he turned his hand over and the grisly hunk of ragged muscle fell back to the ground. He wiped his hand in the grass, then stood.

That doesn't prove anything, he told himself. *It's a chunk of meat, sure, but not a goddamned dog's heart. Probably a leftover bit of rabbit or squirrel killed by a cat, or maybe even an owl last night. It has to be something else* . . . anything *else* . . .

Then he heard a noise that sounded like a muffled scream. Too much like. And, unless he was mistaken, it had come from inside the garage. He hesitated for an instant – but only an instant – then started walking. He didn't want to go look, he really didn't, but he couldn't help himself. Besides, he had to; he was her Daddy, wasn't he?

The door was down, and windowless. But there were windows on the side of the garage, and that's where Gordon headed. As he drew closer, he realized that the windows, which he had first thought merely dark because the garage was closed with no lights on, had instead been covered over on the inside with black paper. So no one could see out? Of course not. So no one could see *in*.

Except that wasn't entirely true, was it? The paper had folded back at one corner. Not much, hardly at all, in fact. But enough.

He placed trembling hands on the smooth wood of the door to steady himself and leaned forward, squeezing his left eye shut and looking through the tiny opening with his right. The interior of the garage wasn't exactly lit by klieg lights, but Gordon saw far more than he wanted to. Saw that Sarah *was* playing a game with her friend's older brother, only it wasn't the kind of game that entailed interacting with a computer-generated image on a video screen. The boy's sister was playing too, as was the remaining girl. There were two adults present as well – Mr. and Mrs. Syler, he presumed – but they weren't chaperoning. They were right in the thick of things. Black leather, metal studs and zippers. Chains hanging from the ceiling. Drain in the middle of the concrete floor. Blunt objects, sharp objects, objects to bite down on, objects to be struck with, objects so complex and nightmarish, they made Kathy's fish-lure dildo look like it had been designed by the good folks at Playskool.

Gordon only had to watch for a few moments to know that the cry he had heard a short time ago had been one of pleasure, though undoubtedly mixed with pain. Still, it hadn't been a cry of distress. Not if the expressions on the girl's faces (on his *daughter's face*) were any indication.

He watched several seconds longer before turning and heading for the still open gate. He walked through and down the Sylers' driveway, into the street, turned to his right and began walking back toward his home, past houses with closed doors and murky windows, each one a mask that could be hiding almost anything.

* * * * *

He didn't question Sarah when she finally came home, looking tired but happy. In fact, he didn't say much to either his daughter or his wife. He busied himself with all the handyman jobs he'd neglected – fixing leaky faucets, replacing the air filter in the furnace, putting on a new hose for the dryer vent, and more – anything that kept his body in motion and his mind silent.

Toward evening he finally ran out of work, and he found himself standing in the space between the dining room and the kitchen, wondering what he should do next. Sarah was sitting at the table doing math homework, and Kathy stood at the stove, working on dinner.

Kathy glanced in his direction. "You know the problem with you, Gordon? You just don't work hard enough." She smiled to show that she was joking, but when Gordon didn't react she said, "Why do you sit down and rest, maybe watch a little TV? I'll have dinner ready in just a little bit."

He didn't feel like watching TV, but he didn't want to rock the boat, did he? So he walked into the living room and sat on the couch. He turned the set to the local news, though he kept the sound muted and paid no attention to the forms and colors that moved across the screen. Paid no attention, that is, until these words appeared in blood-red letters next to the news anchor's head: *Two-Year-Old Disappears from Park.*

Gordon unmuted the sound, turned it up several notches so he could hear better.

The anchor, a chisel-jawed man in his late twenties with a stylish blond hair helmet and an expensive navy blue suit, relayed the details with professional dignity and gravity, though he couldn't quite keep a gleam out of his eye as he spoke. A toddler had disappeared from Indian Creek Park earlier in the afternoon. No one had seen anything and the police had no leads. It was as if – as the toddler's tearful, quavering-voiced mother put it – "My baby vanished in a puff of smoke."

The news drone started to give a number for viewers to call if they had any information on the missing child, but Gordon turned off the TV before he'd finished. He sat for several minutes, staring at the blank screen and the tiny, vague reflection of himself sitting on the couch.

Eventually, he stood and walked into the dining room. He pulled out a chair and sat at his usual place opposite Sarah, who looked up from her homework and gave him a little smile (a little *knowing* smile?) before returning her attention to her math.

Gordon heard Kathy open the refrigerator and take something out. Her listened as she put a plate down and unwrapped cellophane. Seconds later, a hiss came from the stove as she tossed something into a pan to fry. The sound was almost instantly followed by the smell of searing meat.

"We're having stir fry tonight," she called. "How does that sound?"

No one had seen anything and the police had no leads. "Chicken or beef?"

"It's a surprise. A little something I picked up today."

Gordon turned to look at her, watched as she tossed vegetables into the pan on top of the meat. The features of her face had become smooth and hard.

"Of course it is," he said softly.

Sarah looked up from her textbook and gazed at him with dry, painted eyes that didn't blink. "Did you say something, Daddy?"

Gordon didn't have to work up a smile; his plastic lips were already doing the job for him.

"No, Sweetie, I didn't." He took a deep breath, inhaling the scent of cooking food, and sighed with contentment. The good ship Markley was running nice and steady, and it looked like smooth sailing from here on out. Smooth sailing all the goddamned way.

The Great Ocean of Truth

Laws of Thermodynamics:
1. You cannot win.
2. You cannot break even.
3. You cannot stop playing the game.
– Anonymous

"What are you doing here? What are you *doing* here?"

The man's voice catches your attention as you walk into the coffee shop. He speaks too loud, like someone with a hearing problem, and there's a strident urgency to his tone that borders on alarm. The man sits alone at a corner table, his back to the rest of the room, an ancient laptop open in front of him. The man's body blocks the screen, and you can't see what he's looking at – and presumably, talking to. It almost sounds as if he's interrogating the machine, demanding an answer to his question.

The man wears a threadbare army jacket just like the kind your father had, along with faded jeans and scuffed work boots Your father left that jacket to you when he died, but you can't remember where it's at now. Too bad. You always liked that jacket. The man's overlong hair and untrimmed beard are both whitish-gray, but given the angle he's sitting at compared to where you're standing, you can't make out any of his facial features.

You dismiss the man from your thoughts as you continue toward the serving counter. Ghostlight Coffee is located downtown, not far from the VA hospital, and the place attracts its share of colorful customers. Some more so than others.

Ghostlight is housed on the first floor of an old building, with bricks walls, a wooden floor, and exposed heating duct system. You enjoy coming in here because of the place's age. You love the sound and feel of wood giving slightly beneath your weight as you walk, love the smell of dust and mildew. This is a real place, an *authentic* place, built for practicality, as well-worn and comfortable as a favorite shoe. Not like the faux neighborhood business effect that pre-fab coffee houses like Starbucks strive for. This is a place that satisfies both parts of you: the environmental science major you'd been and the construction-company owner you've become. This is urban repurposing at its best. The original structure remains, and the only modern touches are the lighting, the serving counter, and of course the computer register, cappuccino and espresso machines behind it.

Take that, Entropy! you think, and smile.

There's no one else in line, or in the shop, for that matter, except for you, the muttering man, and the kid behind the counter.

"Can I help you, sir?"

The barista is a skinny kid in his early twenties, with short black hair and an eyebrow piercing. He wears a gray T-shirt with *Ghostlight Coffee* on the front, and a white apron wrapped around his waist, as if he's afraid of getting stains on his jeans. Maybe he's clumsy and prone to spillage. Or maybe he just thinks wearing the apron makes him look cool.

You want to tell the kid to skip the *sir* shit. You're only forty-six, for god's sake. But then again, forty-six probably looks ancient to someone as young as the Amazing Apron Lad.

"Just a medium coffee. Black." You hesitate, and then add, "Decaf."

The kid nods and turns away to fill your order. As he does, you pull out your smart phone and check the time. 3:21. You need to get a move on. Lizzie's school lets out at 3:40, and you don't want to be late to pick her up. You haven't seen her since Sunday, when you dropped her off at Beth's, and since you're only going to get two days with her this week – Wednesday and Thursday – you don't want to miss a single minute.

You start to slide your thumb across the screen, intending to open the phone's camera roll and look at a picture of Lizzie – one of your favorites, the one where she's grinning, tongue stuck out, eyes closed as if she's embarrassed by her pose, or perhaps trying to foil your attempt to capture her image by denying you her eyes. But your thumb encounters resistance as you try to unlock the screen. Instead of a smooth surface, the phone feels sticky, as if soda or jam has been spilled on it. For an instant, it seems as if your thumb actually sinks into the screen, and you imagine that if you press harder your thumb will penetrate all the way through and out the back. But then the sensation is gone, your flesh moves easily across the phone's surface, and the screen unlocks. But before you can open the camera roll, the barista returns with your coffee.

You tuck the phone back in your pants pocket and reach for your wallet.

"That'll be one ninety-five," Apron Lad says in a disengaged tone.

He sets the coffee down on the counter, the wood sagging beneath the cup's weight as if it's filled with lead. Soft cracking noises that remind you of breaking ice rise to your ears, only to be drowned out when the man in the army jacket shouts, "What are you DOING here?"

The barista doesn't look in his direction.

"Ignore him. He's in here a lot, and he knows that if he gets too loud, he'll get kicked out. He'll settle down."

True to the kid's prediction, the man quiets, his voice lowering to an unintelligible mutter.

You remove your debit card from your wallet and give it to the barista. The kid swipes the card and hands it back. "Do you want your receipt?"

You shake his head as you replace the debit card in your wallet and return it to your pants pocket. "No thanks."

You pick up your coffee and see a small depression in the counter's surface, tiny cracks fissuring outward from it, like a miniature blast crater. "Looks like you need to get a new counter."

You look up at Apron Lad and start to smile, but the expression dies before it can be born. The kid's right ear is sliding down the side of his face, as if he's a wax dummy in the first stages of melting.

"What?" The kid frowns and his right eyebrow sags, the skin drooping down to occlude the eye.

"Nevermind," you say, taking a step back. The cup's cardboard surface is hot against the soft flesh of your palm, but you scarcely register this fact. A tightness spreads across your chest like constricting bands of iron, bringing with it a surge of ice-cold panic. You force yourself to walk slowly to the closest table, doing your best to ignore the cracking sounds beneath your feet.

You take a seat, set your coffee down, and then take your keys from your pants pocket. You unscrew the lid of the pill fob on your key ring and shake a single nitro tablet onto your trembling hand. You place it under your tongue, close your eyes, and wait. The tablet dissolves within twenty seconds. It's supposed to work fast, but if the pain doesn't go away after five minutes, your cardiologist has instructed you to take a second pill. If that doesn't work, then you're to take a third. And if *that* doesn't work, it's time to call 911 and start praying.

It takes almost a minute and a half for the bands around your chest to loosen, but they do, and you let out a slow sigh of relief. Your head starts throbbing – an unfortunate side-effect of the nitro – but you don't care. You'll take a migraine over a heart attack any day. You look toward the serving counter, expecting to see the barista staring at you with a concerned expression on his face, maybe even hear him ask, *You all right? Is there anything I can do?* But the kid's looking down at his phone, reading a text, maybe playing a game, his right ear and eyebrow back where they belong.

You pick up your coffee, stand, and make your way toward the door. Your head feels like it's going to explode at any moment, but you do your best to ignore the pain. Headache or no headache, you're determined not to be late to get Lizzie. No matter what else happens, you're not going to let her stand there outside her school, alone, wondering where her daddy is. The floor is reassuringly solid beneath your feet as you walk, the wood barely creaking. Good.

As you reach the door, the man in the army jacket – still facing his laptop screen – once more asks, almost conversationally, "Why are you here?"

"I'm not," you say, and walk out.

* * * * *

You get in your pick-up, the words Pinnacle Construction painted on the side. You put your coffee in the cup holder, although you doubt you're going to drink it. Even though it's decaf, you don't like the idea of putting even the minimal amount of caffeine it contains into your system right now. Not so soon after your heart hiccupped, and not with the way your head is throbbing. You turn the engine over, listen to its spastic rumble-knocking, and you know you need to get it serviced as soon as you can afford it. You put the engine in gear, pull away from the curb, and head in the direction of Oakgrove Middle School. The traffic is light this time of day, and you figure you'll make good time, but really, it never gets much heavier than this. Downtown is dead, has been for years. A collection of old, empty buildings, crumbling brick and rotting wood. There are a few signs of life. The Cannery District has a couple funky art galleries and some renovated loft apartments, and there's Ghostlight Coffee, of course. But there isn't much more. It's a small Midwestern city whose best days are long behind it. Kind of like you.

You think about what you saw in the coffee shop. The cracked depression in the counter, the kid's melting face . . . You don't remember the doctor saying anything about hallucinations being a potential side-effect of your surgery. Three months ago you started feeling tired, short of breath, and you went in for a check-up. A week later you were on an operating table, getting a triple bypass. You weren't really surprised. Heart disease runs in your family – both your father and grandfather had bypasses – but it hit you at a younger age than you expected. The surgery went well, and although the recovery wasn't fun, you were back at work three weeks later, feeling better than you had in years. You get angina every now and then, but it's nothing that a nitro tab can't handle. So far, anyway. You suppose it's possible that for some reason you're not getting enough blood flow to your brain. That could cause hallucinations, couldn't it? But then again, it might just be good old-fashioned stress. Heart surgery caused serious psychological repercussions – a newfound awareness of your own mortality, a sense that your body was fragile, that if you weren't careful, it could shatter like glass.

Or crack like rotten wood.

And there's plenty of non-health-related stress in your life. The divorce. Only getting to see your daughter part-time. And business hasn't been all that great. Right now, Pinnacle Construction has more creditors than clients, and the former have been after you like a pack of drooling hyenas circling a choice piece of carrion.

You have a good job. And you worked hard to get your degree. Why would you want to walk away from that – and to start a construction business, no less? In case you hadn't noticed, this isn't the best time to get into building houses.

Beth had been right on that last point. Given the state of the economy, the construction industry wasn't exactly booming. And while your job testing water quality for the county wasn't exciting, it did pay the bills. But you were burdened by a deep-seated dissatisfaction you hadn't been able to fully explain to your wife – which was one the reasons she's now your ex-wife. Even though this all happened long before your surgery, you sometimes wonder if on some level you were aware of what was coming, that your remaining years might number fewer than most, and you didn't want to waste whatever time you had left running test after boring test on water samples. Yes, it was necessary work, maybe even important work, but it hadn't felt as if you were truly contributing anything. You were testing, measuring, assessing, when what you really wanted to be doing was making, creating, *building*.

You think about when you received your first glimpse into the true nature of the universe. It was in eighth grade – one grade higher than Lizzie's in now – in Mr. Gillespie's science class. The man was better suited to teach college than middle school. Most of what he taught went over his students' heads, and his tests were a real bitch. But you'd loved the class. It was the first time you'd felt challenged in school, and there wasn't a day that didn't go by without Mr. Gillespie giving you at least one awesome insight into the way the world worked. But no day had been more mind-blowing than the day he introduced the laws of thermodynamics to the class.

It had all been fascinating, but the second law chilled you.

Put simply, Mr. Gillespie had said, *the second law can be stated as "entropy increases."* He'd smiled then. *Or to phrase it another way, damned if you do, damned if you don't.*

He'd gone on to explain further, using such cheerful phrases as *the ultimate heat death of the universe*, but you'd only been half-listening. You were too busy trying to wrap your mind around the second law. If entropy always increased, you reasoned, then anything anyone did, no matter how constructive it seemed, only helped to hasten the process of breaking the universe down into nothing. And there wasn't anything anyone could do about it.

In the years afterward, you'd come to a deeper understanding of the three laws, and you know that they're far more complex than you'd first thought on that afternoon in Mr. Gillespie's class, but the basic core of your initial insight still holds up.

But Mr. Gillespie's class wasn't all existential angst. He'd hung a number of inspirational posters around his classroom featuring great scientists throughout history. Your favorite had been the poster of Isaac Newton, not because of the man himself, but rather the quote beneath his image: *Whilst the great ocean of truth lay all undiscovered before me.* You loved the poetry and mystery of the line, and that, perhaps more than anything else, spurred you to seek a career in science.

Of course, running tests on river water wasn't exactly exploring the "ocean of truth," was it? And as you grew older and became more aware of the ticking clock that was your heart – a poor defective organ that would eventually need tuning up as badly as your pick-up's engine – you had to do something to give entropy the finger. You knew it was going to win in the end, but you had to at least make the attempt to leave something more behind when you were gone than file after file of test results stored on some office computer. Building houses – building *homes* – where families could raise children, who in turn would grow up to have their own children, had seemed like a perfect legacy. Too bad it didn't pay the goddamned bills, not enough of them anyway.

You decide not to worry about what you saw at the coffee shop. You've got a check-up with your cardiologist in a few days, and you'll ask her about the hallucinations – if they were even serious enough to be called that – then. Thinking about Ghostlight reminds you of your coffee, and you reach for it, only to withdraw your hand. You're still not sure if you want to risk the caffeine. You turn on the radio instead and crank the volume despite your headache. You always turn the volume high; it helps to mask the distressing sounds coming from the pick-up's engine.

An old Bob Segar tune's finishing up, and you catch a bit of lyric about autumn closing in. Nice. Just what you want to hear right now. You leave the radio tuned to this station, though. The song's almost finished, and they play a wide variety of music here. You like not knowing what sort of artist is going to come on next.

It could be anyone from the Big Bopper to the Beatles to AC/DC. *Predictability is its own form of entropy,* you think.

You're driving down Jefferson Avenue. It's the most direct route to Lizzie's school from Ghostlight Coffee, but it takes you through one of the skuzzier parts of town. The buildings here are so old they're on the verge of collapse, and for every business that's open, three have been closed and abandoned. Flaking paint and weathered brick, unintelligible graffiti spray-painted on walls, broken glass and discarded fast-food wrappers scattered on the sidewalks. The people here walk with slow shuffling steps, heads bowed, faces expressionless. Whenever you come this way, you can't help thinking about all the work there is to be done here – buildings to refurbish, businesses to reopen, people to save . . . But it's work you know will never be done.

The song ends and the DJ comes on the air. The prerecorded voice is usually that of an old sitcom actor you recognize but whose name you can never remember. But this time someone else speaks.

"Everything winds down, like an uncoiling spring."

This voice you *can* put a name to: it's Mr. Gillespie.

"So before it's too late, listen to these messages from our fine sponsors"

A commercial for a bartending school comes on, one you've heard many times before. You pay no more attention to it now than you did the other times you've heard it. You tell yourself that the DJ can't be Mr. Gillespie. You were in his class thirty-four years ago, and he hadn't been a young man then. He's bound to be retired now, if not dead. And even if he *is* still alive, why would he be spending what remains of his golden years providing prerecorded patter between songs on a small Southwestern Ohio radio station? It didn't make sense.

But the uncoiling spring was exactly the kind of image Mr. Gillespie would've used when talking about the Second Law. Weirder yet, the line seemed to come in response to what you were thinking. *Coincidence,* you tell yourself. *That's all.* But you don't believe it, not deep down where it really matters.

The commercials, all of them comfortingly mundane, continue for the next couple blocks. As you approach an intersection, you see the lights of emergency vehicles, and you slow down. The traffic light is blinking yellow, and there's a police officer standing in the middle of the intersection waving cars through. As you draw closer, you see there's been an accident, a bad one. Three vehicles – an SUV, a Ford Taurus, and a minivan – all appeared to have attempted to pass through the intersection at the same time, from three different directions, all traveling at surprisingly high speed, the drivers heedless of another well-known law of physics: two objects (let alone three) cannot occupy the same space at the same time. You first reaction is relief. It looks like the accident, bad as it is, isn't slowing traffic down, and you won't be late to pick up Lizzie. Guilt comes next. You should be thinking of the poor bastards who got hurt in this crash – and given the state of the vehicles, let alone the two EMS vans on the scene, you're sure no one's walking away from this clusterfuck unscathed – but your first thought was a selfish one. It's not that you're uncaring. You have a responsibility to Lizzie, that's all. This may be true, but it doesn't make you feel any better about yourself.

It's your turn to pass through the intersection, and the cop waves you forward, his motions sharp, an edge of impatience to them. You don't want to be one of those people who slow as they pass an accident, eager to sate their morbid curiosity. You'd like to think you're better than that. But you can't help sneaking a quick glance.

You see four emergency medical personnel, all dressed in blue uniforms, struggling to pull a mass of bloody flesh and cloth from the wreckage. Several police officers and firefighters stand by, watching, none of them making the slightest move to help. They seem alert, though, their bodies filled with coiled energy, and you catch what appears to be a look of hunger in their eyes. *They're just itching for some action,* you tell yourself. But that's not the kind of hunger you see. As you draw closer, you realize that the collision must have been far worse than you initially thought, for the twisted, crumpled metal of the three vehicles is so intertwined, it seems as if they've merged into a single solid mass. Last weekend, you watched a nature documentary on cable with Lizzie detailing what happened to the body of an adult elephant after it died. Lizzie was fascinated by the parade of predators and scavengers that worked to devour the dead beast over the course of several days, but it was the maggots that really captured her imagination. She'd seen flies before, of course, but not maggots, and after only a few short days under the heat of the African sun, there were thousands of the wriggling white things, so many that they began to reduce the elephant's flesh to a disgusting liquefied mess. And although the program's narrator pointed out how the energy the elephant had stored in its body over the course of a lifetime would be recycled into the environment, you couldn't help thinking this was a perfect illustration of the Second Law in action. The mass of vehicles reminds you of that elephant, while the EMT's, cops, and firefighters remind you of the lions, leopards, hyenas, and jackals who arrived to feed on the corpse. And the maggots? You suppose they're the looky-loo's driving by, of which you're forced to admit you're one. *Just call me Mr. Maggot,* you think.

You're almost through the intersection when your gaze centers on the bodies the EMT's are working to extricate from the wreckage. No. . . *Body*. Singular.

You tell yourself it's a trick of your eyes (no way you want to consider the possibility you're having another hallucination.) The bloody, broken thing the men and women pull from the crumpled metal can't be one large form with multiple heads, arms, and legs. It only looks that way because of the angle from which you're seeing the bodies, the quality of the afternoon light hitting them, the unreal nature of any horrific accident scene. Or most likely, a combination of the three.

Oh, it's a combination all right, you think. It seems like three objects *can* occupy the same space at the same time – after a fashion, at least.

The iron bands around your chest return, bringing with them ice-cold knives of panic. Fresh pain erupts inside your skull, so intense it's nearly blinding. You fumble for the pill fob on the end of your keys, but it's difficult to get the lid off with the keys in the ignition. As you struggle, the bands tighten, the panic intensifies, and you feel your airway begin to seal shut . . .

Pull over! you tell yourself, Wave down the cop, get him to bring one of the EMT's over here. Maybe they'll throw you in the back of one of their vans and haul your ass to the nearest ER.

The car behind you honks, startling you, and you realize that you've slowed to a crawl. The cop is waving you forward, his motions sharper now, more insistent, an angry scowl on his face, and other drivers start honking. *Pull over, pull over, pull over!* But you ignore the voice in your head and force yourself to press down on the accelerator, and move through the intersection. Your head still pounds, but the bands around your chest begin to loosen, your throat opens up, and you're able to breathe again. Not easily, but at least you can get some air. You think you're going to be okay.

You're tempted to look in your rearview to check if you really saw what you think you saw, if there truly was one body with multiple heads and limbs, but you keep your gaze fixed firmly on the road in front of you and continue driving. The pain in your chest eases, but this time it doesn't go away, not entirely.

* * * * *

"Daddy, is that what's going to happen to me when I die?"

Her question catches you off-guard, and you try to make a joke out of it. "You mean getting eaten by jungle animals?"

Lizzie gives you a look that says, Don't be stupid. "I mean being turned into nothing but bones. And those will be gone too someday, won't they? So they'll be nothing left of me." She pauses for a moment to think before adding, "It'll be like I was never here at all."

You've never lied to her before. When she was much younger, she asked you if Santa Claus was real. You wanted to tell her yes, to give her imagination the push it needed to believe that there was magic in the world, at least for a little while. But when you saw the unquestioning trust on her face, you could do nothing but tell her the truth. You quickly followed up by telling her the usual bullshit, that Santa was the spirit of Christmas that lives in everyone, but you could tell she wasn't buying it. Worse, you could tell he was disappointed.

So now, sitting on the couch, both of you looking at a picked-clean elephant carcass on TV, you think of how you'd wished you'd lied about Santa years ago, and you want to tell her that it'll be okay, that God is in his heaven and all's right with the world. But you can't, so you just keep your damned mouth shut and pray she doesn't press you for answers you don't want to give, and you wish like hell that there was someone around to lie to you.

* * * * *

Mr. Gillespie's voice comes on the radio once more. You listen as you rub your chest with your free hand, as if you might be able to massage your now-mild – but still present – chest pain away.

"Here's something to ponder, boys and girls. When the universe begins to break down, space and time will too. It only makes sense, right? After all, that's what the universe is made of. So if time no longer functions – if, for lack of a better word, time dies *– then how is it possible for the universe to truly end? In order to have beginnings, middles, and ends, you need the passage of time. No time, no end. So imagine that the universe is on the verge of giving its last gasp, and in that instant time stops. That means*

the universe would continue to exist in a kind of a frozen eternity, forever on the edge of death but unable to ever reach it. And since time is no longer a factor, there's nothing to separate one moment from the next. Everything that ever happened will basically continued happening forever, but all at once, in one great big jumbled mess. And not just events, either. Thoughts, emotions, dreams, nightmares . . .they'll all be in the mix, too, kids. And we'll be there, every single one of us, in that last forever non-moment of existence. We might even be conscious of what's happened to us, at least partially. Can you imagine what that would be like? I can't, but it sounds a lot like Hell, doesn't it?" A pause. *"That's enough for you to chew on for now. Let's have some more music. I was going to play Blue Oyster Cult's 'Don't Fear the Reaper,' but I decided it would be too cliché at this point. Instead, how about some Steely Dan?"*

You recognize the beginning of "Do it Again," a much lighter song than the BOC tune, but hardly a more comforting one at the moment. But you don't turn the radio off, nor do you lower the volume.

Just get to Lizzie, you tell yourself. *That's all that matters.*

The neighborhoods are supposed to improve as you get closer to the school . . . at least, that's how you remember it. But today this part of town – which used to contain middle-class suburbs with well-kept lawns and warm, cheerful homes – looks like a bombed-out war zone, the road cracked, buckled, and filled with potholes, sidewalks crumbling, houses lopsided skeletal frames, their yards barren patches of lifeless gray dirt. The cars and trucks driving by are rust-eaten wrecks belching black exhaust as they judder along on decaying tires. You see signs everywhere that proclaim this to be a DECONSTRUCTION ZONE, and despite yourself, you laugh.

By the time you reach Lizzie's school – which is now called Oak*grave* Middle School, according to the tarnished metal letters bolted to the crumbling brick façade of the main building – your head feels like there's something inside trying to claw its way out, and your chest is on fire. But you don't care. Take a nitro pill, don't take a nitro pill . . . You know the end result will be the same.

You try to check the time on your phone, but the device deforms in your hand like warm taffy, and you drop the useless thing to the floor. You don't need it anyway. You know you're not late because while the buses are lined up in front of the school, there's no sign of kids getting on them yet. The final bell has yet to ring. You made it.

The buses don't *look* like buses, though. They resemble large gray elephants, a dozen in all, lying on their sides in two neat rows, their massive bodies bloated with decomposition gas. There's a small lot in front of the school where parents are supposed to pick up their kids, and there are a number of vehicles parked there, even more lined up in a single row, engines still running, the drivers impatient to collect their progeny and get on with what remains of their day. Their cars are all of a kind: roundish vehicles encased in green shell-like metal, headlights crosshatched like multifaceted eyes, engines emitting a droning buzz. Your pick-up is the only normal vehicle, and you pull into an unoccupied space and park. Before you can turn off your engine, the song on the radio ends, and Mr. Gillespie comes on again.

"When you think about it, boys and girls, the universe's only real function is to devour itself. It's an ouroboros, tail in its own mouth, chewing and swallowing, chewing and swallowing. And no matter how much it eats, it can never finish the job, and it will never, ever be full. So . . . dig in and join in the feast, kids, and remember to tip your servers on your way out. Bon appetite!"

You turn off the engine and the radio goes silent. Your pulse is beating trip-hammer fast, and sour-smelling sweat rolls off of you in waves. Your headache is so intense that tears stream from your eyes, and the pressure in your chest is so tight you expect your ribs to burst out outward in splintered shards. But as you exit the truck, you leave the keys in the ignition, the pill fob untouched. Let your heart explode like a flabby, rancid, fat-filled balloon. What possible difference could it make?

Now that you're outside, you find the insectine drone of the other cars deafening. Vibrations thrum through your body, and your heart and head try to match the rhythm. It hurts like a motherfucker, but you don't really mind the pain. In fact, it's kind of pleasant in an *Oh my sweet Christ I'm dying* kind of way.

The front doors of the school – glass broken, metal frames rusted and bent – slam open and a tide of children surges forth. Flesh spongy white, eyes flat obsidian, mandibles in place of mouths. The vast majority of children race toward the elephant carcasses, fall upon them, and begin to feast, mandibles cutting away chunks of rotting flesh with machine-like precision. Not all of the kids head for the elephants, though. Those whose parents have come to pick them up run toward the parking lot, and even though her face isn't exactly like you remember it, you recognize Lizzie as she comes toward you. She throws herself against you as if she hasn't seen you in years, and you hug her close, ignoring the way her mandibles catch on the fabric of your shirt. As you hold her, you watch the other children – the ones devouring the elephants – writhing in thick clumps over the carrion, covering it completely in a mass of white. Within moments, dead flesh becomes a foamy, liquid goo, and this, you think, is the real ocean of truth.

Your headache vanishes, as does the pain in your chest. Your pulse falls silent. Your heart is no longer beating, or perhaps it's on the verge of its final beat, unable to complete it. You wonder if Mr. Gillespie was right, if endings are no longer possible here at the penultimate instant before the final entropic collapse of the universe. Maybe, you think. But that doesn't mean you should stop trying to find an ending. To *make* one.

You push Lizzie gently away from you and gaze down upon her with a smile.

"Go ahead," you say. "I'll wait."

She gives a little jump of excitement, lets out an inhuman squeal of delight, and then runs off to join in the feast.

* * * * *

The next day – or perhaps the same one (as if it matters) – you enter Ghostlight Coffee. The old man, the one wearing your father's army jacket, is sitting at the same table, staring at his laptop screen, still muttering, "Why are you doing here? Why are you *doing* here?"

This time, instead of going to the serving counter, you walk over to his table.

You see that he – and by he, you really mean you, because now that you're standing next to him, you can see that this old man is you with a few more decades under his belt – is looking at a picture of you and Lizzie on his screen. It was taken after one of her soccer games when she was younger. You're standing in front of a goal, she's wearing her uniform, her hair tousled, face sweaty, and you're both smiling.

You want to tell your older self not to worry, that you know why you're why – why we're *all* here – but your mandibles aren't capable of speech. Instead, you decide to show him. You grab hold of his jacket, pull him to his feet, and begin to eat your own tail.

ACKNOWLEDGEMENTS

Thanks to Eric Beebe for all his hard work and support. Thanks also to my agent Cherry Weiner, half wilderness guide, half pitbull, one hundred percent awesome.

Made in the USA
Charleston, SC
29 October 2013